APOCALYPSE, HOW?

DAKOTA ADAMS
BOOK I

Galen Surlak-Ramsey

TinyFox
PRESS

A Tiny Fox Press Book

Cover design by Tek Tan.

Library of Congress Control Number: 2019905137

ISBN: 978-1-946501-14-1

Tiny Fox Press LLC
North Port, FL

For Aria

CHAPTER ONE

I don't know how everyone didn't die of boredom a thousand years ago.

I mean, back in the 5th century PHS (Pre HyperSpace), you only had a handful of channels to watch, and the farthest anyone had gone was the moon. To top it off, it took them three days to get there. I'd rather let a Ferrean dust worm gnaw my arm off than spend that long twiddling my thumbs in a cramped cockpit with nothing to do.

And while I'm ranting about ancient history, I can't even imagine being stuck on a tiny blue planet that at least one guide listed as being mostly harmless. I need to sail the Horsehead Nebula! I need to speed dive the event horizon of KT-124! I need to go spelunking at the Venetian poles!

I know. I know. Billions of people have already done all that, but my true passion is finding lost alien technology and prehistoric civilizations that even time doesn't remember. So, after a lot of research, a few hot tips, and calling in three solid you-owe-me's, I got a hold of a good lead on what would hopefully be an ancient crash site on a backwater planet.

How much would a find be worth? Anywhere from junk to untold riches, obviously, but I had hopes that the salvage there would get me enough to buy a brand-new Hermes '64 Intruder. With its seven-point-eight cubic meter warp core and six-barreled displacement drive, I'd lap the galaxy faster than gossip laps a locker room. When I could do that, I'd put all other treasure hunters to shame.

And if I got mega-trillions-jackpot lucky, I could even find something the Progenitors left behind. For those of you who slept through history class, they're the guys fabled to have been the most advanced species ever to exist. They created worlds on a whim and popped in and out of any dimension they pleased.

What I wouldn't give to be the first to prove their existence. Becoming the most famous xenoarchaeologist in the Milky Way would be a nice touch, too, and I'm pretty sure I'd get my PhD on the spot, even if I haven't technically finished my undergrad. Then I'd be able to introduce myself as Doctor Adams. Doctor Dakota Adams.

Yeah, I like the sound of that. Sounds a ton better than Miss Adams, doesn't it? I like it so much, in fact, if I ever get home with my skull intact, I'm going to order a nameplate the first chance I get.

CHAPTER TWO

When I first landed on DD-3123—a small, lush planet on the outer rim—things got off to a slow start. I spent an entire day wandering around trying to find my local contact who promised he could guide me to the crash site.

While wandering, I checked in with my live-stream channel, and I was depressed to discover my usual ten to twenty viewers had dwindled to two. Though I was grateful I still had a couple of names tuning into my show, I soon suspected they were bots.

My search for my native guide eventually led me inside a festival filled with balloons, mud huts, and plenty of odd games ranging from wibblet ball (sort of a soccer-freeze-tag hybrid) to death stick (horseshoes meets hand grenades, not for the faint of heart).

Eventually, I found the guy, whose name was Ryx, near the food vendors. He was snacking on a bag of palafels (think giant caterpillars, deep fried and dipped in honey) and listening to a traveling musical group with vocals strong enough to shatter steel. Once the show finished, we blazed a trail together to a large crater about ten kilometers away. The terrain was scrubby and flat, for the most part, until we reached the crater's outer edge and needed to scale the ridgeline.

After hiking most of the way up, I finished the climb with a short hop and swing of my ice axe to grab the top and pull myself up. Though it was easy, I was jealous of how fast Ryx scaled the terrain. His seven spindly arms were long enough to grab plenty of holds at once, and the suckers covering the palms of his hands were strong enough that he could sleep suspended from an overhang. That said, he was also two and a half meters tall, which meant he'd be smooshed in any cockpit. I've always said I'd take zipping through the galaxy in comfort over pretending to be a bat any day. His furry body and arachnid face weren't appealing either.

Standing next to me, Ryx pointed into the giant crater. The meemar forest obscured everything inside its five-kilometer span with bright orange leaves, but there was a dark blotch that he was drawing my eyes to close by.

"Down there," Ryx said. His natural language was a slew of squeaks, but the 3C-bug in my ear (fluent in over six million forms of communication) made the translation.

"Awesome," I said, plugging the location into my datapad. "I really can't thank you enough for the help. Are you sure you won't come with?"

Ryx made a circular gesture with his left appendage, the equivalent of us humans shaking our head. "Haunted place. Dangerous. Rats went in earlier. Never came out. Beware the glow floor and the one with the red eye."

"Glowing floors and red eyes are bad, got it," I said with a friendly pat on one of his shoulders.

There was a grunt from behind, and Oran, a guy I'd hired to help, pulled himself up over the ridge to join us. Sweat and dirt caked his sunburnt forehead, and the shirt under his brown jacket was soaked so badly I was sure I could smell his reek three planets away. Stink aside, he'd also failed to dress for the occasion. He wore casual weekend attire consisting of tailored pants and a collared shirt, instead of something more suited to exploration like the khaki pants, loose shirt, and wide-brimmed hat that I had on.

"Almost there," I said to encourage him. "Don't have a coronary on me."

"Guess I'm not as young as I used to be," he replied with a weary smile.

I almost made a quip about him only being a few years older than I was, but decided to let him save face so he didn't have to admit a girl was in better shape than he was. "Well, no time to dawdle," I said, starting my way down the crater.

"Yeah. Let's wrap this up," Oran replied, though with far less enthusiasm than me.

I practically had to pull Oran along. I think the talk of the area being haunted concerned him more than the steep, rocky terrain we were descending. After all, if the ship we were looking for had a split reactor, that could be the source of superstition for Ryx's villagers.

We pressed through thick foliage. More than once, thorns and branches snared my sleeves and pants. I kept quiet about it, but Oran complained. "This place is terrible," he said. "We should've waited for Tolby to finish working on your ship. Could've saved us a lot of walking."

"She's due for her thousand-hour maintenance," I replied. "You don't want to skip that kind of stuff unless the idea of breaking down between system jumps appeals to you."

Oran snorted. "Yeah, but waiting a few more hours wouldn't have killed you. It's not like this crash site is going anywhere."

"There's no room to land around here," I explained as I hacked away at the Yubjub bushes with my nanomachete. They'd gotten so dense that I'd have given my firstborn for a flamethrower or a herd of vegetarian land piranhas. "And if we wait much longer, it'll be twenty-nine hours since we've been on this world."

"What's wrong with that?"

I stopped. "I don't like twenty-nine. It...makes me feel uneasy." I couldn't explain it other than that. It's not because it's a prime number. There are some I like (like the numbers three and eleven), but certain numbers are wrong, four especially. Four is scratchy and sounds like a faster-than-light drive when it's about to go supercritical and scatter your atoms across the galaxy. Twenty-nine isn't that bad, but it smells like musty socks and is lime green. If you're not a synesthete, this sounds kooky, but if you are, you know what I'm talking about.

I pushed on, not wanting to think about bad numbers anymore. "God, these trees are huge. No wonder I couldn't see anything from orbit."

Oran let the conversation die. A few hacks later, we broke through the brush and found ourselves at the edge of a small river. It moved at a fast clip, and I paused to wash my face. Once cleaned and refreshed, I checked my datapad to see how much farther we had to go. That's when I realized it said we were less than fifty meters downstream of where we wanted to be.

I looked up, and my breath left me. Ahead there was an exhaust port as tall as I was. I couldn't see the rest of the ship, but what I saw looked intact. Thankfully, the crash was on our side of the river. Trying to cross such a swift body of water wasn't appealing.

I wondered how long the ship had been there. Given the forest growth around it, it'd probably crashed hundreds of years ago. Thousands maybe. Millions? Was it Progenitor?

I chuckled, knowing I was getting carried away. It was a human ship, five hundred years old at the most. As I drew closer, I could see the engines were original Pratt & Taiki FTL drives. They had the company's signature egg-shaped design that early engineers had erroneously thought was more reliable. It also had slanted, atmospheric stabilizing fins made from a plasti-titanium compound (the goldish sheen was a dead giveaway) that had only seen limited production in the early- to mid-first-century AHS.

The ship itself was lying on its belly, sunken a couple of meters into the ground. That said, it was still two stories tall, so I was mostly looking up at it.

"This is amazing," Oran said. The awe in his voice was palpable.

I touched the micro-button on the side of my thin-rimmed glasses and opened a communication line back to my ship. "Tolby? We scored."

"Great One guides us! I knew it!" His deep, rough voice was filled with energy. "What did we find?"

"It's—"

"A Porellian battle cruiser?"

"No a—"

"A Weyani medship?"

"No, it's—"

"By the Plancks!" Tolby boomed. "Tell me it's a Progenitor! It is, right? No...don't tell me. The gods will smite me for the amount of blaspheme I'll utter if I'm stuck here working on this bucket of bolts of yours."

My face soured. "Hey!"

"Sorry," he apologized. He took a deep breath and exhaled slowly. "I'm centered now. You may inform me of this Progenitor ship you've discovered."

At the time, I could picture the serious, slightly adorable look on his tiger-like face and couldn't stay mad at him for calling my ship a piece of crap. "Human origins. Looks like an old exploration ship. Early Odyssey? Still walking up to it."

Tolby grunted. "That's...disappointing. Perhaps it'll have something good inside? I mean salvage on just the ship..."

"Will barely cover costs getting out here, but there's no telling what it was carrying," I said. Remains of ships this old weren't worth much. It would be like expecting the rotting wood of a sunken Spanish galleon to fetch a prime price to a carpenter. No, what we needed to find was some rare cargo.

"Inform me of your progress as things develop," he said. "I'm going to take our ship out for a test flight and make sure everything's running smoothly before we head home."

"Of course," I said. "Hey, rub my elephant for good luck."

Tolby grumbled over the line. "Really?"

"Yes, really!" I said. "He's part of the reason we got this lucky!"

"He's a piece of plastic suction-cupped to your dashboard," Tolby replied. "He can't do anything but decrease warpcore efficiency by 0.00002%, rounded of course, due to his minimal mass."

"Remember what happened last time you didn't rub the elephant? We had that strut malfunction, and it nearly ruined my landing gear."

"That had nothing to—" Tolby stopped midsentence and cursed (knowing I was right). "Fine. There. Happy now? I rubbed your elephant, just how he likes it."

"Perfect. Thanks. Talk to you soon."

"Dakota?" Oran said, drawing my attention. He stood near the aft of the ship, inspecting a large identification plate welded on the side. "This isn't an Odyssey. It's the colony ship of the NTS *Vela*."

I squealed without shame and bolted to where he was to get a look. The fifteen meters that separated us felt like a kilometer. But once I was there, it read as he'd said: COLONY SHIP – NTS VELA.

Tales about the *Vela* had been spun for centuries. No one knew what had happened to it half a millennium ago, but every legend said it had been on its way to unearth a treasure trove of Progenitor technology before vanishing. And while this wasn't the *Vela*, obviously, it was the colony ship that would detach from the *Vela* to land on a planet and well, like the name says, colonize it, since the *Vela* wasn't meant for anything but pure space travel.

My heart pounded against my chest, and I hopped around with unbridled excitement. Technology from the first spacefaring race was at my fingertips! Technology that could power a galaxy or jump ships halfway across the known universe in the blink of an eye! Technology that would firmly write me into all the history books from here till the end of time!

I playfully punched Oran in the arm and smiled brighter than I ever had before. "What the hell are we waiting for then? Let's get in there!"

CHAPTER THREE

Getting inside the colony ship took a bit. For several minutes, I played with the brim of my fedora as we skirted the outside, looking for an entrance. The damn thing was longer than a sandworm, and unfortunately, the main ramp extended from its belly, so it was buried. As we circled, I wondered how much of a ghost ship it would be, but then I squashed the images of an undead crew roaming the decks and addressed my viewing audience (a total of six now).

"For those following, we've found what's likely to be the best find of the century, a lead to the NTS *Vela!*" I paused for dramatic effect and briefly took off my glasses so I could use them to pan around the ship. I ignored the one "*yawn*" in chat, as well as a request for a boob shot (go creep somewhere else, galactic_sized_531), and carried on. "As you can see, it's huge—typical for a first-century colony since they had to be self-sustaining for years should the planet they landed on require atmo refineries to be built. Sadly, we're having trouble finding an entry point, but stay tuned and see history in the making!"

I killed the feed display on my glasses so I could focus on what was in front of me. Though I was ecstatic I'd tripled my viewers from two to six, I prayed I'd find a way inside before my audience vanished.

We found a secondary hatch on the port side, partially obscured by three-spined gornipal clovers. As a side note, the Ipanati were the ones responsible for seeding the three-spined gornipal clovers over multiple star systems, as they believed their holy text had ordered them to do so. Turned out it was all a huge mistranslation, and instead of the prophet Korbal wanting the stars dressed with clover, he really wanted to retire on a little island and work on his gem cutting. Funny how one misplaced dot in their language could cause such a huge mistake, don't you think?

Anyway, the hatch we discovered was about a meter off the ground. To my pleasant surprise, the lights on the control panel next to it were still on. Clearly rubbing the elephant had bestowed us with good fortune.

I glanced at Oran and caught him with an unsettling look in his eye. I couldn't tell if he was nervous or contemplating taking me out and stealing this find. I had to remind myself that he hadn't been anything like a serial killer thus far, and he did know he was being filmed, so people would know who'd killed me if he tried something. Had to be nerves.

"Well, we've got power," I said. I pulled the handle and the door groaned. My nose wrinkled at the smell of mildew. I distracted myself by opening a comm to Tolby. "Good news, bud, might stumble on something Progenitor after all."

His shriek left my ears ringing. "Oh please, please, please wait till I get there!"

"It won't be here," I replied. "But we did find the *Vela*'s colony ship. If the logs are intact, we can see where it came from."

A ruckus blasted through the line along with a flurry of curses. I grinned, certain he'd toppled over in the pilot's seat. "Deep breaths...deep breaths..." he said, returning to the line. "You better not be joking."

"Nope."

"Then why are you still talking to me? Get those logs!"

"I'm going! I'm going!" I said, laughing. I ended the call and hopped inside the airlock. Once Oran climbed in, I used a panel inside to get the system to cycle, which closed the outer hatch and opened the door leading inside.

"I can't believe this is happening," I said.

"Me either," he replied. "If I wake up, I'm going to cry."

"Same."

"Do you think we should be worried?"

I cocked my head, not following the question. "Why? Place seems structurally sound."

"Yeah, but the power is on."

"Isn't that a good thing?"

Oran shrugged. "Don't know. But this boat's fuel cells should've bled dry centuries ago. Even without a system drain, they'd never last this long."

I gnawed on my lower lip. "So, power is a little odd..." My voice trailed, and I wondered who or what was responsible for keeping systems operational. But I couldn't bore my viewers with more downtime as we got some probes to scout the interior. Besides, someone could jump in and lay claim. "Well, let's hope whatever is in here turns out to be friendly."

Oran and I moved down a hall that was bathed in red emergency lighting that ran along the lower wall panels. We passed through a door and came to a T-junction. As we went left, I yanked Oran back a split second before he made a fatal mistake.

"Don't move," I said, keeping a death grip on his forearm.

Oran's fright faded after a few seconds of nothing happening and pulled free. "What?"

I pointed to a missing floor tile. The air above it shimmered and distorted like reality couldn't make up its mind if it wanted to be there. "Grav tile is broken," I said. "Nowadays they stop working, but these old ones tended to do bad things."

To further illustrate the point, I drew his attention to the ceiling where there was a large dent and a brown splatter stain. "Whoever that poor guy was found the ghosts of the ship," I said.

"You sure it's still malfunctioning?"

I nodded. Nearby there was a tool belt with a flashlight attached. I tossed it on the broken tile. The belt rocketed upward, punching a hole through the ceiling. I wondered if it made it through to the next deck. Part of me wanted to see before we left.

"Damn," Oran said, eyes wide. "Let's tiptoe around."

"I'd rather not. The ones up ahead look suspect too. We'll have to double back," I said. "There's got to be more than one way up front."

We snaked our way back the way we'd come. We kept trying to get to the cockpit, but between a slew of broken floor tiles and jammed doors, I feared it wouldn't be possible without an industrial plasma cutter. But then we stumbled on hydroponics, and those thoughts vanished.

The hydroponics bay was well-lit, and the beds were overgrown with plant life. The bay stretched nearly half the ship's length, and at the far end was an open door. Standing between us and that door, however, was a large robot that looked like it was put together from the bargain-bin section of a junkyard.

Its head drooped, and its arms hung limply at its side. At the end of one was a hand with three digits and a thumb, while the other ended with the barrel of a gun. Scattered around it were remains of Ratters, a species of spacefaring rodents. Sometimes they worked for others as mercenaries, scouts or cheap labor, but mostly they kept to themselves and scavenged for anything they could find. I could recognize their ilk a kilometer away, even in the torn-apart state they were in. These must have been the rats that Ryx had mentioned.

"Crap." I crouched and covered my mouth, mortified the robot had heard me and was about to turn its weapon on us both. When it didn't, I looked to Oran, who was as pale as I'm sure I was, and whispered. "Maybe it's offline?"

He shook his head. "Do you want to chance it?"

"For Progenitor tech, you're damn skippy." Though my words sounded brave, I was hardly eager to die. I did have to will myself forward. I needed that flight log, and on some level, I didn't want to fail my viewers either. I could already hear them calling me all sorts of names if I backed down. Coward. Fake. Boring.

I eased into hydroponics, and the robot remained statuesque. Since there were three rows of walkways between the plant beds and it was in the center one, I hooked left and waved Oran over. He hesitated but followed.

We got halfway down the bay when a low hum filled the air followed by heavy thuds of metal on metal. I deluded myself for a full nanosecond into thinking that the robot wasn't powering up, but then its synthetic voice cut through my soul.

"Oxygen consumption irregularity detected. Guests have arrived." It said this three times over, and I could hear it shifting in place, probably trying to decide which way to go. Then its voice blasted throughout the ship from unseen speakers. "All guests are welcome. All guests please report to hydroponics for cake. And ice cream."

Oran dug his fingers into my shoulder. I shrugged him off with a glare. Neither one of us dared to speak, and neither one of us had breathed a lick since that monstrosity had come to life. I wasn't sure which way to go, but when I heard it plodding toward the rear of the ship, I scurried quietly toward the front. I peeked around the edge of some plants and saw the robot disappear down the aft corridor.

"Come on. We don't have much time," I said.

"Are you crazy?" he hissed, brow furrowed. "You want to stay with that thing looking for us?"

I gave him an incredulous look. "We're not leaving the way we came in. Where else are we going to go?" He didn't reply, so I finished the argument. "Exactly. Let's get to the cockpit, grab the logs, and find another way out."

"I hope you know what you're doing."

"Me too." With that, we darted out of hydroponics. The passage turned a few times, and along the way to the cockpit, we saw a lot of missing wall sections, jury-rigged systems and ransacked rooms. Though we didn't hear the robot's heavy steps, it continued to promise cake and ice cream at regular ten-second intervals over the ship's speakers.

A dozen such announcements later, my sanity waned, but it found a bolster of strength when we reached the cockpit. I even got a glimmer of hope for an awesome discovery and kickass story to tell.

Once inside, I was surprised at how little of the original cockpit remained. Seats for the crew, controls, and navigation computers had all been ripped out. There was a mattress nearby, along with a dusty makeshift table and scattered personal effects covered in dirt. The ultra-plex windows had been covered with metal sheets and welded into place. Why someone wouldn't want to look outside was beyond me, but the two most puzzling things were the skeleton and an artifact sitting on a pedestal next to it.

This device had a white surface with a high-gloss finish. Numerous indentations in the outer skin exposed black metal underneath with electric-blue circuitry all across. A barrel protruded from one end, and there was a handle with a trigger at the other. As intriguing as this find was, my immediate focus was on the body.

"I wonder who this guy happened to be," I said, inching forward.

"Pilot?" Oran replied. "Careful. You don't want to turn something on and have that robot know where we are."

His point was a good one. There were a few intact computers on the walls, but if I tinkered with them, it could bring unwanted attention. Instead, I turned my attention to a dusty backpack next to our deceased friend. From it I pulled out a small box about as wide as my hand is long.

"Score," I said with a large grin. "Flight recorder."

"Can you bring it up?"

I tried the buttons on its side, but as I feared, the recorder's screen stayed dark. That wasn't surprising, given its age. But it did look in good shape overall. As I stuffed it into my satchel, I said, "It's dead for now, but Tolby might be able to work his magic and get it running."

"Hang on a minute," Oran said. "Why do you get to hold it?"

"Because I found it."

"And I'm standing right next to you."

"And?"

"And you were about to head off in the completely wrong direction this morning. You wouldn't even be standing here if it weren't for me."

His tone bordered on hostile, and for a moment, I thought about unhooking my axe. "Relax," I said. "I said you'd get a share of what we found, but someone has to carry it. If it makes you feel better, you can hold that thing on the pedestal."

"Maybe I will," Oran said after a grunt. He whipped out his omniscanner, and the little green box went to work. A blue light shot out of its top end and bathed the artifact in light. "Don't touch. It'll take a moment to get a detailed scan."

"I didn't plan on it," I said, circling the device and noting that its skin was as blemish-free as I'd ever seen on anything else. Not a single nick or scratch could be found, which wasn't something I would've expected in such a dump of a ship.

"Got anything yet?" I asked.

"The back is hollow," he said. "I'm not sure how you open it, but since it's not giving any power readings, I'm guessing it's missing fuel or a battery of some kind."

"Any idea how old it is?"

"Not a clue. But as far as tech goes, it's beyond anything a crew five hundred years prior would have had. Honestly, I wouldn't be surprised if it surpasses our own tech. The intricacy of what I'm seeing inside is mind-boggling."

"There's no telling what this is worth then," I said, my eyes locked on the find. "Maybe there will be some logs on the flight recorder that can shed some light on this thing."

Oran nodded. "Hopefully, but we should get moving before that robot finds us."

He reached for the artifact, and he was only a hair away from taking it before I grabbed his arm and pulled it away. Oran's eyes were as big as a spiral galaxy, and I directed his gaze to a set of wires running from a plate underneath the artifact to a computer just underneath. "Sensor pad."

Oran whipped out his omniscanner again and put it to use. "It's taking weight measurements about every second."

"Weight? What for?"

"Maybe he was expecting something to change."

"Or maybe it's an alarm," I said. "That psycho robot back there was hell-bent on guarding the place."

"What do you want to do?"

"We can't leave it," I said. "It could be worth a fortune. A fortune's fortune."

The robot's distant voice interrupted our conversation. "Please note unaccounted guests will be reprimanded. With death. And no ice cream. All guests should now report to hydroponics for proper disintegration."

"No point then in forming a committee. I'm grabbing it," Oran said. "If there's an alarm, we'll have to hightail it."

I held up a finger. "One sec. I've got an idea."

I bolted over to the boxes of junk, and after briefly rummaging around them, I found an old coupler attached to a servo that looked like it was about the same size as the artifact. I tossed it in my hand a couple of times as I visually compared the two. Then, in one smooth motion, I snatched the artifact while at the same time rolling the coupler onto the scale.

My hands trembled as I realized I was holding the device, and even better, the world hadn't exploded.

"Cake," I said with a smile brighter than a supernova.

Alarms blared, and the door to the cockpit slammed shut.

CHAPTER FOUR

I stuffed the artifact into my satchel and rammed the cockpit door full steam. Though I pushed with every fiber of my soul, the stupid door didn't open. It didn't even budge when I screamed at it to do so. Locked doors never did seem to listen to a good screaming, so I probably should have tried something else.

"Oh god, we're going to die," Oran said before biting down on a knuckle and freezing in place.

"Gnawing your fingers isn't going to get us out of here!" I yelled. My eyes frantically searched the area for something I could use. Then I noticed one of the wall panels near the door was missing. I lunged for it, hoping the door's opening mechanism could be reached. Sadly, it couldn't, but I did see the next best thing: the hydraulic lines.

I had my ice axe readied in a flash. It took a few tries with it, but I managed to puncture the lines. Black, viscous liquid squirted out of the wall, and thankfully, the sight of it spurred Oran into action. Together we pushed against the door, and it slid open.

We raced down the corridor as I called Tolby. "I hope you're done because we've got trouble."

Tolby's reply was filled with static. "Are those alarms? What did you do?"

We rounded a corner, and at the other end of the corridor stood the robot. It stared at us with a bright red eye, and its barrel pointed at our heads. We both lunged back the way we'd come an instant before the wall behind us was showered with metal slugs.

"Might have pissed off a homemade sentry bot," I said as we took off in the other direction.

"Have you tried talking to it?" Tolby asked. "Maybe it's misunderstood."

"It's not misunderstood!"

"Well if you haven't talked to it, how do you know? I mean, you did set off the alarms. Maybe it was trying to sleep."

"It's trying to kill us!" As wonderful of a pilot and friend that Tolby was at the time, his inability to see the bad in anyone couldn't have picked a worse moment to drive me crazy. "I need a pickup like yesterday!"

"Copy. I'm on the way. Try not to die."

"Believe me, I'm trying."

Oran and I reached a junction, and not knowing which way to go, we arbitrarily ran left. The robot's loud thumps pounded in my ears and grew louder every second. For such a pile of junk, the damn thing moved fast. With each stride and large gulp of air, I anticipated being shot through the back.

"I told you we should've brought our guns!" Oran yelled.

As much as I would have liked to have one at this point, wishing for mine wasn't going to make it materialize in my hands. "Ryx never would have helped us if we had," I said. "His culture thinks they're tools of evil spirits."

"Yeah, well, we're going to join those evil spirits soon if our luck runs out."

I couldn't argue with that. We rounded another corner, and I took it as gracefully as a newborn fawn cast out on a frozen pond. Water had pooled on the floor, and my feet came out from under

24

me. I managed to push myself up, but a single stride into my run shot lightning pain up my leg.

The robot came into view. "Ankle sprain detected. Lobotomy subroutine initiated. Please standby."

"The hell I will." I limped down the hall as fast as I could. Oran was easily fifteen meters ahead of me, and other than a sympathetic glance in my direction, he didn't come to my aid.

The droid leveled its gun at me. I turned away, gritting my teeth. A loud whirring sound blasted down the hall, but no metal slugs flew, and I didn't gain a new ventilation system in my body.

"Guests are not allowed to exit without proper incineration. Containment procedures initiated." It started moving toward me again, but within a step or two, it slowed dramatically, and its gait made it look as if it were drunk.

Whether the robot was suffering from degraded power cells or some other malfunction, I didn't have the slightest clue, but I was grateful nonetheless. Ahead of me, the hatch at the end of the corridor began to slide shut. It moved slowly, with deep groans and a horrid screech. Oran made it through, but it didn't look like I would. I redoubled my efforts and ignored the fire racing through my ankle. As the door was about to close, I jumped forward as if my life depended on it.

Guess it was a good thing I never did track.

The door clamped down on half my chest and my shoulder, pinning me to its frame. Talk about rotten luck. Maybe I shouldn't have broken that chain letter. Anyway, I tried squirming through the door, but it was useless. "Oran! Help!"

Oran spun around and dashed back to me. "Why'd you have to go and do something like this?" he said, pulling my arm hard enough to nearly take it from its socket.

"Needed more of a challenge."

Oran didn't even crack a slight grin. Guess he was devoid of any morbid sense of humor. He tried to pull me through, but when he checked over my shoulder, he stopped, and his face drained of color.

"I'll cut your satchel," he said, whipping out a knife. "Maybe that will give you enough room to get through."

I cringed, hoping he didn't miss. "Be fast."

It was over in a flash. He sliced through the leather strap, and my satchel slipped from my shoulder and landed a hair behind my feet. He whispered an apology; I didn't understand why until he snatched the satchel and ran away.

My heart dropped, and my eyes watered. I hated that I couldn't wipe away my tears and hated even more that I was going to die sobbing. Not the way I'd ever expected to go. Then again, I thought I'd at least make it to thirty—hell, twenty-five.

"Thank you for your cooperation," the robot said. "Ice cream will be served after deboning is complete."

With a set jaw, I used my feet to push against the door and launched myself backward, freeing myself of the pin. I yanked my axe free of my belt and spun to meet my killer. If I was going to die, I decided I'd at least die defending myself instead of being a hapless victim.

The robot was only a couple of meters away when I came around. It stretched its clawed hand toward me, and I took a swing at it with my axe. Instead of a satisfying dismemberment, or even a good debilitating chop, all that resulted from my attack was the clang of metal against metal as the blade bounced off.

"Well, that didn't work," I said, backpedaling.

"Violence is not nice," the robot said.

It lunged forward with surprising speed. I drove forward, ducking as I went by to get under that claw. I was fast, but not quite fast enough. The robot managed to get a small grip on my collar, but fortunately, it tore as I went by.

The robot whirled around, and I took off running back the way Oran and I had originally come. Sadly, with my gimpy ankle, I wasn't fast limping through the ship. I made it past the cockpit without incident, but when I entered hydroponics, my day went from terrible to total crap storm.

At the far end of hydroponics, another junkyard robot lumbered at me. It moved faster than the one I'd ditched, and although it didn't sport a gun, it looked strong enough to rip apart a bulkhead like tissue paper. Worst of all, I knew I'd never outrun it.

"This is so not fair!" I said, backing and wishing that somehow reality would change and I'd instantly wind up safe in bed or my gun would appear in my hand.

I caught a glimpse of a loose floor panel to my left. I darted to it, worsening my ankle in the process, and using my axe, I popped it out of the fittings that held it down. Beneath was the safety grate that sat above the grav tile, but there was enough room in the gaps to slide the point of my axe down into it. I never was a believer in any sort of god, but I'll be damned if I didn't pray my little heart out that this idea would work.

I kept a half pace away from the grav tile while resting my foot on my axe's handle. I don't know how I managed to stand still and not pee myself as that robotic killing machine came stomping toward me, but I did. As the robot stepped onto the exposed tile to tear me limb from limb, I slammed my foot down on the axe handle.

The point dug deep into the tile's delicate circuitry. Sparks flew in all directions, and the robot crumpled on the tile as if the unseen hand of God had smashed it from the heavens with a vengeance. My axe flew to the center of the tile as well and fused together with the robot's remains. The entire twisted mess then shot straight up, punching a hole through the ceiling.

I staggered back, grateful I hadn't been yanked into the mess. I hadn't planned on losing my axe, but it was a small price to pay for staying alive. I limped out of hydroponics, thankful I was almost at the airlock.

On the next corner, I nearly fell face first when I stopped as fast as I could. My satchel was lying next to the wall nearby, but more important, there was a large section of floor missing and bloody goo dripping from the panels above. I wasn't sure if I was sad or glad that Oran had met such a grisly end, since he'd left me to die. Maybe both.

I snatched my satchel off the ground and checked the contents. The flight recorder was still inside, along with the artifact we'd found on that pedestal. Off I went again, my heart singing with joy as I was close to the exit.

The moment I reached the airlock, I pounded on the controls to get it to cycle, but nothing happened. A new, digitized, feminine voice echoed through the halls, and what it said struck far more fear in me than that first stupid robot ever had. "Warning. Airlock cycling not permitted with alien artifact missing. Please stand by and a sentry will be with you to assist."

"What?" I screamed. "There's more of you?"

To my shock, the female answered. "Negative. There is only one of me. There are, however, three operational sentries headed your way. Please have artifact available and free of blood, bone, and gore. Have a nice day."

"Oh god, this can't be happening."

"God says that yes, this is happening."

I swore at the voice and swore again when the panel went dead. I furiously punched the controls again, but it only took a dozen panic-filled hits to realize they'd been remotely disabled.

I darted to the outer hatch and tried to push it open, but it didn't give. Maybe if I'd had my axe I could've pried my way out or hacked away to get to the hydraulics, but I didn't. All I had was my nanomachete, and it was made for vegetation, not steel.

I opened a comm to Tolby and prayed he'd have an answer. "Tolby, I'm stuck inside, and there's a ton of homemade robots trying to kill me. Where are you?"

"On the way," he replied. "Five minutes. Tops."

"If you don't get here in sixty seconds and somehow rip this hatch open, I'm going to be torn limb from limb!"

"Your ship won't go any faster!"

"Rub the elephant!"

"I rubbed your damn elephant already!"

I groaned and wished rubbing it more would help. Sadly, luck doesn't work like that. I'm not sure about the minimum required amount of time between luck recharges, but I know it's more than a half hour. "Any chance you know how to hotwire an old airlock?"

"No, but I'll have the computer look it up and send you the instructions. Colony ship from the *Vela* was a Gorgon series, right?"

"I think so."

Five agonizing seconds later, my data pad lit up as the message came in. It stopped my heart: Manual cycling of airlocks on a Gorgon Series IV colony ship can be accomplished in forty-two simple steps. Approximate time to completion: eighteen minutes.

My throat tightened. "Airlock is out, Tolby. I need something else."

"Give me half a second," he said. His voice felt as tense as the muscles in my back. "Okay. I've got an idea—might work."

"Tell me!"

"Engine room," he said. "Overload the reactor. It'll open all hatches to the outside in an effort to vent the heat. AI can't override that."

"You want me to make the ship go critical?"

"You have a better idea?"

I shook my head and ran my gimpy butt toward the aft of the ship. Along the way, Tolby was kind enough to send my datapad the fastest route to get to the engine room, which had to be updated twice because of broken grav tiles.

Thankfully, the door to the engine room slid open without a fuss. Between the loud thuds of my heart in my chest, however, I was pretty sure I could hear the faint thumps of incoming robots echoing down the hall.

Once inside the engine room, I spent a hot second at the door's controls and locked the door behind me. I figured the ship AI could unlock it but hoped Fate would smile upon me enough that it couldn't.

"All right. I'm here," I said, taking in the scene before me. "What do I do?"

"Reactor controls should be—"

"Got a problem here," I said, cutting him off. "The reactor isn't online."

"What do you mean it's not online? That's not possible."

"Well, it is," I replied. "The fuel cells are dark as can be, but there's some sort of battery-looking thing hooked up to them."

"Hooked up how?"

I hurried over to what I was about to describe. Next to the reactor was a haphazardly slapped-together system that was obviously made from a number of parts from inside the ship. However, plugged into the middle of that system was a cylinder as long as my hand and half that thick. Across its surface was an intricate web-like pattern, and I knew right then and there that it was related to the artifact we'd found earlier.

"Tolby, you're never going to believe this," I said, amazed at what I was looking at. "I think this ship is powered by Progenitor tech."

"Just get out of there, and we can talk about it later!"

"How?"

"If whatever you're staring at is powering the ship, it should still be able to cause the reactor to meltdown if you turn up the juice."

"Are you crazy? I'm not blowing this thing up. It's got Progenitor tech!"

"No, you think it does," Tolby replied. "And is that worth your life? Besides, the AI will try to stop the explosion, but not before venting procedures are initiated. It should be fine."

"I'm not losing this thing on 'should,' Tolby!"

A heavy thud against the engine door ended the conversation. Whatever hesitations I had quickly went out the window when I realized a robot was on the other side, trying to get in.

I darted to the nearby engine console and prayed it still worked. Did it? Of course not. So, I moved on to the contraption that housed the alien cylinder, searching for something I could use. Thankfully, there was a dial near the base that looked like it was part of a regulator on the makeshift power supply.

I twisted the dial as far as it would go. Instantly, the engine room sprang to life. Long-dead lights shone with the fury of a thousand suns before exploding. A loud hum filled the air, and the viewport into the reactor's heart was a swirl of blue energy. The cylinder glowed a bright orange, and the air around it shimmered.

A klaxon blared, and the female AI spoke. "Warning. Danger. Reactor critical. You now have sixty seconds to reach a minimum safe distance."

"What did it say?" Tolby shouted, his fear palpable.

"It said in a minute this place is going to be a vapor cloud the size of Nebraska."

I caught a glimpse of movement out of the corner of my eye and jumped sideways. A robotic claw flashed in front of my eyes, nearly taking my head from my shoulders. My robot assailant recovered, and though it was smaller than the other two robots I'd encountered, it looked no less deadly.

Two hatches at the rear of the engine room shot open before it could advance. Light and fresh air poured in from the outside and gave hope to my soul.

"Ciao," I said, sprinting for the exit for all I was worth.

The robot bolted after me. Stabs of fire raced through my leg with every stride, but I didn't dare slow. I jumped out the hatch the moment I could, only to sail through the air, three meters above the ground.

"Oh sh—" was all I got out before I hit the ground and tumbled. I rolled, bruising every bit of my body. When I stood, my vision wobbled and blood ran into my eyes and down my face. The world felt muted and surreal.

"What's going on?" Tolby asked. "I'm two minutes out."

His words snapped me out of my daze. "Stay clear, Tolby!"

"But—"

"I said stay clear!"

I glanced over my shoulder to see the robot standing at the hatch. It faded back into the ship a moment later. Perhaps it didn't think it could get down safely, or perhaps it was going to try to stop the reactor from exploding. Either way, the impending mushroom cloud was my biggest concern. Sadly, my ankle could no longer support any weight, and I was reduced to hopping on one foot. I wouldn't get far on that.

Since I couldn't run, I decided to do the one thing I could: float. I threw myself into the river and allowed myself to be swept downstream. The current was faster than I'd anticipated, not that I was complaining. I did my best to keep my feet pointed in the direction I was traveling, but as the river twisted and built into rapids, that was easier said than done.

I was about to look behind me when the world turned white.

CHAPTER FIVE

Death is the black hole of life. There's no escaping it. You can never actually see what it's like without crossing the event horizon. And ever since death's discovery, beings from across the universe have had countless thoughts on what the afterlife would be like, assuming there was one.

The Uraki of Silmar VII believe that this life is a play and we've all forgotten our lines. Sadly, they say that our director is out to lunch. Death is simply exit, stage left, where we get to see the script before getting tossed back on stage, only to suffer from stage fright so badly that we forget our lines yet again. Repeat ad nauseam.

I'm not sure how much I buy that, especially when a large portion of their religious views revolved around talking stars—and not the entertainment type. I mean the giant fusion reactors hanging in the sky. I mean, really, talking stars? What would they chat about anyway? What galaxy has the best supermassive black hole? Who can burn through hydrogen the fastest? Silly.

Anyway, if the Uraki's view of death were even partially correct, it would explain why I couldn't remember a thing when I realized I was lying on my back, watching fuzzy clouds drift above. I'd died and been reborn and somehow lost my script.

After I realized I didn't believe in reincarnation, I briefly entertained the theory that I must have slipped and knocked my head while hiking somewhere. That theory, however, crashed harder than a whale hitting the ground at terminal velocity when I noticed my legs were partially in a river and a water-logged satchel was attached to my hip. At that point, it all came flooding back.

"Tolby, I'm alive!" I said, laughing. "Can you believe it?"

He didn't answer, and I quickly realized why. My glasses were gone, and with them, my primary comm with him as well as my feed. The foremost annoyed me, but the latter dug at me a hundred-fold more. Hopefully, I could re-establish a link to my channel. Maybe the explosion and my sudden offline status would grant me more viewers as word would spread that I might have been atomized, but I really feared that by the time I got reconnected, everyone would have left.

I dug into my satchel and pulled out my tablet. I was about to establish a comm with Tolby to tell him where I was when my ship flew overhead, made a sharp U-turn, and landed nearby. I'd barely limped a couple of paces before my ship's ramp descended and Tolby rocketed out.

Powerful legs drove his half-ton of feline bulk faster than I'd ever seen the big guy go. The wind swept back his white, tiger-striped fur from his face, and his emerald-green eyes glistened with worry and relief. Before I got a hand up to stop him, he hoisted me over a meter off the ground so our eyes were level before he assaulted my cheeks with a massive tongue bath that was equal parts scratchy and slobbery.

"I thought you were dead!" he shouted. His eyes went fierce and his ears flattened. A growl escaped his lips, and he tightened his claws in my hair. "Don't ever do that again!"

"You said to blow the reactor, remember?"

"I said start a meltdown so you could escape, not nearly blow yourself up by not giving the AI time to shut it down."

"Yeah, well, that part wasn't intended. Is there anything left of the ship?"

Tolby shook his head. "Not from what I could see. Just a huge, smoldering crater. Did you at least manage to save anything other than yourself?"

I pulled out the artifact from my satchel and showed it off. "Got this."

Tolby's striped tail went wild. "By the Plancks! Do you really think it's Progenitor?"

"I think so, but we'll need some help checking it out," I replied, starting for the ship. "Let's get out of here and see what we can do about that."

Tolby helped me along as my ankle throbbed. I knew I only had to suck up the pain for a little longer until I could take some medinites to help repair the damage and stick the thing in a boot for a day.

A couple of minutes later, we both took our respective places inside my ship. Tolby jumped into the pilot's seat (which, thankfully, was highly adjustable to account for his three-meter height), and I plopped down in the space for the copilot. Yes, I can fly, thank you very much, but Tolby really likes my Raptor, and as long as he was happy playing chauffeur, I was happy to pass the time chasing leads on the computers or working on building up my orbital station on my game of SpaceVille.

"I'm so enthused I should compose a symphony worthy of the gods," he said, head bouncing to whatever magnum opus he was working on in his head. He stopped his moves suddenly and turned toward me. "What happened to the human you'd hired earlier?"

"He took a wrong step, and a broken grav tile killed him."

Tolby cringed, and I cringed, too. I still wasn't sure if Oran had left me because he felt he couldn't save me or if he was an opportunist that took advantage of the situation I'd been in. I mostly leaned to the latter.

"Maybe we should've taken this slower. I could've helped after working on your ship."

"There were Ratters. Might not have found anything if we'd waited."

Tolby's ears twitched. "Ratters? Odd for them to be this far out."

"Dead ones, but I'm sure more are on the way. We should get out of here before they think we killed their friends." My gaze drifted to the floor where there was a mini bottle missing its top, with remnants of a glowing, orange liquid inside. "You amped?"

"You mean did I enhance my wit and reflexes after getting a dire distress call from my adoptive family?" he said, eyes flashing over to me with energy. "Damn right I did."

"I thought those were expensive."

"Losing you would be more so," he said.

I didn't say anything.

"What's wrong?" Tolby asked.

"Nothing," I said, which of course was categorically untrue.

"So, everything," he said with a grin.

"Can't be good for you is all," I said. "I mean, have you seen the people—"

"We've been down this before," he said, waving me off with a laugh. "I'm not a person. Don't be jealous that my impeccable physiology lets me partake in things you can only dream of."

"Fine," I said.

"In other words, you're still irked," he said, still grinning. "Look, we've—I've been making this stuff and more since before your great-grandparents were even alive. And if we're ever being attacked by a herd of Crysthian dragons, you'll thank me for my lightning-quick reflexes."

"I don't plan on going to that place," I said. "Too cold for my likes, not to mention the atmosphere that'll eat through a spaceship in under an hour if your shields fail. That just doesn't appeal to my sensibilities. I don't care what rumors treasure hunters cook up about the place."

The conversation died, so I popped open a compartment to my left and pulled out my spare pair of glasses. They had dark brown rims instead of the light grey my originals had and that I liked better, but if I were going to update my audience, I couldn't be picky about what the camera was built into. A few micro-button pushes and voice commands later, I was logged back into my channel.

My jaw dropped when I saw my audience had grown to well over three hundred. The chat display was a whirl of speculation. Most positive. A few hoped I'd been vaporized and my last vid feed would end up on a new dumb streamer award reel.

I sucked in a breath to compose myself. I had to be professional, but still fun. This was a golden opportunity to give my audience what they wanted—excitement, adventure, and to be part of something historic. I flipped on the feed as Tolby took off. "Well, that's one to write home about," I said, pointing my glasses at my face and smiling for the camera. "First off, Mom, Dad, I'm okay. Little wet, as you can see, but I promise to be more careful next time."

"We are not doing that again, Mr. and Mrs. Adams!" Tolby added.

I chuckled. "Okay, so he's probably right about that. But we did come away from our find with a healthy appreciation for swift rivers and—drum roll please—we scored ourselves a Progenitor artifact!"

Chat was less impressed than I'd hoped, though I did catch a few people thinking I might be the real deal. One user, however, rutabaga113, managed to not only spam the chat with the same message a dozen times over, but also convinced a few more of what he had to say. His words were, and I quote with misspellings and all, "fake fak faek fake. lets c the wrekage like shed relly blow up a ship."

"Fine," I said with a growl. "I'll show you proof. Tolby, circle the crater."

My furry pilot immediately banked my ship and made a wide circle about two kilometers over the lifeboat, or rather where it hadn't been. There was a good-sized hole in the meemar forest almost a hundred meters across. The trees along the edge were stripped of their bark, and in the center of the hole was a crater that still smoked.

"See?" I said, proud that I'd survived but annoyed I had to prove it. "That's the real deal right there. Tolby, how big do you think the mushroom cloud was?"

"Big enough to give me a heart attack. I'm glad I have three."

Rutabaga113 and his detractors remained silent, and I leaned back in my chair with a smile. Dakota one, naysayers zero. But my euphoria faded and an unsettling sensation gripped my stomach and threw itself a big enough party that I felt sick. That crater was more than the remains of a colony ship; it had nearly been my grave.

"Be back soon," I said with a heavy sigh and killed the feed to my channel.

Tolby looked at me with concern. "What's wrong?"

"This was supposed to be more adventurous."

"If this was boring, I don't want to see what you had in mind."

"No, I mean, more fun."

Tolby smiled, showing off two rows of sharp teeth. "Let's celebrate. This find is worthy of one."

"There's something else," I said, drawing back the corners of my mouth. "Found the flight recorder. If we can get it working, we might be able to use it to find the *Vela*."

He never said it, but I was pretty sure at that point he would've married me in an instant if he could have.

CHAPTER SIX

When people first figured out how to blast themselves into outer space, they had a lot of funny thoughts about it. First, they thought they'd find aliens quickly. That, of course, was nonsense as every spacefaring race knows to play hide-and-seek with upcoming species, and when your technology is light-years ahead of the seeker, it's always been easy to stay hidden until you can jump scare a hapless astronaut in the funniest possible way. Six hundred years later, the video of Xibbich plastering his blobby body across Captain Dack Piaga's cockpit, causing the poor man to shower his navigator in a cold double latte, still wins best comedic short at the Persean Galactic Comedy Festival.

Second, there was a lot of speculation as to what constituted must-have gear for sailing the stars. There was talk about everything from towels to cyanide capsules. The latter was for stranded situations, obviously, and while the foremost was a bit of a joke, it's turned out to be a handy thing to have, though I'd argue my fedora is more so. But in the nineteen months I've zipped around the stars—on account of Dad making me wait a full year from learner's permit to license—the most important piece of equipment I've carried with me has been my PEN (Personal Environmental Nano-manipulator).

Well, I usually carried it with me. I'd accidentally left it in my ship when we got to DD-3123.

Anyway, it's a handy little thing that looks almost exactly like the fancy ballpoint pens of the late 5th century PHS, but instead of only being able to scribble notes on paper, this bad boy can make changes to almost anything on the molecular level. Not only can it do that, but it can do it very quickly. Need to fuse some wiring? Piece of cake. Locked yourself out of your cockpit and the entry pad AI is giving you trouble? Zap the circuitry and force open the door. Catch your little brother rummaging around your room when you're gone? Jab it through his skull. Okay, don't jab it through his skull, but you can at least threaten him with it.

Best of all, if you have a compatible tablet, you can hook your PEN up to it and perform detailed scans on anything in the galaxy to get an idea of what it is and how it works. Unless, of course, it's a Progenitor artifact. In which case it's useless, and that was something I was coming to grips with as Tolby and I flew back to civilization. Sadly, my channel viewers weren't as understanding and once again, their numbers were dwindling. I couldn't blame them. It wasn't very exciting watching someone play with half a ball.

"Gah, still nothing," I said, tossing my PEN into the cup holder next to me with disgust. For the last hour, I'd been studying this blaster-looking thing with nada to show for my efforts. My foot was killing me, too. I couldn't wait to get home so I could tend to it properly.

"Take a break," Tolby said as we came out of subspace. The view outside shifted from a swirling vortex of greys and arcs of yellow and green to a gorgeous view of Uranus. I'd always liked how its red rings contrasted against the blues of both the giant and the outer rings. But what I've loved the most about the place was that it has long been the home of Midd's, birthplace of the best root beer floats this side of the galactic bulge.

Now there are some who foolishly argue that the root beer float is not the best beverage available (let's not even get into the heretics that don't like it at all). But what other drink has stood the test of time like it has? Beer? Wine? Water? Yeah right. There's a reason why President Janson, 72nd president of the United States, demanded one at every staff meeting. There's a reason why Napoleon lost the Battle of Waterloo when he didn't have his. And there's a reason why that Christ guy kept changing water into floats when he'd crash parties. Because the root beer float is the ambrosia of the gods. That's why. So, it's plain to see why I had insisted on us dropping by to get one.

Tolby slid our ship sideways and into range of one of the two hundred docking arms coming off of Midd's. They latched onto our starboard hatch with a muffled thump, and Tolby hit a button to power down the engines. When they did, the interior lights flickered.

"Still haven't figured out why it's doing that," he said apologetically, but truth be told, the lights had been doing it for so long I barely noticed. Besides, it wasn't his job to fix every little thing in the ship, even if he liked to play mechanic. "I'll go in this time. Would you enjoy the usual?"

I flipped him my credstick. "Yeah. Colossal Float. French Vanilla. Two cherries on top. Thanks."

"Anytime." With that he left the cockpit.

"Two cherries!" I repeated as the door slid shut. I leaned back in my seat with a satisfied smile. As I waited for my best furry to return, I turned the device over in my hand, wishing I could learn something about where it had come from and what it did.

I went back to using my PEN on the artifact to pry its secrets and hoped that if I could find the *Vela*, I could find even more treasure like the one I was currently looking at. I mean, surely there was more Progenitor tech on board, right?

"Root beer is served."

I twisted in my seat with a stupid, elated look, but it quickly fell when I saw that the cup Tolby was carrying wasn't even a half liter. "Why does that colossal not look very colossal?" I asked, trying not to sound crass. I was sure there would be a good explanation for it. Like they ran out of cups. Or root beer. Or there was a shootout and this was all Tolby could save before diving back through the hatch. Then I noticed his other paw was empty. "And why didn't you get yourself something?"

Tolby handed me the float. "All I could afford. Your stick was declined."

"That can't be right," I said after a slurp. I logged the computer into my bank to check. "I paid...last month...I think. Besides, there's like five accounts on that stick."

"I tried all five," he replied. "All maxed. I used what little I had on me to get that and refuel the warp core."

"Oh damn. I'm sorry you had to do that. I'll get it straightened out and pay you back."

"I know."

I was glad he let me save face. We both knew I'd been hurting for work and the mistake wasn't on the bank's end, but mine. My stomach rumbled, and I knew I was probably going to lose a kilo or two this coming week as my meals were going to be lean, especially if I wanted to make rent—and if I was being honest, I wasn't sure I was going to make that either.

CHAPTER SEVEN

If you take an extended hiatus from bathing, there are varying levels of stink you can have ranging from a mild funk after a bit of running all the way up to "Who left the heat on in the morgue?" Personally, I don't like to be on the scale whatsoever, but going on expeditions into hostile ships and thwarting the plans of a lobotomizing scrapbot tends to work up a sweat. So, you can see why I insisted on going to my apartment, so I could soak in the tub before we did anything else. It also gave me a chance to put my first aid skills to good use and tend to my ankle.

My apartment was a cozy place built on the outskirts of Briggs City, Mars. It had the most gorgeous view of the circular plain, Chryse Planitia, I'd ever seen. Sometimes I would wonder how my neighbor, Norm, managed to live in his tiny little nine square meters of space with no view whatsoever. I mean, that's barely enough for a standing shower, let alone room for an end table. Course, the people one floor above who lived in apartments double the size of mine probably wondered how I managed, too. But since they also had four times the rent, I wasn't at all jealous.

After my interlude in the tub, I threw on some new clothes and joined Tolby in my living room. He sat on my yellow pullout sofa and had the popup table extended from the floor (awesome space saver, by the way). On that table were a handful of gadgets he'd hooked up to the colony ship's flight recorder as he tried to get it to work. On his face, Tolby wore a jeweler's loupe, which only solidified the fact that he was without a doubt the cutest spacefaring giant feline in the entire galaxy.

"Get anywhere?" I asked.

Tolby dropped the flight recorder and bounded across my mansion of an apartment. He came at me with such vigor, if we didn't have a long, established history together, I probably would've died from fright, thinking he was about to make me his midafternoon snack.

Before I could react, he grabbed me by both sides of my face and leaned his head down so his forehead touched mine. "Guess. What. I. Did!"

His eyes had more energy than a blue hypergiant, so I didn't have to guess. "You got it working."

"I GOT IT WORKING!" He lifted me off the ground and spun us around. "Do you know what this means? Do you have any idea?"

"Yeah, if you get any more excited, you're going to tear through my back," I said, realizing his claws were about to draw blood.

Tolby set me down. "Sorry. But this might be the best thing to have ever happened to me. To us!"

"So, what's on the flight recorder?"

"I don't know yet. I wanted you to be here when it was accessed for the first time."

"Thanks," I said, scratching his side. I darted to my mini-fridge, grabbed a root beer, and popped its top. "Okay. I'm ready for greatness. Let's see what there is."

Tolby fired up the flight recorder as I sat down next to him. Faded green words scrolled faster than I could read as the device booted up, and after a few seconds, the screen went blank aside from a small, blinking cursor.

"Here goes," Tolby said, sucking in some air.

I watched him type the commands with bated breath.

> *>Load FlightData.mnf*
> *Data encrypted. Input key:*

Tolby blinked. "What? That's not right."

I stared at the recorder's request thinking the Universe was playing some prank on me. "Tell me you can hack this. I mean, encryption five hundred years ago has nothing on what we can do today, right?"

Tolby's shoulders slouched. "I don't know. This thing is ancient. Not sure there's anything out there that can interface with it anymore. We'll never guess the key. It's probably sixty alphanumeric digits long."

I groaned but tried to remain positive. "Well, at least that's a step in the right direction."

"Got any ideas on what to try?"

"Not a one."

"Think Logan would know?" Tolby said.

I shrugged. "Couldn't hurt to try."

Using my tablet, I called my brother. Thankfully, he picked up the line. The hologram was tiny, but I could still see he was dressed in red-and-green plasti-armor and sporting his newest toy, the TrippMag 4000—finest stun rifle to ever grace the game fields of AllOutWar™.

"What is it, sis?" he said. "We're about to start a new round. I don't have a lot of time."

"I found a flight recorder from like five hundred years ago," I replied. "I want to see what's on it, but it's encrypted."

Logan rolled his eyes. "Please tell me you didn't 'borrow' that from a museum."

"No, thank you. I didn't," I said, feeling my skin flush. "And that was a onetime deal before. And I was eight. And it's not like I didn't give it back the next day."

"After Dad found out."

"I was going to give it back!"

"After you had already broken it."

"It's not like I meant to."

"And Mom and Dad had to pay a fortune to get it restored."

I gave a half snarl. "I thought you were about to start a game or something. Can you help me or not?"

Logan glanced over his shoulder to someone unseen and held up a finger before returning to the conversation. "Yeah, probably. What do you have?"

"It's a flight recorder from a Gorgon Series IV colony ship. Says Kiodenne on the side. Guessing it's from around the year 52 AHS." I paused for a second as Tolby whispered the next bit that I relayed to Logan. "Tolby says we need something to interface with it to decrypt the files to get by the encryption key."

"Wow, really? A Kiodenne?" Logan replied. He ran his hands through his spikey blue hair as he talked to himself, trying to figure out what to do. "Well, I've never actually worked on one of those. That's some seriously old tech. Can't believe you even have one working. Are you sure this is important? A workaround won't be cheap."

"Yeah, I'm sure," I said. "I think it'll lead to the *Vela*."

Logan shook his head and looked at me with the same sort of pity I reserve for those who can't change the positron filter on their warp drive. "Oh god. Not you too. The *Vela* is a pipedream, sis. I could probably count a dozen fake recorders I've heard about this year without trouble."

"And how many of them came from the *Vela*'s colony ship?" I said with a Cheshire grin.

"Seriously? That's where this recorder came from?"

"Yeah."

"How do you know?"

"Because I was at the crash site and the boat had *Vela*'s registration stamped on it."

"You're lying."

"I'm not."

"You're mistaken."

I beamed. "Nope."

"Damn. I don't know what to say."

"Say you know how to crack this thing's security so I can find that ship."

Logan yelled at some teammates behind him before replying. "I've got to go, but go see Pizlow. He's the owner of the Remoran Club at Callisto. He loves all things antique and is usually scouting the galaxy for new finds to add to his collection. I'd wager he can work with that flight recorder. He's a little seedy, but he owes me a favor after I debugged his inventory systems. I'll give him a call if you want and let him know you're coming by, but watch your step."

"Awesome," I replied. "Thanks for the help."

"One more thing," he tacked on. "Like I said before, cracking that flight recorder won't be cheap, and whatever you do, don't tell him where it came from. If it's really from the *Vela*, he'll want it for himself."

CHAPTER EIGHT

Finding a spot to bring my ship in at Wilan Space Station was a nightmare. The station looked like a bloated top with sixteen arms at the base for private docking, and all of them were full. There were also four massive hangar bays for personal craft like my own, but three of them were designated for use only by crew or those staying at the hotel-casino inside. That meant anyone wanting to go to the Remoran club who came from the outside like ourselves had to wait for a slip to open in the last hangar bay, and that meant Tolby and I spent nearly two hours sitting in my cockpit, staring at the crater-filled surface of Callisto and admiring the swirling clouds of Jupiter. The gas giant had always been an impressive sight, but I could only watch it so long before I was ready to eject myself into space to deal with the boredom.

"This is guest control," said a rough voice over the comm. "You're cleared for landing in Bay Four, slip 36-D. You are hereby ordered to relinquish control of your ship to our tower so we can bring you in. Understood?"

"Understood," Tolby replied. After he gave autopilot permissions to Traffic Control, he looked at me with eager eyes. "I'm joining you this time, right?"

I clutched my chest and feigned a deep hurt. "I can't believe you'd think I'd make you wait in here alone."

"Well, you did make me work on your ship while you explored the colony ship."

I reached over and patted his shoulder. "That was before I knew what it was. Anyway, from here on out, we're doing everything together. Promise."

We touched down inside the hangar bay and nestled between a couple of other ships that were larger, cleaner and more expensive than mine. My beat-up Raptor looked out of place, and although she was a fine ship, I couldn't help but feel a little jealous of whoever owned the ships next to mine. But as soon as I tracked down the *Vela* and my channel was the most popular one of all time, all that would change. Course, at that point I wouldn't have to land in a public hangar either. I could get a slip on a high-class, private docking arm. Hell, I could have my own nightclub if I wanted.

The hangar bay itself was a couple of hundred meters across, bathed in a perpetual blue light that came off the shield that allowed ships to pass in and out while at the same time protecting everything inside from the vacuum of space. The exit was at the far end, but having just hiked through treacherous jungle and dashing about a wreck filled with unstable robots, a little peaceful stroll didn't bother me one bit.

Out of the bay, we traveled down a white, circular tube toward the club. It had windows on one side that offered the same view of Jupiter I'd seen from my cockpit. We had to take a turbolift up near the top of the station, and once we exited, it wasn't much of a walk to the club. Along the way, the faint smell of exquisite food drifted in the air, and if we weren't hot on the tail of ancient tech—not to mention broke—I'd have insisted on stopping for a bite to eat at one of the fancy restaurants on this level of the station. Heaven knows my rumbling stomach would've appreciated it.

"Oh, I like this place already," Tolby said, bouncing along to the beat that came from ahead. "Can we stay a bit?"

"I don't think that will work," I replied, double-checking that my emergency cred stick was still in my pocket. "I've got to stretch this last bit of money as far as it will go. Otherwise I'm going to be selling everything I have just to eat and make rent, let alone fund an expedition."

"I find that disagreeable to say the least."

I bumped him with a hip. "When we're rich and famous, we can buy the place."

"You can have it. The only thing I want is my catamaran," he replied. The glint in his eyes told me he was serious too. He was already plotting where he'd sail it for the next three years. Given the fortune the Progenitor tech would rake in, I also wagered the catamaran he was going to buy would double as an aircraft carrier.

We passed through the double doors and took in Remoran in all her glory. A high-energy scene, with pulsating lights of orange and purple and a steady pounding of music assaulted us. The crowd was thick, and creatures from across the known galaxy filled the dance floor and vied for a spot at any of the four bars. Creatures with lots of eyes or no eyes. Creatures with spikes on most of their body or cybernetics for all of their body. But my favorite were the J'nars—a.k.a. red angels. The short ones were easily two meters in height with gorgeous shimmering tones on their wings and glowing tattoos that circle the top of otherwise bald heads (making them look like they have halos).

"Any idea where you're going?" Tolby asked as we pushed through the crowd.

"Not a clue."

"Try not to get separated then," he said, taking my hand in his giant paw.

It felt a little silly at first, as if I were a little kid being toted around by a parent, but I soon understood his concern. With all the jostling, it wouldn't take much for us to get separated, and even if he was a vertical overachiever, he could easily lose sight of me.

I stood on my tiptoes to get an idea of where some offices might be, but the crowd was too tall.

Seeing my plight, Tolby temporarily hoisted me over the crowd so I could get a better look. "What do you see?" he asked.

"I think it's over there," I said, pointing. "There's a hall that people are being kept away from. That's got to be the management offices."

Once he put me down, we pressed through the crowd, and by we pressed through, I mean Tolby used his enormous bulk to part everyone and I followed closely in his wake. When we broke free of the crowd, we found what we were looking for: a passage leading away from the main club area. It made a short run before ending at the bottom of a spiral staircase, but between us and said hall, however, were two bouncers that could easily give Tolby a run for his money. They had tree trunks for arms, on account they were part plant, and I was pretty sure either one could tear a rocket nozzle in two with their colossal hands if they wanted.

"Off limits," the one on the left said with a growl. His yellow eyes, four of them, all narrowed in unison. "Step back."

"I'm here to see Pizlow about this," I replied, whipping out the flight recorder. "He'll want to see me."

The other one chuckled, but his tone was anything but amused. "Direct. I like it. I like it enough not to smash you where you're standing. Now go."

I stood in silence, weighing my options for a response. I didn't think he was exaggerating on what he was about to do, but at the same time, I knew if I left, I wouldn't get another shot at seeing Pizlow short of sneaking in, and disco ninja I was not. "I'm Dakota Adams," I said. "Logan's brother. Pizlow is expecting me."

"Is that a fact?"

"It is."

The bouncer on the right grunted. He tightened a fist, but his friend put a hand on his shoulder. "Stay. I'll check. If I come back and she's lying, you can use her head for a tetherball."

"I'm not lying," I said as the bouncer walked off. Tolby shot me a wary look, and all I could do was shrug in return. "What? I'm not lying."

"I know, but I get the feeling he might want to make you a tetherball for the hell of it."

"Good thing I have you around," I said, smiling and nudging him with my shoulder.

A minute later, the bouncer returned. "All right, Bornu. She's telling the truth. Boss wants to see them now."

Bornu's face soured, and he thumped one fist into the other before mumbling under his breath. "Fine," he said. "You take them up."

And so the other bouncer did. Tolby and I followed him up the stairs and down another hall until we got to a sliding door at the end. Our bouncer-escort waved his hand in front of the biometric scanner, and after a pleasant, three-note set of beeps, the door whisked up and out of sight.

We stepped into an office that felt as big as a cruise ship. It was a half circle with full-length windows that looked out to Jupiter. Cool blue lights illuminated the space while soft classical music— like fifteen-hundred-year-old music—carried through the air. Scattered around the floor at regular intervals were display cases, some holding obvious artifacts from civilizations lost long ago, and others showcasing antique robots. The walls were lined with actual bookshelves, and aside from a few spaces holding sport trophies, the shelves held actual books. And since no one had real books anymore, I guessed the most recent copy Pizlow owned was at least four hundred years old.

Pizlow looked up from his desk at the far end of the room. He was so enormous he made his bodyguards look anemic. If you took a polar bear from Earth, mated it with an applegar from Urlan IV (to get the translucent claws and horns on the head), and then had him swim in a pool of steroids for a year before dipping him into some old brown paint (got to get that rust-color fur somewhere), you'd get Pizlow.

"Come, sit," he said in a surprisingly refined voice.

Tolby and I walked toward him. I tried not to gawk at everything on display along the way so I could appear professional, but when I spotted the camera from *Voyager 1*, I stopped.

"One of my prouder pieces," Pizlow said. "Dates back before your kind even set foot on another planet."

"That's an incredible find." I tore myself away and started toward him, but I didn't get far. I stopped after a few paces when I saw his marble statue of Brunah, the three-headed, warrior-hero who won freedom for his species from the gods. Well, according to the legends, that's what he did, anyway. I wasn't so interested in the myth, other than it did make a good bedtime story, but the half-meter chipped statue had to be five times as old as the pyramids. "This isn't a replica, is it?"

Even from a distance, I could see the gleam in Pizlow's eyes as he replied with pride. "Took me a while to acquire that one."

"It's amazing," I said. "There must be a hundred stories behind this piece."

"And then some."

"May you keep night away from me and day forever upon my face," I said to the statue, touching my forehead and then twice again on each shoulder. It was more for my own amusement, remembering a bit more of the mythology and customs surrounding Brunah, but I'll admit, I was thrilled to see Pizlow nod in approval out of the corner of my eye when I did all that.

"You probably get this all the time, but I'm in awe of everything you have," I said as I sat down in a black leather chair across from him. Tolby joined me in the other to my left.

Pizlow smiled with a razor grin that would make any great white jealous. "This isn't even a tenth of what I have, but certainly many of my favorites."

"And here I thought you were going to be a strict businessman."

"Business pays for the interests," he said. He leaned back and tapped a little box on the side of the desk. The classical music faded away, and sounds from an alien orchestra took its place. The music reminded me of the rainforest at night, full of insect activity. It was strangely calming, almost hypnotic.

"Let's get down to business, shall we?" he said. "I appreciate that you are genuinely interested in my collection—unlike others that pay it lip service and have no idea what they're looking at—but time is money, and I'd like to make more of it before this day is done. I understand that you are the favor Logan wants to cash in on."

I nudged Tolby, and he gently placed the flight recorder onto his desk. "We found this a little bit ago," I said. "There's some encrypted flight data I want access to. I've got nothing to do it with since it's so old."

Pizlow picked it up like a mother would her first child. His eyes were awestruck. "A Kiodenne. I haven't seen one of these in a long, long time. Before you were born."

"As you can see, it works, but I can't get to anything on it."

"What are you expecting to find?"

I shrugged. "Something. Anything. Trying to work backward and see where it came from."

Pizlow looked up from the tablet with a hefty dose of skepticism. He even grunted. "You expect me to believe you got your brother to cash in a favor with me and you don't know what you're looking for?"

"No, that's not it at all," I said. "I found it in the wreckage of a colony ship. I'm hoping it can point me back to the main ship it came from."

"A colony ship, huh?" Pizlow set the flight recorder to the side and drummed his claws next to it. The tone in his voice said my words had triggered something inside his head, and I had a bad feeling I wasn't going to like what it was. "You know, I sent some Ratters to investigate a lead I had on a crash site not long ago— could've been a site for a colony ship that this Kiodenne would've been used on. Haven't heard back from them in a while. I was going to see where they were after this."

I chuckled, nervously. So did Tolby, but he was even more obvious about it. "Small galaxy I guess," I said.

"Care to fill me in on what you found and where?"

I shrugged and whipped up a fast lie. "Dead boat near the Ghost of Jupiter. Two crew, long gone, obviously. Computers were shot so we didn't get any data. No cargo—we're hoping the good stuff is still on board where it came from."

"You seem anxious about this."

"Because I don't want you to think we had anything to do with your missing Ratters."

"What makes you say they're missing?"

The air grew stifling, and I wondered how long it would take before my skin glistened with sweat. "I don't know. I assumed is all. You did say you hadn't heard from them."

"Mmm," he said. After a bit more drumming of claws on the desk, he slid the recorder in front of him and said, "I can break this recorder's encryption without trouble. I've got an old T-800 that can act as a junction between it and a crackerjack. Should take about thirty seconds to finish. But it's going to cost you two thousand, due right now."

Even if the price was nearly all I had left, and I'd have to sell some stuff to eat later and pay rent, I was so happy I felt like an angel ushering in the heavenly host. "Thank you, from the bottom of my heart."

"There's more," he said, leaning forward. "In addition, I get half of the salvage you find and first pick at that. I'll send a couple of robots with you to keep things honest."

I jumped out of my seat and spoke before my brain caught up. "What? There's no way that's fair. I nearly died for that recorder. You can't take half my salvage."

"Truth is, Miss Adams, you're not going anywhere without that data decrypted," he said. "If you don't like my terms, find someone else. I promise they'll want ten times what I do in credits plus the same portion of salvage."

I forced myself to settle in the chair. Tolby looked worried, and truth be told, I was anxious myself. We both knew when we found the *Vela*, Pizlow would want in on the action immediately, if not outright take it all. Maybe he'd honor the business arrangement, and honestly, I couldn't be sure anyone else would be any more trustworthy either. I stuffed my hands between my legs to keep them from shaking. "Point taken," I said. "I guess splitting something is better than not finding it at all."

Pizlow grinned and stood. "That's the spirit. Follow me."

I did, and he led Tolby and me into a side room where he had a massive bank of quantum computers that lined three of the four walls. I wasn't sure what they were doing, other than making a symphony of beeps and showing a ton of programs and real-time status updates of stuff on five separate screens. He opened up a mini wall vault on the far right and from it pulled out a half-meter cable attached to a black box. He then placed it and the flight recorder near one of the computers and started playing with the black box's micro buttons. In a flash, the cable sprouted what I could only describe as three spindly, wire fingers that danced across the tablet while a fourth inserted itself into the flight recorder's one and only port.

"Looks as if this will be over even quicker than I thought," he said. "Let's take care of the rest of our transaction while we wait. Two thousand, due now."

"Sure, no problem," I replied. I reached into my pocket, and my heart stopped when I couldn't feel my emergency cred stick in it. I patted both sides of my pants several times over, and then again and again even faster as if the act would conjure the card—the money I needed—into existence. But it never materialized, and I felt my face drain of color.

"Is there a problem?" he asked.

"No."

"Because you look like you can't find something, like monies."

"I swear I had it coming in," I said, searching my pockets yet again. "We came from the ship straight through to you—"

"And nearly got trampled by the crowd," Tolby added. The fur on his back bristled, and his ears went flat before he leaned in close to me. What he then whispered I'd thought of only a nanosecond before. "Someone pickpocketed you."

"I don't take kindly to hustles," Pizlow said with a scowl. His computer beeped, and he looked down at the flight recorder. "You best pray the information on this is worth something because my fee just went up to ninety percent of your salvage."

"Ninety?" I shrieked. "That's not fair!"

"The only thing keeping it from going to a hundred..." His voice trailed as he started flipping through the recorder's encrypted data. A deep growl came from his chest, and he looked at me like a shark eyeing a wounded seal. "You didn't find this near the Ghost of Jupiter. You found it at my crash site."

God, how dumb was I? Of course, he'd know where I found it once he had the log. "Your Ratters were already dead when we got there, I swear. We didn't steal anything."

"You're chasing down the *Vela,* and you expect me to believe you wouldn't do anything to find it?"

I shook my head and held my hands up defensively. My words spilled out of my mouth faster than I could think about them. "Honest, the ship had some psycho robot sentries inside that killed them all. I had to blow it all to get away from them."

Pizlow stepped forward. His already massive bulk seemed to increase tenfold. "You destroyed my find?"

"Not me as much as the reactor did," I said, cringing.

Tolby immediately put himself between Pizlow and me. "That's far enough."

"Don't think for a moment you're the one keeping this civil," Pizlow said, glaring at Tolby. "If I wanted you as a rug, I'd have you skinned in a heartbeat."

"Try," Tolby said, flicking his claws open.

"Easy guys," I said, grabbing my bud's elbow and pulling him back. Not that I didn't appreciate his white knight attitude from time to time—especially times like this—but it did dawn on me we were still very much on Pizlow's home turf and he had a slew of bodyguards that could make things ugly, really fast. As such, negotiations were in order. "So, now that the flight recorder is ready, what do you say we split the salvage on the *Vela* fifty-fifty? That should be more than enough for both of us."

"I think not, Ms. Adams," he said, still keeping an eye on Tolby. "You've cost me a considerable sum of money already by destroying what was rightfully mine. The way I see it, not only is this flight recorder mine, but you owe me the costs of that boat and everything inside it. And since I doubt you're in a financial position to make such monetary restitution, you can work off your debt in my club. Thirty years ought to do it."

I lunged for the flight recorder. Though I managed to grab onto it, I was no match for Pizlow's vice grip. Thankfully, Tolby struck the brute across the face an instant later. His claws raked across Pizlow's cheek, drawing blood and causing the club owner to reel back and roar as he relinquished his hold.

Tolby struck out again, but this time there was a flash of light, and he bounced back, striking a force field that suddenly sprang up between him and Pizlow.

At that point, I pivoted on my heels and dashed for the exit with Tolby right behind.

"I want their bloody heads on my wall!" Pizlow bellowed.

The bouncer that had led us in was still standing by the office exit. He looked confused at first, but his brow knitted and suddenly he had a gun in one hand and was talking into a communicator with the other.

Tolby ran at the bouncer full steam as I grabbed a vase off one of the displays. I had no idea what it was worth but guessed it was more than I'd earned in my life.

"Catch," I said, tossing it at the bouncer.

The bouncer, looking more fearful at the incoming vase than if it were a charging omni-rhino, dropped both his gun and his communicator to make the catch.

Tolby and I were out the door before the bouncer could recover. I grinned and shot my big tiger buddy a glance as we raced down the stairs. "Nice swipe by the way."

Tolby snarled. "The coward would have a personal forcefield."

Once we hit the bottom of the stairs, my hope for an easy getaway sank. At the far end of the hall came two more bouncers, looking about as cordial as Pizlow had moments ago. There was no way we were getting by them, so I took the only option we had. I barged through the one and only side door between us and them, pulling Tolby along with me.

The hall we were now in stretched for twenty meters or so before ending in a set of double doors, which we blasted through. On the other side was a kitchen, full of chefs slaving away over steaming pots and mixing a plethora of doughs, sauces, and bowls. They all looked at us with shock, and one even demanded an explanation for our intrusion, but I sure as hell wasn't about to stop and give it to them.

Tolby and I dodged around counters and cooks, racing for the doors at the other end of the room. Right as we got to them, a bouncer burst through the door we'd come in and made a beeline for our position. Thankfully, the kitchen was tight, and with the cooks scrambling about, the bouncer had to slow his pursuit considerably.

We darted through the restaurant with ease. It was a lovely place with vintage wood floors and teak panels on the walls. I would wager the dim lighting usually added to the intimate ambiance, but a girl dashing by tables, tripping up two waiters with full serving trays no less, and being followed by an intergalactic tiger, probably killed whatever romantic mood the patrons were looking for. Sorry, not sorry.

When we got out, fate smiled upon us, and we bolted into an open turbo lift. It was supposed to be a fast trip down to our hangar, but I swear the thing could sense our desperation and slowed to a snail's pace. And did it have to stop on every other floor? Apparently.

By the time we got to the hangar, it was nothing short of divine intervention that we weren't immediately grabbed by security. I saw three of them detaining a girl a couple of dozen meters away who looked enough like me to warrant a stop. I felt bad that she was simply in the wrong place at the wrong time, but I wasn't about to rush to her defense. Tolby and I seized the opportunity and slipped by in all the bustle.

Unfortunately, while we'd dodged the previous group, there were at least two other pairs of security guys (and one gal) roaming the bay. We slinked. We sneaked. We even hid in landing gear housing of three separate ships to slip by, and eventually we made it to my ship and quietly got in.

"How is the whole station after us?" Tolby said as we took our spots in the cockpit.

"Pizlow owns the nightclub. I'm sure he's buddies with station security."

Tolby shook his head with a sigh. "We'll never get out of the bay. If they haven't already, they'll harden the shield so nothing can get through."

"I know," I said. I popped open the compartment to my right and held up the Progenitor artifact. "But we have this."

"What are you going to do? Throw it at them?"

"Bargain our way out."

"But—"

"Trust me on this," I said. "Start her up and take off. I'll handle the rest."

Tolby's face took on a myriad of stress. "I hope you know what you're doing."

"Me too," I replied with a half grin.

Tolby hit the button to fire up the engines, and our ship leaped five meters off the deck. In an instant, the usual blue tones to the shield ahead turned red, and our comm came alive.

"Raptor class vessel in 36-D. Return to deck immediately. The shield is hardened and a lockdown is in effect."

Tolby started to reply over the comm, but I hit a button and quickly took over. "Negative," I said, buckling the five-point harness to my seat. "This is an emergency egress. We're leaving right now."

The next reply wasn't from one of the station's traffic controllers, but Pizlow. I wasn't surprised. I was counting on it. "You're never leaving, Dakota, without full payment to me on what you owe," he said. "Don't take anyone else with you in your stupidity."

I opened a video stream to go along with our conversation and held up the Progenitor artifact so everyone on the line could see it. "Check this out," I said. "That recorder wasn't the only thing I found. We're leaving, and if that shield doesn't give and we blow, you're going to lose this, too, genuine Progenitor tech."

"Looks like a piece of junk to me," Pizlow said. "I'm calling your bluff. You're not getting away."

"Well, you know where I'll be headed so you might as well let us out now and not destroy everything," I replied. "But we're going through this shield in ten seconds."

61

At that point, Tolby cut in. "Is that what made the ship explode?"

I could've kissed him right there, and although we were stretching the truth a bit as to what made the reactor on the colony ship go critical, they didn't know that. "Ha! That's right, Pizlow. This baby is what caused your find to go nuclear. You guys got five seconds to drop that shield."

"Not going to happen," Pizlow growled. "You're not the type to kill a bunch of people anyway."

"That's on you. I'm leaving."

"Sir?"

The last voice wasn't Pizlow's or Tolby's. It was the guy from Traffic Control, and he sounded like he was walking a tightrope stretched across the Valles Marineris canyon on Mars. I had to seize on his fear before Pizlow scared him into compliance.

"Punch it, Tolby!" I shouted as I reached forward and rubbed my plastic dashboard elephant.

My big bud only hesitated a moment, but he pushed the throttle all the way forward. We raced toward the shield with its angry red glow. I screamed over and over in my head for it to turn blue as time slowed to a crawl, but the shield stayed hardened.

I clenched my teeth, squeezed my eyes shut, and braced for impact.

CHAPTER NINE

I slammed hard against my harness, but instead of opening my eyes to a fiery death, I was greeted with a wide view of space. I hit a button for one of my monitors and popped on the rear view. The station was rapidly shrinking behind us, and a glance at the scanners showed no one was apparently in pursuit. I exhaled sharply and leaned back in my chair, laughing.

"Told you rubbing the elephant works," I said. "Thank him for getting the traffic guy to drop the shield."

Tolby groaned, and his eyes rolled a bit in his head. "I wish he'd have dropped that shield sooner," he said. "I think it was still softening when we went through it."

"Probably need a new paint job, huh?"

"You've needed that for a while."

The corners of my mouth drew back, and I shrugged. "Maybe. My financial situation hasn't helped that much."

"It still isn't."

"All the more reason we need to get to the *Vela* before Pizlow."

"You sure that's a good idea?" Tolby said. "He's going to send an army after us. That artifact we've already got will likely set us up for life."

"I know, but it'll take him a little bit to organize any sort of group," I replied. "Hopefully that will give us enough time to think of something because I don't want to give up whatever's on that ship."

"Think of what, exactly?"

"I don't know. Move the ship. Hide it somehow. Maybe just board and grab the good stuff and be gone before he gets there. We'll think of something."

Tolby tilted his head to the side, and his eyes filled with skepticism. "That doesn't sound like the best of plans. Maybe we should think about this more."

"I can't let him have what we've worked so hard to get. Besides, if we gave up now, aside from losing out on a Progenitor find, I'd be doing a great disservice to my loyal fans." When Tolby still didn't look happy, I said something I thought I'd never say since he'd always gone with me everywhere. "If you don't want to go, I'll drop you off at your place or mine. I don't want to force you into something you obviously hate."

Tolby shook his head. "No. I'm going where you're going. I wouldn't let you do this alone, but if you get me killed, I'm going to haunt you for the rest of your life."

"Well let's try to avoid that then. I don't do ghosts."

"What now?"

I handed him the flight recorder and got ready to make a call to my brother. "Put us on course to wherever this thing started its log at. That'll be the last known location of the *Vela*."

"Got it. What are you going to do?"

"Warn Logan," I replied, grimacing as I pictured Pizlow's enraged face. "I'm afraid Pizlow might go after him if he can't reach us."

"Probably a good idea," Tolby said. "I feel like I should advise you on something, however."

"What's that?"

"We need to have better plans in place," Tolby said. "This is the second time in less than twenty-four hours you've winged things, and it almost turned out disastrous."

I rubbed his head, but he didn't look amused. "I know I worried you back there—"

"And on the planet."

"And on the planet," I conceded. "But sometimes you have to improvise."

"And sometimes a little extra time prepping is good too," Tolby said. "I hate having to fight, and I imagine if Pizlow and I went at it, I'd end up biting him. I bet he tastes like moldy socks."

"Eat a lot of those?" I replied with a chuckle. To that, Tolby laughed, and the tension melted between us. "I promise I'll be more careful. Now let's find that ship and give Logan a call."

CHAPTER TEN

The coordinates the flight recorder gave were about eight thousand light-years away and headed toward the Cat's Eye Nebula. As Pizlow had alluded to when he first saw that data, the area was devoid of anything but hefty sums of nothing. That said, the log explicitly stated that those coordinates were where the colony ship had launched from, and thus, as we flew through subspace, I was sure the *Vela* would be there.

Well, I hoped at least. How bad would that suck if it had moved? Maybe we could at least pick up its trail.

I tried calling Logan over and over, but he never picked up the line, and I was instructed to leave a message. Since I couldn't come up with a good way to tell him I might have screwed up and endangered all our lives, I just told him to call me back ASAP. In between attempts, I browsed the rest of the flight recorder's data. There was a pilot's log that was about as interesting as scrubbing grout. It basically gave a day-by-day account of ship supplies, gauge readings, and countless doodles (none of which were good), and it had no commentary whatsoever as to what had happened on the

Vela or why the colony ship had made a controlled crash landing five hundred years ago.

I tried Logan one last time when we dropped out of subspace, and to my shock, he picked up the line.

"What's up?" he asked.

"Uh, nothing, you know, just wanted to talk about my meeting with Pizlow."

"He couldn't help?"

"Yeah, I mean, no, he got it." I was stammering like an idiot, but the more I tried to rein myself in, the worse it got. Soon as I told him, I knew he'd groan this awful noise that sounded like a wounded wildebeest. I've always hated it. "It's just that, well..."

"What did you do?"

"I might have pissed him off," I said, cringing. "He found out about the *Vela* and tried to take the flight recorder."

"Ugh." And then he groaned, and I cringed again. "I told you to be careful."

"I was! Let's not forget you sent me to him. Some friend you have."

"I wouldn't call him a friend," he replied. "He was someone I knew could help."

"Well, that's good, about not being friends. I'm pretty sure he wants to kill me now. And you, too, maybe. He was going to enslave Tolby and me, but then Tolby clobbered him, and we ran, and well, it was a bit of a mess after that."

Logan cursed over the line, loudly. "Where are you at now?"

"A little under a thousand light-years away from the Cat's Eye Nebula in the middle of dead space. The *Vela* should be around here somewhere."

"Really think it's there?"

"Somewhere. Hopefully, Tolby compensated for five hundred years of drift around the galactic core. Otherwise, we might be out here a while."

"Look at the math if you want," Tolby said, sounding insulted. "But what I came up with using that data is dead-on."

Logan laughed. "Your big guy sure took that personally. I wouldn't double-check that if I were you."

"Not yet at least. Last time I did, he—"

"There!" Tolby yelled, pointing an excited claw at a scanner with a triumphant look on his face. "I told you I nailed the jump!"

I glanced down at the scanner, and sure enough, our systems had picked up a blip. Not a rock blip, or a planet blip, or a speck of goo when you didn't clean the monitor after a sneeze, but a bona fide blip of a spacecraft. I mashed the button to put up the blip's image on our view screen and magnified. At first, I had to squint, but eventually, I made out a faint twinkling of light. My heart skipped a beat and then jumped into overdrive as the more detailed scans came back. There was a ship out there, all right, maybe a thousand meters long by computer estimates, but it was dwarfed by a gigantic, oblong structure next to it that made the ship look like a bathtub toy.

"Holy snort," was all I could get out.

"What did we just find?" Tolby said.

"I have no idea." I fired up the KT band sweeper for a detailed readout of what was ahead, and when the scanner finished its work, the readout was so unbelievable, my first thought was that the damn thing was broke—which figured since it was now out of warranty by three days. "This can't be right."

"What?"

"There's a massive dark energy signature coming from that structure."

"How massive?"

"Enough to give a small star a run for its money."

"This is good, right? Or are we in trouble?"

"I have no idea." I shook my head and blew out some air and forced myself into a better perspective. "It's good. It's got to be good. It's not like there's a graveyard of ships around here, right?"

"Hey!" Logan said, tearing me away from the scanner. "What's going on there? You guys okay?"

"We found it," I said, praying I wasn't about to wake from a dream.

"The *Vela*?"

"Maybe. There's a ship out here, and it's saddled up next to a BFA. That rock might as well be a moon it's so large."

"That's no moon," Tolby said. "It's not even mineral."

My brow furrowed and I checked the scanner. "Nothing on the sensors. What else would it be?"

Tolby shrugged. "It's too symmetrical for something natural."

I watched with bated breath as the ship grew bigger on the screen, and I soon had to reduce the zoom to keep it all in view. The ship was slender for its length, about a hundred and fifty meters wide altogether, and it was tall, a good three times in height what it had in width if you included its numerous tower-mounted arrays.

"Dakota?" Logan said. "What's going on?"

I flipped on our searchlight and swept it over the old ship. Its skin was white for the most part, but there were plenty of spots where the paint had been chipped, scraped, and scorched off due to the general wear of time. Cosmetics aside, the entire ship looked intact, so it wasn't obvious why the crew had to abandon it.

"Dakota!"

"Hang on, Logan, sheesh," I said, still looking. I panned the light until it caught some bright orange lettering near the top. The words burned brightly in my eyes: NTS VELA.

"We found it, Logan," I said, my voice cracking and my eyes tearing. "We actually found it."

Something heavy and noisy dropped on the other end of the line, and my brother cursed. "I'm coming. Send me your location. I'll help."

"Probably not the best idea," I replied. "Pizlow is coming, and we need to be long gone before he gets here."

69

"Cripes, Dakota, bug out while you still can. You can't search an entire ship that fast."

I felt my stomach tighten as my determination set in. I checked the time to get a gauge on how the universe felt, too. It was a little after fifteen hundred hours, and since fifteen is extra lucky and feels like a blanket fresh from the dryer, I knew we'd be just fine. "I'll be careful. Don't worry. See you soon."

I killed the comm before he could protest any further. Maybe I ended the conversation too abruptly, but Tolby and I needed to work fast, and arguing with Logan would only slow us down. I glanced at Tolby and saw he had the same wide eyes I had, and he could barely contain his energy as he squirmed in his seat. I half wondered if he'd light the cushion on fire with his butt from all the friction.

"This is so exciting!" he said, slowing my ship down. "I'll pull along port side. Do you want to hail it before we board?"

"Why? It's a ghost ship."

"It has power."

"Nominal at best," I replied, glancing at the scanner. "Why would people still be aboard if they had to abandon ship? And we're talking five hundred years later."

"Maybe they didn't want to go home," he said with a shrug. When my facial expression didn't match the reply he wanted, he tacked on, "Look, it might be a good idea. What if you were floating around here for centuries and someone suddenly barged into your home unannounced? You'd probably be a little cross, don't you think?"

I sighed and flipped the comm to X-Kermit, a protocol that broadcasted over a spectrum of frequencies and was a prime choice for communicating with outdated equipment. "NTS *Vela*, this is Dakota Adams of the *Fram*. Do you copy?"

Static was our only reply, so I flipped from X-Kermit to J2-Modem and tried again. "NTS *Vela*, this is Dakota Adams. Do you copy? Do you require assistance?"

This went on a few more times as I tweaked our broadcast settings until Tolby gave an approving nod. "Guess it's dead."

"Told you," I replied. "How should we go in?"

"I don't think we can dock," Tolby answered. "At least not without cooperation from its bridge, which isn't going to happen."

There was a tension in his voice, like he was talking about having to swallow a bitter pill without actually naming it. "EVA time, huh? Got to love those spacewalks."

Tolby shuddered. "Afraid so. I can park us a few meters from a hatch, but we're swimming in vacuum one way or another."

"Sounds fun, but just make sure it's anything but four meters away. I hate that number," I said.

"I will. Got an entry point in mind?"

"Pull us up to where the colony ship used to be. Maybe the airlock will be friendly there."

Tolby nodded as he skirted us alongside the ship. As he pulled up the ship's schematics to find the airlock I wanted to use, my comm sprang to life with a new call.

"Logan, really," I said, hitting the button. "We'll be gone long before you get here."

But it wasn't Logan on the line. It was Pizlow. "I see you've arrived at my ship," he said. "Nice live feed you have there."

"Got to keep my audience happy," I said. I probably shouldn't have been so blasé given what he'd want to do to me, but since I'd just checked my channel and was up to a thousand viewers, I was feeling pretty damn good about it all. "Something I can do for you?"

"Actually, there is," he said. "I'm sure you think you can get in and out before I catch you. Maybe you can. Maybe you can't. Do you really want to chance it?"

I laughed. "Not much of a choice at this point. Need to make my trouble worth something."

"That you do," he replied. "What's your life worth? Leave now, and I promise I'll forget the trouble you caused me in my own club.

But if you're still there when I arrive, or if you've left and taken one scrap of metal off that ship, all bets are off. Understand?"

"Perfectly."

Pizlow terminated the call, and I looked to Tolby for input.

"Do you think he's serious?" Tolby asked.

"Completely," I said. I drummed my fingers on my thighs, trying to decide what to do. "He must be far off to make that offer since he doesn't seem like the kind of guy to forgive and forget. He might even have an idea what's aboard."

"We're still going in then?"

I nodded. "Yeah, and when we're rich and famous, I'm sure we'll be able to afford plenty of protection from the likes of him."

"Then we better hurry," Tolby said.

He continued to move us down the port side of the ship. As we made our way to the hatch we were going to use, I could see plenty of recesses in the hull where portholes were, but all of them had their protective shutters closed, so I couldn't see inside the ship. Given it was abandoned, that wasn't surprising, just annoying. I would've liked a peek inside before we went rummaging around. You know, in case there were any hazards to be aware of, like psychotic, half-working bots that were intent on lobotomizing every person they encountered.

"That's odd," Tolby said, ducking his head a little to get a better view out of the cockpit. "Look at that."

"What?"

"That," he said, sliding the ship a few meters to the side.

"That...is odd," I replied. Now that we'd shifted position laterally, I could see an antique umbilical cord used for boarding that stretched from the *Vela* to the asteroid. "What were they doing? Mining?"

"If they were, why use the umbilical?"

"No idea. Let's find out."

Tolby parked the ship a moment later, next to one of the hatches. "That should do it," he said. "Think we should take anything special?"

I shook my head. "Usual bag of goodies should do it. I can't imagine we have the time to lug around anything else."

"Here," he said, handing me my pistol from inside a storage compartment. "Might need this."

"Hope not," I said, strapping the holster on my waist.

Tolby nodded as he grabbed his sidearm, too. "Well, if we run into another set of crazed droids, you'll be happy you took it along."

"True, though I'm hoping the entire place is as dead as space."

With that, we hurried to the airlock. A few minutes later, we were both standing inside, fully dressed in EVA suits. It was hard not to giggle at my giant furball. He looked like an enormous astronaut plushie.

"Ready?" I said, hitting the depressurization button. The air in the lock whisked out, and the usual white lights inside the airlock switched to a deep red.

Tolby bounced up and down, but it wasn't out of excitement. He looked like a prizefighter getting ready for his next big match. He'd never been big on spacewalks. "Yeah. I got this. I got it."

"Awesome sauce. Let's get famous."

I smacked an open palm onto the big green button to cycle the lock, and the exterior hatch slid open. It's funny how such a huge thing made only the faintest of sounds, and that was only because its movement was captured in a small amount of vibration that ran through the floor and up my feet. I didn't think about it much, however, as I was more focused on our entry point to the *Vela*. As a testament to Tolby's piloting skill, it floated in space less than three meters away, a mere hop across the void. Next to the hatch, I spied the access panel, and my heart pounded. The panel's buttons glowed, and I knew with a little luck, it would let us right in.

"I'll do it," I said with a smile. Relief immediately spread across Tolby's face. On the one hand, I thought he was silly not trusting our suits, as they were capable for full spacewalks, but on the other, there has always been something unnerving about literally having nothing under your feet, especially when you're almost a thousand light-years from anywhere.

"Thanks," he said.

My ship rolled to the side as the space around me erupted in flame and chaos. Something heavy hit my back and sent me flying out of the airlock. Head over heels I spun, and as I looped, I caught sight of a barrage of glowing red bolts slamming into my ship, blazing a fiery path as they easily blew through the hull, shooting out the other side with a shower of sparks.

"Tolby!" I screamed. "Where are you?"

I hit the controls on my armband to my EVA's jetpack, and my tumbling became even faster and more erratic. My mouth dried and my throat closed as I tried to regain control. Everything was unresponsive. God, why didn't I rub my elephant before we left?

"Tolby! I can't stabilize!"

Stars streaked, and the *Vela* along with my burning ship flashed by as a blur over and over. The air inside my suit became stifling, and I thought I'd choke to death each time I remembered to breathe.

"Hang tight," Tolby said. Though I was thrilled he was alive, his next words chilled me to the core. "Oh damn. You've got a busted nozzle."

"What?"

"It's spewing all over the place," he said in a pseudo-calm voice. "Don't worry. I can reach you."

The *Vela* grew smaller with each spin I made. I balled a fist and cursed. It wouldn't be long before it became a speck in the void, and then nothing at all. Could Tolby find me then? I didn't know, so I did the only thing I could think of. I turned the dial on the five-point harness on my chest and pushed the quick-release button. My EVA's pack ripped away a moment later, and I heard the faint click of connection hoses cutting themselves off.

"I've got about five minutes of air," I said, trying to be optimistic. "Time for you to be the hero."

"I can't believe you did that! What were you thinking?"

"That I didn't want to be lost in space," I replied with a chuckle. "At least I'm not picking up speed anymore, right?"

His huge body impacted mine, and I felt his arms clamp around my chest. Our meeting slowed the spin, I assumed due to the increase in mass (yes, I remember my physics, thank you very much), and a dozen mutters later from my furry friend, we stabilized. That didn't help my mood, because it gave me a good—albeit distant—view of my ship exploding.

"Okay," he said. "Hold your breath till we get inside. Hopefully, there's atmo still in there."

"There will be," I said, not willing to consider the good chance that that wouldn't be the case.

Tolby shot us back toward the *Vela*. The ship grew, but not as fast as I'd have liked. While he flew, I brought up the schematics on my armband. "There's a hatch near the stern that's closer than the one we'd parked at," I said. "Let's try that."

"Send me the location."

I hit a few buttons on my arm and put the schematics on his HUD, all the while wishing I was back in the normal world, sipping a root beer float and thinking about something other than an I'm-about-to-suffocate-and-die situation. "Got it?"

"Got it. Now stop talking. Save your air."

"But can you see it?"

"Still talking!"

"If you can't, let me know!"

Tolby bopped me on the back of my helmet. "Quiet!"

I shut my eyes and sang the only song I could think of in my head. "Mary Had a Little Lamb." It was on the childish side, yes, but it did conjure imagery that had nothing to do with my current predicament. After about the umpteenth round, my lungs burned for air, and I realized taking in new breaths was barely helping. Carbon dioxide saturated my suit.

"Tell me we're almost there," I said. I opened my eyes, but things were dark, and the *Vela* looked like a blurry shadow. Oddly enough, in all that haze, I could make out another ship that looked like a boot knife with fins, a dozen times the size of what mine used to be, heading toward the bow.

"Ten seconds to the hatch," Tolby said. "Stay with me."

I counted to ten, but it felt like a million. We thudded against the hull, and I shut my eyes as I heard Tolby try and work the controls. He started cursing about something, but with my lungs screaming for air, I didn't focus on him too much until he swore loudly.

"Damn it," he said. "Jaws of a vortabeast are easier to open."

"You can still get it though, right?" I whispered. Before he answered, I felt him yank us away, presumably to another entry point. The closest one I could remember off the schematics was a hundred meters away.

I blew out all the air in my lungs, unable to hold it any longer. When I gasped for fresh air, I got none. My body heaved trying to find oxygen in my suit, but there was none. Despite my every mental protest, I thrashed in my suit.

Pinpricks covered my skin, and my thoughts went to mush. In the last few seconds of consciousness, I wondered what my tombstone would say. Maybe something like:

Here lies Dakota
She turned a lovely blue
While she was on a spacewalk
But never thought—

CHAPTER ELEVEN

There's something strangely comforting about being woken up by the patter of furry paws to the cheek. When I roused, it took a few seconds for my vision to return. First, there were shadows and a bright light, but after a few seconds and a huge gasp of air, there were lots of shadows and a bright light—only everything was sharp and clear again, and my faceplate was retracted. Tolby knelt over me, green eyes wide and then filled with an enormous amount of relief.

"Thank the Planck," he said, flopping his ginormous head on my chest. "You'd gone limp. I thought I was going to have to give mouth to mouth."

"Sounds like a cheap excuse to smooch me," I said, patting his head.

"Not a fan of the smooth skin, sorry," he said. "I'd have to shut my eyes and think of something more pleasant, like sipping gasoline."

"Hey!"

"You started it."

I pushed myself up and looked around. The air was freaking cold, for starters. My breath hung in the air, and thank god the heater in my suit still worked. Behind me was an airlock, and stretching left and right was a corridor that reminded me of the ones I'd run through in the colony ship on DD-3123. The only illumination came from our helmet-mounted lights, and those lights revealed dozens of missing panels on the walls along with broken and cannibalized parts and systems, though a few places looked like someone had taken a gigantic drill to them and bored holes nearly a quarter meter wide. As charming as our surroundings were, my thoughts were elsewhere. "How long do you think it will take us to fix my ship?"

"We're not going to be able to," he said, though he didn't have to. "I saw it blow as I pulled you into the airlock."

I felt my lip quiver and my eyes get puffy. I wasn't going to cry. I wouldn't let myself. I guess because I felt like I needed to hold it together till we were safe. In hindsight, a good breakdown then and there would've made me feel a lot better. So instead of crying, I beat up the wall. "Damn it! I love that ship!" I said punching metal a few more times. "It was the only one I'd ever bought on my own."

Tolby looked at me with sympathetic eyes. "I know. I'm sorry."

I dropped my fists at my side and laughed. "I still had Logan's birthday present in there, too."

"The telescope he wanted?"

"Yeah."

"Wasn't his birthday a couple of weeks ago?"

"Yes, but it didn't get to my house until the other day. I kept saying I'd really gotten him something and it hadn't come yet, but he thought I forgot. Kept saying I should've just said it got blown up in the mail if I wanted a better excuse."

Tolby cracked a half grin. "Sounds like Logan...well, to be fair, sounds like you, too."

I nodded and glanced around. "Where inside the *Vela* are we?"

"Deck three, about a hundred meters from the port engine room."

"Think it's still operational?"

Tolby shrugged, but I knew that it was far more optimistic than what he was thinking. "No telling. Thinking about flying this baby home?"

"Not sure what else we can use," I replied with a shrug. "If it can't get us home, maybe the comm station still works and we can send out an SOS. Don't suppose you saw who shot us?"

"Pizlow, I'd wager. Those weren't standard plasma bolts, by the way. Those were PCAM rounds."

"What?" I said, staring at him with the same face I make when trying to wrap my head around how quantum time tunnels work.

"Plasma-capped antimatter rounds," he explained. "The plasma burns a hole through the target's armor so the antimatter detonates inside. More effective that way. You could tell by the red tinge they had—that's the effects of the field used to contain the antimatter. Fleets abandoned their use though, for the most part, because of how unstable they can be."

"How do you know all this, Mr. Sun Tzu?"

"My kind knew war, and I still pay attention to what's out there," he replied.

Though his voice spoke matter-of-factly, I could see hints of sadness in his eyes. Moreover, he never talked about his species, or where he even came from for that matter. I guess nearly getting blown up changes what you're willing to talk about. "Fill me in?"

Tolby shook his head. "Later, maybe, when we're off this derelict and not getting shot at. Survival seems to be paramount now."

"I'm going to hold you to that conversation later," I said, realizing that was the best I'd get for now. I wanted to pry, but he was right. Survival trumped anything else, but at the same time, since we were here, I was really hoping we'd find more out about the *Vela*'s past and score the greatest find of history in the process.

"Try the bridge?" Tolby asked as we made our way down the corridor.

"Good a place as any," I replied. "But Pizlow would probably be headed there, too. I imagine when he sees us, it'll be a shoot-first-and-ask-questions-never type of encounter. These ships had a security station, right? Maybe we should raid it for weapons. Might be nice to have something bigger than our pistols."

Tolby shook his head. "Guaranteed way to get into a firefight the moment we see Pizlow if we do that. He'll see that as an act of aggression, not self-defense."

"News flash, Tolby, he's already trying to kill us. At least this way we'll have a fighting chance."

"And if we aren't armed to the hilt, we won't be tempted to fall back on them as a crutch. We'll have to find a peaceful solution."

I stopped dead in the hall. "I think we can safely say a peaceful solution with Pizlow is out. Tolby, he just nuked my ship."

"He might not have known we were on it," he said. "Or maybe it was a misfire."

"A misfire. Really? That's what you're going with."

Tolby shrugged. "I'm saying I don't want to see anyone killed over an honest mistake."

"I can't believe you're being like this. I'm not saying we should go to war with the guy. I'm saying let's give him a good reason not to pick a fight with us."

The corner of Tolby's mouth twitched, his telltale sign when he was deep in conflicted thought. "Fine, let's check the security station," he said with a huff. "But only for protection and only as a last resort. Trust me, Dakota, you don't want to know what it's like to see someone die up close."

"You're right. I don't," I replied. I punched up the *Vela*'s schematics again and flipped my faceplate down so I could see them on my HUD. "There's a lift up ahead that will take us close to where we want to be. Hopefully, there's no lurking horror on board between us and it."

"Yeah, but that would explain the missing crew," Tolby said as he chuckled nervously.

We traveled another fifty meters through the winding corridor and came to a starboard-side lift that the specs said would take us near the security station. I hit the panel to call it to our deck, and a whole bunch of nothing happened. No sounds. No lights. No lift.

"No power," I said, depressed at the obvious observation.

Tolby whipped out a multi-tool and went to work on the panel. "Might be able to flip it on if I can find whatever relay switched it off and run a bypass."

I waited a few minutes before asking how much longer it would take. All I got in response was a shush and wave of his paw. Well, okay, that was after the third time I asked. The first two were a generic "Soon."

"Pizlow is going to have looted this place and be long gone by the time you get that going," I said.

"If the whole ship is this run down, he's probably having as much trouble moving through it as we are."

I grunted and tried not to think about it anymore. I knew Tolby was right, and I knew he needed to concentrate. But I also knew we had to go up three decks to get to the security station. I needed to do something, anything, to help make that happen sooner rather than later.

"Got an idea. I'll be right back. Don't get eaten while I'm gone."

"From what?"

"From whatever."

Tolby shot me an unamused look.

I hurried back the way we'd come until I reached one of the machine shops we'd passed. I wanted a crowbar or something I could pry the door open with, but what I found was almost as good and might prove better down the road. In a foot chest next to a pair of lockers was a handheld plasma cutter that even had a handy D-ring I could use to attach it on my EVA suit's utility belt. I snatched the tool and ran back.

"We can cut the locks with this," I said, showing off my find.

"Too late," he said after he stuck out his tongue and twisted a pair of stripped wires together. The panel sprang to life, and he hit the call button. "Next time, don't doubt the Tolby."

A low hum came from the other side of the door, but then it stopped and nothing more.

"You were saying?"

"Figures," he replied. He undid the wires, stripped a few others and then twisted new pairs together. "That should do it."

And it did. Sort of. The door slid to the side, but on the other side, there was no lift, only the shaft. I shook my head, frustrated but no longer willing to stand and wait. "All right, let's go."

"Where?"

"Up," I said. "We can use the maintenance ladder."

"I can get the lift to come. Give me a second."

"I gave you plenty. I'm going. Stay here if you want."

I eased myself into the shaft and looked for the ladder. It took me a moment to find it in the dark, even with the light on my helmet, but once I did, I pulled myself over and started my climb.

Tolby poked his head inside the shaft. He looked up, down, and up again, and in both directions, the beam from his light was swallowed by darkness. "This could get messy."

"Only if you fall," I said with a half grin. "So if you don't want me scraping you off the bottom, don't."

Tolby muttered something I didn't catch, but he came nonetheless, like I knew he would. The thought crossed my mind that I might've been pushing him too much, or being reckless with both our lives, but we'd both made harder climbs in the wild, and we did need to get something to defend ourselves with before we ran into Pizlow.

We ascended two and a half decks without trouble, but right before we got to the third, we reached the bottom of the lift, which blocked any further progress. If that wasn't bad enough, the door to the deck we wanted had about a dozen centimeters showing.

"Seriously?" I said, leaning against the side of the ladder. "Can't something go right for us just once on this stupid ship?"

"What's the matter?" Tolby said. "I can't see from down here."

"The lift is in the way."

"I told you we should have waited for me to get it working."

"Yeah, yeah," I replied. I hooked my elbow around the ladder to keep me from falling and brought up the *Vela*'s schematics. After searching the deck below, I found an alternate route we could use. "Can you get the door down there? We can go through the galley and use the service lift to the officer's dining hall on the next deck."

"I think so," Tolby said as he stretched and grabbed the manual lock release for the door. I thought he'd fall for a second, but he didn't, and he managed to pull the lever before opening the door and hopping through.

We entered a hall that ran twenty meters before dumping us into the galley. Rows of metal tables filled the room along with a host of flimsy chairs. Some were neatly placed alongside the tables, but far more lay scattered around the room as if a small tornado had ripped through while a few diners patiently sat in their places for it to pass. Well, minor correction, a tornado that somehow missed the plates, trays, and food that were still on the tables.

"What happened here?" Tolby said, eyeing the nearest setting.

"No idea, but this place is creeping me out," I replied, dropping my faceplate for an extra layer of protection.

"Me too. I wouldn't touch anything if I were you."

"Why's that?"

"Poisoned, maybe. Or contaminated. Why else would they leave it all like this?"

"Point taken," I said.

We entered the kitchen where there was still frozen food in heating trays and pots filled with ice on stoves. We ignored it all and hurried to the other end where the service lift was. I hit the call button, and nothing happened. Out of annoyance, I hit it five more times, and on the last hit, to my utter surprise, it lit up. Thank goodness for that, too, because my eyes were picking out a blood-dripping horror lurking in every shadow.

The door to the lift opened with a ding, and my breath caught in my chest. My eyes locked on a bot that looked like it was one of the better-put-together brothers of the bots I'd encountered on the DD-3123. Its torso sported four arms, two with hydraulic claws meant for cutting, one with a blowtorch, and one with a four-digit hand. Before we could exchange any meaningful communication, it used the latter to punch me in the faceplate.

CHAPTER TWELVE

Believe it or not, I've aced every anthropology course I've ever taken. And while I'd occasionally score less than stellar on the odd exam, there was never anything about any culture that used robotic punches to the face as a way to giving merry greetings to new visitors.

That thought repeated itself several times as a crack rang in my ears, and my faceplate cracked like a spider web. I staggered from the blow, and Tolby instantly pulled me back and whipped out his pistol and pointed it at the bot's head.

"Get away!" he yelled.

The bot didn't. It drove forward, mechanical claws outstretched. Tolby fired off a couple of quick shots, but the bot immediately threw up a force field they skipped off of. Even though Tolby's attack had failed, he forced the bot to go defensive long enough to push me aside and get us both running.

"Which way?" I said as we bolted out the kitchen.

"That hatch looks like our only option," Tolby replied, pointing to a door near the elevator shaft we'd come up.

Tolby had barely finished when the bot came pounding out of the galley, fresh on our heels. The damn thing seemed faster than a Reerok racing horse and probably ten times crueler than those that trained them. As such, I knew I didn't have time to run around the tables, and so I opted to vault over them, using my hands for an extra boost. Tolby, ever more athletic than I was, easily bounded over them without assistance.

I cleared the first row of tables without trouble, aside from sending some trays laden with frozen food sailing through the air. The second row, however, not so much. Apparently hurdles in dark conditions weren't something I was made for, and I ended up tumbling to the ground and ramming my side into the legs of one of the next tables. Thankfully, this turned out to be fortuitous as a jet of flame from the robot's torch sizzled past my head.

"Get that door open!" I shouted, rolling under the tables before coming to my feet.

"I'm trying! It's not responding!"

I got to him a split second later, and we probably only had twice that before the robot caught up with us. As such, I grabbed Tolby's arms and yanked him toward the elevator shaft. The loudness of my heart smashing against the wall of my chest was second only to the voice in my head screaming how we were about to die.

"Not the shaft! We'll fall!" Tolby yelled.

"Better odds than staying here."

I half ran, half jumped into the elevator shaft. Using one arm to catch the doorway, I swung myself onto the ladder. Tolby was a heartbeat behind. He didn't wait for me to make room, not that I blamed him. He hit me with such force that I lost my grip on the ladder when I grabbed him with my free arm to keep him from tumbling into the dark.

Falling three decks and landing on my back at the bottom of an elevator shaft was every bit of fun as one could imagine. Somewhere between my terrified shriek and subsequent impact, I had enough wits to try and grab the ladder as I fell, but the most I managed was to slide-slash-bounce off the rungs with my arm. That was probably the only thing that slowed me enough that I didn't break every bone in my body when I hit, but the entire ordeal did knock the wind out of me and left me with a sore back and a tingling arm.

"Dakota! Please, please, say something!"

I could see from the movement of light above that Tolby was scurrying down as fast as he could. "I'm alive," I said. "Don't fall trying to get to me."

"Praise the Great One," he said, tension melting from his voice. "Can you move?"

I sat up slowly right as Tolby dropped to my side. "I feel like a terrosaur's chew toy, but yeah, I can move."

Screeching metal followed by a dull whine drew our attention up. The lift descended a couple of meters and stopped at the galley.

"I think it's time to go," Tolby said, helping me to my feet. "I don't want to be a pancake when that thing comes down here."

"Me either. Help me with the door."

The lift started to descend as we pulled the manual lock release. Though that went easy, the door opened much slower than I wanted, regardless of my swears. You'd think knowing I had about five seconds before going from one-point-seven meters in height to a solid three centimeters would give me herculean strength to rip them apart, but it didn't. In fact, it took us a full twenty seconds to open the doors, and the only reason I wasn't squashed flat was the simple fact that the lift stopped on the deck above us.

"Why do you think he didn't come down all the way?" Tolby asked, once we were out of the shaft and running down the hall.

"Maybe he didn't want to scrape us off the bottom of the elevator," I replied.

"Or just didn't want to risk damaging that artifact you've got."

87

"Either way, I'm not about to go back and ask. Let's find a place to hole up and figure out our next move before that thing comes down here."

Tolby nodded, and together we hurried our way through the ship. After several turns and a half flight of stairs, we ended up at the ventral communication blister of the ship. The room was an inverted dome on the belly of the *Vela* with double-paned ultra-plex windows lining half the perimeter. I imagine they gave a good view of the antenna array and the outside, but with their shutters closed, I couldn't see anything. Of course, we weren't there for sightseeing, so it didn't matter all that much.

"Think we lost him?" Tolby said, panting and leaning against one of the computer banks that stretched across the center of the room.

"Not sure." I held my breath to try and listen, but it wasn't easy to do. I felt as winded as Tolby seemed to be. For the few seconds I managed, however, I didn't hear anything. "Maybe. Hopefully."

"Why do you think it attacked right away?"

"Probably protecting the ship the same way those other ones were at the crash site," I said.

"They're set pretty aggressive for an exploration ship," said Tolby. "Wonder why."

"Considering they're protecting a ship that's tracking down the greatest find in all of history, we should be glad there aren't a hundred more sporting phase cannons."

Tolby chuckled. "Point taken. So what now?"

"Maybe we should check the Captain's Quarters and get access to the log? That could shed some light on what happened here and if they found anything."

"Good idea," Tolby said, bringing up the *Vela*'s schematics on his HUD. "It's midship. A bit of a hike from us, but far enough from the bridge I don't think we'll run into Pizlow if we're quick."

"Let's move," I said.

I turned for the door we'd come through and literally ran into a carbon copy of myself, right down to the scar I have over my left eyebrow. Well, she was a carbon copy excluding the little fact that she looked more frazzled and lost than I usually do, and her right arm was covered in intricate, glowing circuitry exactly like the Progenitor artifact I had hanging off my belt, but holy hell, she even sounded like me.

"Oh, crap," she said.

"Crap?" I repeated.

The girl whipped out the alien artifact, pointed it square at me, and fired.

CHAPTER THIRTEEN

Being shot wasn't at all what I'd expected. Everything went black. I don't mean in the I'm-knocked-out sense, or even the half-way-asleep sense, but literally black. Fully awake and thoroughly confused for who knows how long, I floated in a void, unable to see, hear, or feel anything. Kind of like one of those sensory deprivation tanks, only terrifying instead of relaxing.

I yelled a few times, hoping Tolby would answer, but I didn't hear anything, and part of me wondered if I'd even yelled at all or if I'd only been screaming in my mind. A pinprick of light drew my attention down. At first, I thought it was something small near my feet, but I soon realized that it was quite large, only far away, and it was rushing toward me—the proverbial light at the end of the tunnel.

With all the grace of a ragdoll spinning in an antique dryer, I tumbled out of that dark world and smacked into a cold, hard floor. The room spun, and my stomach emptied itself. Using the back of my hand, I wiped my mouth and cringed at the lingering taste of bile right as Tolby hit the ground next to me.

"I'm going to be sick," he said, barely on all fours.

"I already was."

The world settled, and my eyes gawked at the L-shaped room we were in. The general feel of it suggested we were still in the *Vela*, somewhere, though I wasn't sure where we were or how we'd gotten there.

I caught sight of a bunk at the far end with a quilted blanket hanging half off it. In the center of the room stood a desk that was doing a fine job of keeping two computers off the steel-plated floor. A mess of cables, most spliced several times over with others in obvious rough patch jobs, ran from the rear of the computers and disappeared into the ceiling. Faded photographs stuck in wood frames hung on the walls that looked like they'd disintegrate if you sneezed a few rooms over, and the faint scent of alcohol lingered in the air.

Behind the desk sat my cyber doppelganger in a chair made from scrap that had been beaten into shape and welded together. It looked about as comfortable as a cactus. Maybe it was due to the spare light in the hall before—not that the three ceiling-mounted fixtures offered much more—but she looked like another ten years had come and gone since she'd run into us moments ago. She rocked in her chair with her hands tightly gripping her face while mumbling to herself. "Shouldn't have. Mustn't have but must. Let it calm, calm, calm, and all will be right."

Tolby and I exchanged glances. I didn't have to ask to know he was all for making a silent exit, posthaste, but I couldn't leave her like that, especially since she was more or less me. "Are you okay?"

Her eyes, looking like she was on her fiftieth expresso for the day, found mine. Her nails dug into her cheeks, leaving fine red lines in their wake. "We shouldn't have crossed. I mean...I knew we were...or had...once before...but this could be really, really bad."

"Okay," I said, retreating a few steps. Unsure what to say or do, my eyes scanned the room. I spied her artifact on the floor near her chair and I forced myself to ask something that sounded insane at the time. "Did that thing bring us here?"

The girl froze as if unsure if she should answer. Eventually, she nodded. "Can fold spacetime. Anywhere. Any when. Handy for coming and going and whenning."

"Whenning?" Tolby asked. "You can time travel with that?"

"I think so," she said. "I mean, yes. It's hard to remember things right now."

My eyes lit up, and I had to ask the obvious question, even though the answer might freak me out. "Are you me from the future?"

"Future?" she said, rocking and laughing. "There's no future...or past. It's not...what's the word? What did he say? Think! Think! Think! No effects and cause. I mean, no cause and effect. It's wibbly."

"Wibbly? What's wibbly?"

"Time!" she shouted.

The muscles in the girl's face relaxed like a nice nursebot had stuck her with a 50cc syringe of hydrapentimorphine. The corners of her mouth turned up. "That's what he said, what we can never, ever forget. Time is wibbly. Wobbly. Like a ball of...stuff."

"Who said that?"

"The man! The box!" The air shimmered around us. And though I hadn't taken an exact inventory of what and where everything was in the room, I could've sworn in that instant the blanket on the bed in the back moved a half meter and there hadn't been an extra chair tucked in the opposite corner. "Damnit," she said. "I did it again. I changed what's next and what's before all at once."

"How?"

"You know something now you didn't know before later."

"Before later?"

She shrugged. "Or later before. Like I said, it's wobbly wibbly."

"Wibbly wobbly," Tolby said.

"That too." I turned back to the girl. "Are you me or not?"

She laughed. "We are very, very different."

"Then why do you look like me? And can my thingy do what yours can?" I said, holding up the artifact that was hanging on my belt.

"There is no mine and yours." Her voice strained, and her face turned red like she was in the middle of another contraction in a four-day labor. When it passed, she said, "So much you learned. Will learn. But not here. I can't be with you."

"Little late for that after you dumped us all here together," I said with an awkward chuckle.

"The Ratters were after me. Couldn't let them catch you, I don't think. Would mess it up too much."

"Can you show me how to work this?" I said, holding up my portal device and praying to whatever gods were out there that the answer would be yes.

"You figured that out, later." Futuristic Cyber Me bit her lip and grunted.

Words failed me at her prophecy. My heart couldn't decide whether it wanted to race like a Tornian wildebeest stuck with a branding iron or stop beating altogether. Was I actually going to command spacetime like she could? "Oh god, I can't wait."

"Dakota, if she's telling the truth, that will literally be the biggest find of all history," Tolby said.

The girl screamed like a banshee before doubling over and falling out of the chair.

Tolby and I were at her side in a flash. I rolled her onto her back. I tried to get her nails away from her face, but with inhuman strength, she kept them dug in her skin. All I could do was stroke her forehead and hope to calm her down, but it didn't seem to work. Her jaw set tight, and her eyes clenched shut.

I looked her body over, trying to find signs of trauma, but other than a few old bruises that weren't very big and scrapes on her elbows, she looked to be in good shape—current affect aside.

"What do we do?" I said, looking to Tolby. When he shrugged, I tried whispering to her and hoped it would be enough to take her mind off things. "You're going to be okay. We'll be safe and out of here before you know it."

The girl came to and staggered to her feet. "You've got to go. Too much future is mixing with too much past and the entire galaxy could crack open."

"Okay, definitely don't want that to happen, but where should we go?"

"Wherever you were going before we—" She staggered back, and when I went to go to her, she stopped me with an open palm. "Every time we talk, my head feels like it's going to explode." Blood trickled from her nose. She wiped it away before straightening. She was trying to look strong and in control, but her body shook, and sweat beaded across her brow. "Just do things like you came the first time, not the others."

"This is the first time," I said.

"No. I mean, yes. Sort of," she said. She cringed, and tears streamed down her face. She spun in tight circles a few times before she grunted and scooped her artifact off the floor. "Go. Me for this hard."

"We were headed for the Captain's Quarters, remember?" Tolby said. "Let's get back to doing that. I think she could use the break."

I watched the girl spin a few more times and mutter to herself before nodding in agreement. "I guess that's our only option."

We were a few steps away from leaving the room when she shouted at us one last time. "No! Wait!"

"You said we had to go," I said.

"Emphatically," Tolby added. "Otherwise we'd split the galaxy, remember?"

"Galaxy, yes, but not the Captain's Quarters," she said. "It's too late for that. You've got to get to the museum, where you were going to go after that."

"We were?"

The girl nodded. When she spoke this time, she seemed much more in control, much freer of pain and insanity. "You'll be searching for Curator. He's the one that will teach you, shape your brain, and give you the interface."

"Who's Curator?"

The girl gritted her teeth and shooed us away; all the while her face turned crimson. "He's the umbilical. I mean over it. Beyond it. Deck five. It'll take you to his home, and you'll see. Or hear, I think."

"What about—?"

That was all I got. She wrapped her arms around her belly as her face filled with a demonic rage. From the top of her lungs, she screamed, "Get out!"

My hands went up defensively, thinking her head was about to turn into a pink mist. "Easy there. We're going."

We left the room, the door sliding closed behind us with a hiss, and we wasted no time hurrying down a dark corridor. Like the first one we'd traveled through when we had arrived on the *Vela*, this one had plenty of ripped apart panels on both the floors and ceilings. After a few turns and passing through a couple of fire doors in the bulkheads, I broke the silence between us. "What the hell was that about?"

"No idea, but I'm beginning to think this might be the start of one of those stories that's filled with a chain of warning signs all pointing to a big ball of crap."

"What are you suggesting?"

"We respect those warning signs, find a way home, and enjoy a big glass of root beer while we still can."

I hit the panel behind us and shut the fire door behind us. "I'm still out a ship."

"Exactly why we start working on that now instead of later," he said. "The *Vela* should have a number of escape pods. Maybe we can get them to work. If not, we're going to have to find a way to steal one off Pizlow's ship, because I promise you, no one is coming here for a long, long time."

I thought about his words. I honestly did. There was a lot of truth to his first comment, and so many tales of disaster could've been avoided if the people who ended up with a quaint obituary had gotten off the crazy train at any number of stops before it plowed through the final stop of Too Late Now I'm Dead Junction. Then again, all the great stories and amazing finds all had one common thread: perseverance.

"You're not going to give up on this, are you?"

"She said I get to time travel," I said. "You really want me to give that up?"

"Yes."

I sighed heavily. "Let me rephrase: do you really think I will?"

"No," he said.

Though that was all he said, maybe I should have listened to his objections, but I didn't. "Exactly. Now don't look so worried. We'll be fine. You'll see. Now let's get to that museum and see what's inside."

CHAPTER FOURTEEN

Tolby and I zipped through a few decks of the *Vela* as fast as we dared. Along the way, we had to dodge three groups of Ratters. Thankfully, they were so busy arguing about what was worth looting and who got what, getting by them was relatively easy.

The airlock hatch that led to the umbilical took a little coaxing to open, a few swear words by yours truly, and a lot of work by Tolby using his PEN. Once we got through, Tolby put the airlock in lockdown mode to buy us a little more time, and we raced across to the museum.

The umbilical had been hooked up to a small antechamber inside the museum, and that opened up into a massive welcoming area. I felt as if we were in an enormous cathedral thanks to the vaulted ceilings stretching overhead and marble floors underfoot. Two things, however, kept that feeling from staying. First, the placed lacked pipe organ music. Second, standing in front of us was the skeleton of a beast with limbs that dwarfed oaks, a coiled tail that looked like it would lap an athletic field, and jaws that probably ate elephants like popcorn.

"Sweet mother of Planck," Tolby said. "What the hell is that thing?"

"Nothing I want to meet," I replied. As frightful of an idea as meeting such a creature was, the real threat was behind us, not in front. I threw a nervous glance to the rear. "How long till the Ratters reach our barricade?"

Tolby shrugged. "Hopefully they'll want to thoroughly search the *Vela* before moving on. That'll give us at least a few hours."

"Awesome," I said, rubbing my hands in anticipation of how much of this place we'd get to explore ahead of Pizlow. "Where do you think this Curator guy is?"

"In his office?" Tolby replied with a chuckle. "Don't suppose there's a museum directory or tour guide around somewhere, do you?"

"Doubt it," I said as I glanced around. On either side of us were several alcoves with wall-mounted pictures and a few halls that stretched off into the distance, and while those gave us options to explore in addition to using the pair of circular stairs behind the super-beast exhibit, they didn't help make up my mind on where to go. "Let's take the stairs, I guess. One direction seems as good as the next."

A metal sphere the size of a grapefruit, white with inlays of black and blue circuitry and a green eye in the center, swooped down to us with a high-pitched screech. I cringed at its noise, but Tolby ended up in a crouch, covering his ears—one of the few times I was grateful my ears were not as good as his. It circled us so quickly I grew dizzy trying to follow it. "Oh my goodness!" it shrieked with a digitized voice. "You are even cuter in the flesh!"

"Uh, thanks?" I said.

The ball stopped in front of my face. "Explanation. Not you. Him."

"Him?"

It bobbed toward Tolby. "Further clarification. The Kibnali."

"How do you know what I am?" Tolby said, eyeing it skeptically.

"Lecture. As Tour Guide, it is my responsibility to know everything there is to know about all our exhibits," it replied. "We have an entire wing dedicated to the rise and fall of the Kibnali Empire. Would you care to see it?"

A whole wing dedicated to Tolby? Was I hearing that right? I didn't even know what species he was, and now I was being presented with the opportunity to learn all there was about him and more. I gripped his arm, and all thoughts of Pizlow and the Ratters vanished. "Yes, we want to see!"

Tolby's shoulders fell. "No, we don't."

"Why not?"

"Because we have more pressing matters, like Pizlow and finding this Curator guy," he said, though I could tell there was more to it than that.

"Indifference," it said. The eye widened. "Oh, that reminds me. May I see your tiny paper devices that serve as a representation of a valid transaction?"

"My...what was that? Tiny paper whatnots?"

"Tiny paper devices that serve as a representation of a valid transaction."

"Tickets?" I said with hesitation.

"Excitement! Tickets! Yes, that's the word!"

"I didn't realize we needed some."

"You're in luck, my dear," it said, spinning around. "We're having a sale on omega-level lifetime family membership, which gets you and your entire family into all wings at all times, grants you access to special theater showings as well as sneak peeks to upcoming events, as well as twenty percent off at the gift shop and all dining establishments. All for the low price of six hundred and twenty-seven brrrrtrppppppt."

"A...brrr...what?" I said.

"Sorry, a brrrrtrpppppppt." The Tour Guide tried a few more times with equal success before taking a different tack. "My translation matrix is a little gummy. I'm looking for a word that roughly means years of being on display in exchange for access to the fantastic Museum of Natural Time."

"I'm not going to be a slave for lifetime tickets! That's crazy!" I said, throwing my hands up. "Even if I wanted to, I don't live that long!"

"Exasperating sigh. Annoyance at self," said Tour Guide. "Note to self: don't assume simple things to basic humans."

"You're complaining about me being basic when you think me spending six centuries on display isn't insane."

"You'll be placed in a stasis tube and won't age a day," Tour Guide replied. "In fact, once you've made full payment, we'll slide you through a wormhole right back to the moment you were frozen, plus or minus a few weeks. Paradox failsafes and all. It'll be like you were on extended brrrrtrppppppppt...brrrrtrpppppppt...holiday."

The entire idea of the transaction left my stomach in knots. Though a herd of questions stampeded through my mind, a simple but poignant one popped out of my mouth. "If this is a museum, where is everyone?"

"You're right here," it said. "And your Kibnali and I are next to you."

"I mean visitors."

"Shame. I was hoping you wouldn't notice."

"Kind of hard not to."

"Owners have been...brrrtrppppt...have been...brrrtrppppt... erased! Yes, erased. That'll do. Still some faint streaks of them left across the universe, but when they vanished, so did our guests. Tragic. Replacing with enthusiasm. That said, you're the second group that's wandered in here the last few centuries. Seems like we'll be back to business as usual in no time. Hopeful worry. Course, that means we need to get Eddie back in his tank."

I looked at the skeleton beast that dwarfed us and forced the question. "Please tell me this guy and Eddie aren't related."

Tour Guide chuckled. "Humored. No. That was a Norphean ragnasaur. They've been extinct for...well, given they're from another timeline, I can't really tell you in years. Eddie, however, is the only cybopod alive and came from a galaxy on the far side of the Virgo cluster. He looks like a giant squid with a fetish for cyber implants, and he's generally a good fella, provided he's not hungry. And doesn't see you. Or hear you. Or smell you." Tour Guide paused. "Reluctant, honest advice. It's best to avoid him altogether until he's back where he belongs. Otherwise, you're likely to soil your leg-and-butt-covering cloths."

"How long will it take to put him back?"

"Unable to determine," it said. "Only three staff available, myself included. Also, we don't have the proper equipment."

"What do you need? A giant tranquilizer?"

"Amused. No, we need a dozen Pangolian armored robots or a pocket universe storage device—" Tour Guide stopped midsentence, and his eye lit up as he saw the portal device hanging off my belt. "Joyous discovery! You brought Jakpep back!"

"This is Jakpep?"

"Troublesome little guy," Tour Guide said. "Always looking to surf spacetime with someone new. Can't be content sitting in a box all day where he's protected from the elements and sticky fingers. Rude. Ungrateful." Tour Guide spun in a circle, his eye changing to a fiery red. "Don't you talk like that to me! I'll send you to the archives if you keep that up!"

Tolby and I each took a step back, but he was the first to speak. "We didn't say anything."

"Embarrassed apology. You lack the interface to hear Jakpep. He's being discourteous at the moment and using language that would make any drill instructor blush."

"So how about we bring this guy back to Curator in exchange for some tickets?" I said, thinking the barter sounded fair to all parties involved—especially since as soon as I got to him, I'd be a time lord. Time Queen? No. Time Empress!

Tour Guide hummed a bit before bobbing up and down. "Agreeable proposition. We can swing through the—" Tour Guide looked over my shoulder and brightened. "Oh, hello! Welcome to the Museum of Natural Time!"

CHAPTER FIFTEEN

I spun around, drawing my Series IV deatomizer right as a dozen Ratters flooded into the antechamber we'd come through.

"Oh damn," I said, faltering at how many there were. However, their numbers weren't the only thing that had me concerned. Each looked hungry for a fight. Their scarlet eyes contrasted sharply against ink-black fur, while dagger-like fangs glinted in the light and two-inch claws gripped rifles that were customized with ten parts duct tape and three parts recycled plastic bottles.

The lead Ratter came to an abrupt halt when he saw us. I guess he wasn't expecting a human and a giant tiger on the other side. He got over his shock quick enough and started shooting at us from the hip.

He didn't hit us, but he did hit Tour Guide square in the eye. Poor little guy exploded, sending red-hot shrapnel everywhere. Bits of metal lacerated my scalp and neck, searing skin and scorching my suit. It was every bit as pleasant as I imagine being sprinkled with lava would be.

Tolby and I dove in opposite directions, finding temporary cover behind the columns that stretched to the ceiling. Quicker on the draw than I ever was, Tolby already had his sidearm out and was returning fire, cursing the entire time. "So much for a couple of hours!"

"Yeah, I know." I flinched as a shot tore a chunk of stone out of the column, but I did manage to shoot back. I was surprised at how shaky I was. I doubt I could've hit the broadside of a cruiser. I guess not being used to a firefight will do that to you—and honestly, that's something I never want to be comfortable with. As awful as my aim was, however, it was enough to keep the Ratters hiding behind their own columns and corners. Good thing they're mostly cowards.

"We can't stay here much longer," Tolby said as he popped off three more shots. The last one connected with a Ratter's forehead. The sewer-covered fleabag dropped faster than a prom dress in a cheap motel. Tolby grinned. "Ooh. That was a good shot."

"Can you do it eleven more times?" I said.

"If I had more power cells," he said. "I didn't pack for a gunfight."

My stomach soured. Though I obviously had a sidearm, too, I never planned on using it in a gunfight, let alone a full skirmish. I only carried it as insurance against creatures wanting a midday Dakota snack—which happened to be plentiful on surfaces of untamed worlds. As such, I only had a spare pack on my belt, and the one in my pistol was already half empty. I was pretty sure we'd run out of shots before they ran out of Ratters—and that would be before the rest of the colony from Pizlow's ship showed up. "I'm up for ideas," I said, firing near blind.

"We make a strategic retreat."

"No arguments here." I peeked around the column. A Ratter from the back popped up from behind a marble counter off to the side and lobbed a sphere that pulsed with angry red light.

I scrambled away from the column before the grenade hit the floor. I stumbled from the ensuing blast but managed to stay on my feet. Ratters intensified their fire as I dashed for more cover, but the only space that looked remotely safe was down a side hall.

"Tolby! You okay?" I shouted, sliding around an upright cross-section of a petrified tree that could double as a landing pad for a blockade runner. I glanced around the exhibit and called again right as four Ratters came barreling into the hall, guns blazing.

I snapped off a few shots in rapid succession. I still wasn't winning any marksmanship awards with my aim—first place in pity at the local youth rifle match, maybe—but as before, I managed to send the Ratters scrambling for cover.

In the brief lull from the chaos, I could see the entrance had three more Ratters running in. And if that's how many I could see given my limited view, there had to be four times that. I couldn't see Tolby, but the vermin kept their heads down and weapons firing at something, so I assumed it was him.

My earpiece came to life with Tolby's voice, but what came across was garbled. "...you...that?"

"Say again?"

"...did...your..."

I cursed, took a few pop shots at Ratters, and cursed again as the comm link continued to assault my ears with static and broken words. "Tolby, get out of there if you can," I said, praying he could hear me better than I could hear him. "Meet me at the—" My words caught in my throat as my eyes fixated on three more grenades arced in my direction.

I didn't do anything heroic like pick them up and toss them back, and then fend off a full battalion of Ratters with my pistol and good looks. Instead, when I realized all three were going to fall short or bounce off the cross-section of the petrified tree I was...cowering behind, I ran.

I ran knowing the momentary lull of gunfire was my only chance to get out alive. I ran with the explosions of grenades ringing in my ears and the overpressure thumping against my back. I ran out of the exhibit, down corridors, up ramps and through rooms that I could have spent a lifetime soaking in all they had to offer. Paintings of foreign lands, suits of armor from empires long gone, and sculptures of creatures I never fathomed existed went by me in a blur of color.

No matter how far or fast I ran, or how many turns I took, there always seemed to be a Ratter or two on my tail. Three times I thought I'd finally lost them in the museum's sprawling layout, only to find myself trading shots after getting no more than a few breaths reprieve from the chase.

The fourth time I lost my pursuers—and it figures it would be the fourth given how much I abhor that number—I'd ducked into the "Life of a Bujbuj" room. As best I can tell since I didn't have a lot of leisure time to take it all in, the Bujbuj was a predatory aviary species that could only see in a much narrower band of light than even people. Thus, to really impart the feel of what it was like to be one, the hall was draped in dark purples and darker shadows, while the displays of its favorite foods—which ranged from scaly bipeds to winged insects with platypus heads and sucker-laden feet—glowed like they enjoyed bathing in nuclear waste.

I figured the darkness would help hide my movements. Hunched over so much that I was nearly scrambling on all fours, I made my way around the various display cases and info panels. I heard the clamor of Ratters from behind and looked back as six stepped through the entrance and into view. They paused, glanced, and spotted me in a flash. I'd forgotten how well they could see in the infrared, and the darkness that I'd hoped would shield me did nothing but hinder me as I scrambled for the back entrance.

"Don't you have anything better to do?" I yelled, squeezing off a couple of shots in their direction. I would have fired a few more, but when I pulled the trigger a third, fourth and fifth time, nothing happened. My power pack was spent.

"Shit," I cursed. I cursed again when a Ratter put a shot through a Bujbuj egg sitting next to me. The thing exploded, showering me with thick, green yolk. Right as I got to the exit, I screamed in fright as the biggest Ratter I'd ever seen lumbered around the corner.

"Squishy," it said in a rough voice.

It swung a heavy, barbed pole that sparked with electricity at my head. I managed to throw myself to the side before my head became a tee ball, but I lost my footing in the process and hit the floor with a thud. Pain raced through my sides due to my already bruised ribs taking another pounding.

The Ratter came at me again. Two strides into its pursuit, it abruptly halted as a bloody, shimmering blade jutted out of its chest. The blade disappeared as quickly as it had come. The beast stumbled twice before collapsing to the floor. Behind him stood a warrior who was nearly as tall as Tolby and clad in graceful, bone-white armor that clashed sharply with the fiery-red, full-face, feral-looking helmet on his head.

My savior sized me up for a split second—though I didn't know why at the time, I assumed now to see if I'd been injured—before blitzing the remaining five Ratters. He moved with such a fleet foot, I wondered if I was dreaming the deadly ballet of death he danced. He moved through the Ratter ranks as if he were in perfect step with their collective whole. Where they shot, he had been ten steps ago, and where they hid, so he appeared before flashing his blade and ending a life. Five Ratters. Five strokes. Five dead enemies.

The fight ended in less than ten seconds, but in reality, it was over the moment he entered the hall. He surveyed his handiwork one last time before running over to me.

"Thanks," I said as I pushed myself to my feet, voice wavering. I hoped he was friendly—or at least, impartial to my presence—since he hadn't sharpened his blade on my neck, but the thought that he was killing his opponents in descending order of threat did occur to me.

"Dakota Adams," he said. "It's about time you got here."

CHAPTER SIXTEEN

Stupefied and feeling like the Universe was playing a practical joke on me, all I could say was, "Come again? Have we met?"

"Yes and no, and all at once."

"Meaning?"

"Meaning I've met the later you in the past, but at this present time, you haven't met me until now."

"Ha!" I said, jumping in the air and clenching a victory fist. "I do get to time travel!"

"In one timeline, yes," he answered. "It is possible to keep that from happening and not create a paradox, however, so we must get you to Empress and then Curator before the rest of those vermin wander this way and change everything."

Aside from the fact I didn't entirely trust him, even if he did save my life, I had more pressing matters. "No, I have to find my friend, Tolby, first," I said, looking back the way I'd come. "The Ratters split us up at the entrance when they attacked."

"I know," he replied. "You'll get to him, I promise, but only after you slip back in time. If you choose to go now, whatever you find will always be."

"What do you mean?"

"I mean as part of the basic laws of time travel, you can't go back to change something you know happened."

"Why not?"

"Because a future event—such as you deciding to change a specific moment in history—cannot be the cause of a previous event," he explained. "The Universe will not allow a paradox, and due to this, it will split you apart to stop you if it must."

"But surely if I time travel, I'll make changes to the past."

"Accidental changes are not paradoxes, but they can still cause problems. Intentional ones are. If you go back to the museum entrance and find Tolby dead, there's nothing you'll be able to do to ever change that."

"But he could still be alive."

"How long do you think he'd last in that firefight alone?" When I cringed, he continued. "Precisely. I'm offering a way that you can snatch him to safety the moment you two were separated."

My stomach knotted. Could I really leave Tolby to fend for himself? I mean, I guess that's not what this warrior said was going to happen, but it sure as hell felt like it. "I don't know," I confessed. "He means more to me than you'll ever understand. Besides, for all I know, you're trying to kill us both and take my artifact."

The warrior nodded to his sword. "I could take it any time I wish, but I'm not brave enough to meddle with spacetime." He then sighed and removed his helmet atop his head, revealing a Kibnali staring back at me with lavender eyes, gleaming teeth, and a bright orange coat of fur. "I am Yseri of the House Eledan and Handmaiden to the Empress and Weapons Master for the Kibnali Empire," she said with a deep bow. "Tolby is the last male alive of our species, and while I don't challenge your love for him, I promise he means more to us than he does to you."

"You're Kibnali," I stammered, shocked that there were more of them and feeling stupid for assuming the warrior was a male. "But how? I thought—"

A series of screeches from not-so-far-away carried through the air—Ratters infighting, I knew. Yseri clearly shared my thoughts as she donned her helmet once again. "No time to talk. Stay close if you don't want to get cut down."

"For the love of everything, I hope you're right," I said, breaking into a run behind her.

We probably covered a full kilometer inside the museum in four minutes. My legs burned and my lungs ached at the furious pace she set. But with god knows how many Ratters pouring into the museum, not to mention Pizlow and his bodyguards as well, I was happy to put a lot of distance between them and us. I could only hope Tolby would be okay, wherever he was.

We took a branch into yet another exhibit, and I had to stop as my eyes feasted upon everything the place had to offer. A myriad of physical and holographic displays filled the area, each one describing various aspects of Kibnali life. There were mosaics showing needle-threading ceremonies, water games with teams of Kibnali and one pissed-off-looking alligator-lion hybrid thing, and schools that taught the kits to write with specialized quills made from amber and to fight with sword, spear, and sidearm from an early age. Given the sheer number of things to look at, I could've spent the next ten years of my life in this place and still not have seen everything it had to offer.

What really got my attention, however, was the gargantuan marble statue that loomed over me. It depicted my feline buddy wrapped in armor, gripping a funky rifle in one hand and hoisting a battle flag in the other. His face was cast in a terrible snarl as his lead foot pressed into the neck of some unknown, alien foe that looked part arachnid and part Komodo dragon.

"Whoa," was about all that got out of my mouth as I stood. I half expected Yseri to stop and explain the statue's significance, but she kept going. I kicked myself into gear and sprinted to catch up.

Finally, she slowed to a brisk walk, and though I wasn't able to read the info panels on each exhibit, I got the gist of it all. The displays had moved on from general Kibnali culture and were now recounting their bloody conquest of space. Over what must have been thousands of years, if not tens of thousands, I watched the Kibnali Empire dominate an entire galaxy before moving on to the next, and the next, and the next.

"Your people," I said in equal parts awe and fright. I wondered if the Kibnali end was the reason why Tolby had never spoken of it. "Such rich history."

"One way to put it," Yseri said.

Goosebumps rose on my skin. Was it just the Kibnali of those countless millennia who were so violent, or were all of them like that? Was my best buddy fit to that mold, too, and he just kept it hidden? I didn't voice those concerns, but I did speak to something else on my mind. "You must have numbered in the trillions of trillions."

"At our height, all that and more," she said with a sorrowful chuckle.

"What happened?"

Yseri didn't answer. Instead, she motioned to a large hologram that was the sole occupant of a nearby alcove. It showed a star going supernova with all the fury of a vengeful god, and the explosion frozen in time was an instant away from engulfing an armada of ships that appeared to be bombarding a planet speckled with thousands of islands. Though I guessed it was the Kibnali homeworld, Yseri confirmed my suspicions.

"The Last Act of Defiance," she said, eyes never leaving the piece. "We fought the Nodari for centuries. But no matter how many we killed, it was never enough. Their numbers were legion compared to ours. Our millions of worlds became ten thousand. Then a hundred..."

"And then one..." I finished. I felt my throat close, and all I wanted to do was hug her. I might have if a tiny part of me wasn't sure she wouldn't mistake the gesture and lop off my hand. "How long ago was this? And where? This can't be the Milky Way, can it?"

"A million years ago and a billion galaxies away," Yseri replied. "Though I can still remember it all like it was yesterday."

"You can't be that old, can you?" I said. There was no way she had lived that long, or so I thought. But then again, I really didn't know that much about the Kibnali, even if I'd been treasure hunting with one for a few years now. Tolby never said much about his race.

"Of course not," she said with a laugh born from disbelief. "Empress is the oldest, almost four hundred and fifty years by your standards of time. I'm not even a quarter that."

"How are you here then if this all happened that long ago?"

"A combination of stasis tubes and wormholes made by the Progenitors," she said. "Had they not snatched us to be exhibits a moment before our world was incinerated, we'd have all died long ago." Yseri shook her head and huffed.

"And Tolby, too?" I asked. "Was he snatched?"

"I'd assume," she replied.

"Why isn't he here with you guys? We bumped into each other on another planet, and he never said anything about being a museum piece."

"You ask a lot of questions."

"Given everything tossed at me in the last few minutes, I think I have the right to a few," I said, not understanding where her edge of hostility was coming from.

"Perhaps you're right on that," she said. "Spies ask a lot, or did, and sometimes I forget we're not living in that time anymore."

"I take it you don't know what happened to Tolby then."

Yseri shook her head. "No, I don't. I assume something went wrong with his transport when the Progenitors took him. It's possible even he doesn't know."

"Yeah, maybe," I said as I made a mental note to follow up on this with him later.

"When the Ratters are gone, perhaps then we can talk more about the past—assuming we're still on speaking terms. Now, however, I have to do the Empress's bidding and bring you to her before time runs out."

"I didn't realize we were on a clock."

"There's a lot you don't realize, unfortunately."

She said no more, and together we hurried to the end of the hall and moved through a set of double doors that slid into the wall on approach. From there we entered a dense forest that had a winding footpath. The footpath only ran a few hundred yards before it came to stairs leading to the Kibnali temple.

The entire thing was surrounded by a stone wall, four meters high. Open doors set in a large archway let us into a barren courtyard. The temple itself, stone as well, was octagonal, squat for the most part, but with a single tower that extended from the center that stretched high over the trees.

"Empress is inside with Jainon, the other handmaiden and our High Priestess," Yseri said. "Though you were before, I feel I should impress upon you that you must be polite above all else. Courtesy is highly valued in the Kibnali Empire."

"I suspected as much," I said, even though that was a complete lie. Tolby and I had always had such a laidback relationship, complete with friendly jabs and on rare occasion, ugly fights. But perhaps that was because we were so close we could do that. Now that I thought about it, he was always very accommodating with strangers, almost to a pathological degree, and hated fighting— which, as I started to think about it, was strange given how good he was at it.

Then again, given the war-loving culture he came from, maybe it all made perfect sense.

Anyway, we slipped through a massive set of double doors and down a short hall until we reached the center of the temple. There, we entered a circular chamber filled with musky incense, colorful lights dangling from the ceiling, and an array of oil paintings stuck to the walls. Inside the room were two other Kibnali. One was dressed in the same white armor that Yseri was in, and looked almost identical to her, save for the fur on her right ear was all black.

The other Kibnali wore ornate, sapphire-colored armor. Though it covered most of her body, I could still see she was thinner than the others. She wore gold rings in her ear that shined brightly against a dull coat of brown and grey fur. She carried herself as if the entire universe would heel at her command, and I didn't need anyone to tell me that this one was the Empress.

"Don't speak unless spoken to. Understand?" Yseri whispered as we approached.

"Can do," I said, though I doubted how true that would prove to be. Despite all the fighting and near-death experiences I'd had as of late, my stomach tightened with excitement. All I wanted to do was pick her brain for the next year and learn all I could about her species, her empire, and everything else she could tell me about the worlds far, far away.

The two Kibnali took note of us and halted the conversation between them. Though I hadn't picked up on what they were talking about, their furrowed brows and crossed arms led me to think we'd interrupted something intense.

Yseri knelt. "Empress," she said, head bowed. "I've brought Dakota, as instructed."

Empress bounded on me in a flash. Though she was the shortest of all, she still was considerably taller than I was. She gripped me by one shoulder and used her other paw to tilt my forehead up so I ended up staring into her starburst, golden eyes. She leaned her face so close our noses touched and held it there for three breaths before she straightened. At that point, she used a paw to pry open my mouth and draw back my cheeks.

"You're dressed differently than when we last met, and you humans all look the same to me," she said, voice full of energy. "But I'd recognize those canines anywhere. As such, I beg your forgiveness for the inspection, but I wanted to make sure it was you and not some imposter."

"Aa ee it owee ow?" The Empress let go of my mouth and tilted her head, so I repeated myself in a much more intelligible manner. "Can we get Tolby now?"

"We will do that and more," she said before spinning me around to face Yseri and Jainon. "Today we rise from the brink of extinction, my dear sisters, and retake our place in the Universe!"

The two handmaidens dropped to their knees and touched their foreheads to the ground. "We are your fangs and claws, and will rend your enemies for your name's sake."

"Rise, then, and seek Hisoshim's blessing as we ready for battle." The Empress then spun me around once more so she could see me. "Your weapons. Where are they?"

"You're looking at it," I said, motioning to the pistol on my hip. "It's out of power, though."

Empress put a paw on my shoulder and squeezed. "I'm pleased to see that despite your limited arms, you have the serenity of a true warrior."

I laughed, though I didn't intend to. I'd never considered myself a soldier. "I'm only this calm because Yseri said I'd be able to get back and save Tolby."

The Empress's eyes narrowed, and Yseri shrunk. "What did you tell her?"

"As my life is yours, I said nothing specific, but she was about to run—"

"You cannot say anything at all!" The Empress barked. I must have had quite the look on my face, too, for when she looked back at me, she softened her tone and posture. "Jumping through the past is risky enough," she explained, "but doing so with ideas on how things must be creates disaster."

"Good job, sis," Jainon said, sticking an elbow into the handmaiden's side. "All that work to save her is going to go right down the tubes when she sucks us down a paradox vortex on her first jump."

"I said I was careful with my words," Yseri said with a growl.

The corners of Jainon's mouth drew back. "At least when we die, it'll be fast. Unless it drags us down into some hellish dimension. There's probably no bright side to that, scorching flames aside."

"Enough," Empress said. "We need to stay focused."

I was glad Empress took charge. Though I wasn't worried about any of what Jainon was ribbing her sister over, I was worried about my best bud. "What does this mean for Tolby?"

"All this means you must forget all expectations you have for what's going to happen," the Empress replied. "The past can be in flux almost as much as the future. But fear not. We will save Tolby, not because it's destined to happen, but because we are stronger than our adversaries."

"You seem sure about this," I said, snapping my fingers in rapid succession and bouncing on the balls of my feet. How insane was all this? I had so many questions, but I figured she wouldn't be answering any of them given what she'd just said. Besides, I wanted to get to Curator and get to the time-hopping. That said, my most worrisome thought popped out of my mouth. "I hope you know what you're doing."

Empress looked me square in the eyes and held my gaze. "As do I, Dakota. As do I."

CHAPTER SEVENTEEN

Curator's office. Not what I was expecting. After a journey to the top of the museum, which was at least a couple kilometers up (and made remarkably fast thanks to a turbo lift), Empress and I stepped through one last doorway and into a dodecagonal room with screens lining each of the twelve walls as well as the ceiling. Playing on each screen was a scene of wanton destruction, straight from the dreams of someone with a heavy demolition fetish.

In the center of the room stood a crescent-shaped desk with a dark, matte finish. Behind that and in a metal chair reclined the Curator. I would've guessed that was who it was anyway, but the Empress whispered his name in my ear the moment I saw him.

Curator was a synthetic being made from overlapping platinum and gold plates and was nearly four meters tall, though at the time he was reclining in a giant, curved chair that looked like it was a distant cousin to a hammock. Two arms sprouted from each of his shoulders, and six eyes were set into an angular face. Long glowing wires flowed from his head. Red and green bands bound them together, giving a cyber-dreadlock appearance. He didn't notice our arrival as his attention was focused on the screens.

"More! More! More!" he shouted, gleefully throwing both pairs of arms into the air as a particularly loud and vibrant explosion took up one of the larger monitors. The picture on another screen—a high-angle shot of the museum entrance—showed the main exhibit littered with fire and debris. It began to rumble before distorting and then simply turned dark. Curator slumped in the chair while mumbling his thoughts. "Note to self: have Patsy screen out all anticlimactic endings."

"Hello," I said, feeling awkward that we were still lurking behind him. "Curator, is it?"

Curator twisted his head, and when he saw us, he half rolled, half flopped out of his chair. "You're finally here!" he said. He started to rush over, but halted as he looked about, and then dove into a desk drawer like a hawk spying a hapless fish over a lake. From it, he yanked out three party poppers and a flimsy, green plastic horn with silver fringe edges. The latter he stuck in my face, and the former he held expectantly.

"Go on," he said. "Blow."

I took the horn with trepidation and eyed it and Curator with equal amounts of confusion. "Blow?"

"Yes! Blow, my dear!" he said, even more excited than before. "How else are we going to start the party?"

I put the thing to my lips and gave a puff of air. The silver fringes jiggled to the sound of a dying duck. Curator looked irked, so I sucked in a deep breath and gave it a full blast. Fringes shot in the air. My ears rang. Confetti from the poppers rained all around. Despite the oddity of such a welcome, I couldn't help but grin. "What are we celebrating again?"

"The End! What else?" he said.

"End of the...?" My voice trailed, and I hoped he didn't mean either me or the Universe.

"End of the Museum!" He exclaimed with a sweeping gesture with all of his hands. "Look at the screens. Each one uses a lens of future knowing to peer down many potential timelines, each one showing what may befall this place in the next few days. Isn't it glorious?"

I laughed because how else could you respond to such a ludicrous statement? I mean, surely, I'd heard wrong. He must have meant somewhere else, or maybe was trying to use a figure of speech to say they were renovating the place. But when I forced myself to take a closer look at the monitors, I realized he was being literal, and he didn't mean somewhere else. Each screen displayed some aspect of the museum, a few I recognized, and all of them were being torn apart. Then I saw myself in one, flung through the air by some unseen force and making a bloody splat on a wall.

"Oh, don't worry about that too much," he said. "You're not in all of them."

"How many am I in?" I said, feeling my stomach churn.

"Enough you've got a chance to get out of here, I think," he said. "Hard to tell since footage always ends when the station goes up. But one thing is for certain. Someone is going to open up a wormhole in the reactor room and start a chain reaction that leads to total destruction."

"Why would anyone do that?"

"They're probably sick of hearing 'Now if you look to your left you'll see...' or 'Please direct your attention to the...' and decided to do something about it."

"Shouldn't you be stopping whoever it is?"

"Can't," he said. "I mean I could try, but it's still going to happen, somehow. Can't argue with the future. Believe me, I've tried."

"Nonsense!" I said. "You can always change the future."

Curator bent double, laughing like a mad man. When he righted himself, he looked at me with sympathy. "Oh, to be young and naïve again...No, strike that. That's how I got trapped in this dead-end job. Look, my dear, take countless eons worth of existence to heart when I say you can't change some things, no matter how hard you try, and what's coming up is one of those things. Besides, even if I did stop whoever wrecks the place from wrecking it, the gaskets around the spacetime folds in the reactor are worn and won't last much longer anyway. So, might as well let someone have some fun playing demolition derby, yes?"

I wanted to argue, I really did. There was something to his tone, however, that spoke to untold depths of wisdom and experience backing his words, and I wouldn't be able to change his mind one bit. "Well, if this is going to happen no matter what, I'd rather not be here when it occurs, if it's all the same to you."

"I completely understand!"

I relaxed a little. "Wonderful. Could you tell me when everything goes to hell? That way I'll be sure I'm long gone."

"Too many potentials too be certain, but soon enough for us to celebrate," he said before diving into another desk drawer and pulling out a bottle of champagne and a few crystal glasses. "Under a week, at the most. I'd wager less than a day."

"Less than a day!" I shouted, eyes wide. "I've got a friend to save and a ship to find in less than twenty-four hours? That's what you're telling me?"

"No, I'm telling you the museum will be destroyed in that time frame. How you interpret that data to drive your actions is up to you."

"Gah! Why are you so happy about this anyway? As the curator, I'd think the last thing you'd want is the destruction of all your exhibits."

Curator popped the cork, sending a huge stream of bubbly goodness sailing through the air before he filled all three glasses. "A small price to pay to be free of eternal servitude, my dear. I can't even begin to relay how nightmarish it is to have to constantly protect the place against every little paw, hand, tentacle, and sucker on all the little hell-bent children who stampede through the museum, completely unsupervised, our current lack of visitors notwithstanding."

"Don't you want to escape at least? Save some of your favorite exhibits?"

"Nope," he replied. "I want sleep. Blissful, eternal sleep."

I think I needed a whole ten seconds to wrap my brain around all he was saying. Even when it had, I still abhorred every bit of it. How could he possibly be okay with the destruction of so many priceless artifacts? How could he sleep knowing so many cultures and stories had been obliterated? I guess the latter was silly since he wouldn't be sleeping at all when he was wiped out with the museum. "Okay, fine. You can stay here. I don't want to, though. Is there anything around here I can use to get home with? A spare ship, maybe? A super webway gate that has a direct pipeline to Mars, perhaps?"

"No, don't think so," he said after some thought. "Things that aren't non-functioning replicas around here are still non-functioning if you get my drift, and if memory serves, we haven't had a working spaceship since one of our more unruly former patrons thought it would be a good idea to test his hotwiring skills on the warp drive. Needless to say, we have neither him nor the warp drive."

"Doesn't that figure," I said before cursing under my breath and turning to Empress. "What about you? Why are you so calm about all of this?"

"We've already been told about this," she said.

"I hope you have a ship tucked away around here because mine got nuked."

The Empress tiled her head to the side, and even though we were different species separated by a bajillion light-years and countless millennia, there was no mistaking the look of abject pity she gave me. "Do you think I'd be like this if we weren't prepared?"

"No. I mean yes. I mean, you know what I mean," I said, exhaling sharply and letting the muscles in my back and neck relax.

"It would be silly of me to make sure you've got room for all of us in this fancy, blazing-fast space hopper, right?"

"As I said, we're prepared."

"Good. Good." I repeated that a few more times to reassure myself things would work out. I snatched the glass of champagne and downed it in a single shot. "That's worth celebrating."

Curator whacked me on the back with enough force to send me stumbling. "That's the spirit!" he said. "Happy times for everyone!"

My eyes drifted to his desk as he set his glass on it. Aside from the drink, there were a couple of circular electronic devices and a pink gem about the size of a vintage baseball, the kind people used to knock around for sport in the 5th century PHS as opposed to the larger, 3rd century PHS version used as a ceremonial focal point for weddings in the House of Cork. However, on closer inspection, I realized what it was, but could scarcely believe it. "Is that a Gorrianian resonance crystal?"

Curator glanced nonchalantly over his shoulder. "It is. Why do you ask?"

"There's like four of them known to exist," I said. "You could buy an entire star system every day for the rest of your life with just one of them."

"I use it as a paperweight."

"A paperweight. Just like that."

"The smaller ones are good for playing marbles, but don't play against Tour Guide. He cheats."

It's a wonder I didn't pull every muscle in my face, given how wide my eyes went. "You play marbles with them? How many do you have?"

Curator opened a drawer in his desk and pulled out a mesh bag that was loaded with the priceless crystals. "Have two more sacks floating around, too. Since I'm feeling generous, do you want one?"

I couldn't reply, verbally at least, I was in such shock. I did manage to look like a stuttering idiot, though. So I had that going for me.

"Here," he said, taking one of the precious "marbles" out, putting it into a little gift box he had in the desk, and dropping it into my hand.

I stuffed it into an inner pocket in my EVA suit before promptly wrapping my arms around Curator and squeezing. "Thank you! I can't even begin to say that enough!"

"The least I can do," he said. "Is there anything else I can help you with? Technically, I'm on the clock for a little bit longer."

"Well, yeah, actually, there is something very important I need help with. I don't suppose you could show me how to use this?" I said, holding up the portal device.

Curator chuckled and backed away like I was holding a loaded baby one sneeze away from a total diaper blowout. "Now that's a toy you might not want to play with."

"My friend is in trouble, or he was in trouble. I need to go back in time and save him."

"You can't undo what's already been done."

"I've been told that already," I said. "But I don't know what has been done yet, so that's allowed, right?"

"It's possible, yes, if that's what you mean."

I nodded. "I can't not go back and help Tolby, regardless of how dangerous it is."

"Dangerous, eh? That's one way to put it."

"What's another way?"

"That," he said, pointing an accusing finger at the device, "single-handedly wiped out its creators by bringing about the Progenitor Apocalypse."

My mouth dried, and I could feel my knees wanting to fold. Abject terror gripped me at how lackadaisical I'd been slinging the object around. It wasn't a nifty toy if his words were even remotely true. The damn thing was a doomsday device on an intergalactic scale. "It brought about the apocalypse? How?"

"Spacetime backlash against a multifold paradox a thousand years in the making," Curator answered.

"A what?"

"They were about to create a massive paradox, and the only way the Universe could keep it from happening was to wipe them out. It doesn't get much more apocalyptic than that."

"No kidding. I take it that's why the museum's empty?"

"Yes. The backlash wiped out almost every trace of what they'd done, save little snippets here and there, like this museum. When your friends from the *Vela* arrived, I was shocked they'd managed to find us since we were floating in the middle of nowhere."

I whistled low and soft as my imagination ran wild. Had galactic clusters been pulverized by some unseen force? Or a rogue wave through the fabric of space scattered the atoms of the Progenitors across the entire Universe? How had that wave removed all the Progenitor history as well? Did other creatures just instantly forget about them as spacetime twisted and rippled throughout the past, present, and future? So many questions, but I didn't have time for that story, sadly. I had to get back on track.

"I'll be careful. I promise. One hop back to save Tolby and I'm done."

"It's rarely one hop back, and good intentions won't save you from paradoxical correction," he said. "Tried to warn that Nathan fellow about that. Didn't want to listen to me, though. Thought he knew it all and ended up accidentally warping himself right into our Juxipode plague exhibit. Got infected in under a minute. Dropped dead a few weeks after that."

My stomach tightened. "That doesn't sound good."

"It wasn't," Curator said, shaking his head. "Didn't feel good, either, I imagine. The guy spent the last bit of his life nuttier than a bin of spare parts."

I rocked on the balls of my feet. I didn't like thinking about the grisly picture he was painting, but still, I needed to get to Tolby. "I promise I'll keep all that in mind."

"Are you—" He stopped when a red portal as tall as me opened a few meters away. "Oh. Never mind. Looks like I show you how to use that after all."

I turned to the left. On the other side of the portal, I could see the same room we were in, with myself, Curator, and the Empress standing in roughly the same positions we were in now. The me on the other side waved, and I returned it, feeling like I was staring through the looking glass as I did.

Curator spun me around. Even though I was being manhandled, I wanted to see what the other me was doing and tried to crane my neck around, but he planted a hand on top of my head and kept me from moving. "Need you to wait a moment," he said.

"What for?"

"You'll know in a few minutes," he replied. "Can't ruin the experiment or risk a paradox."

"Fine," I said. Though I capitulated to his demand, he didn't let go for a full count to twenty. I hummed to myself the entire time, feeling extra silly. When I was free, I glanced over my shoulder to find the portal had closed. "Now what?"

"Right, give me your arm," Curator said, extending a hand.

Reflexively, I pulled both arms to my chest. Maybe I was being overly defensive, but there was something in his voice that put me on edge. "What for?"

"I need to mark your interface sites on your body so the device can properly communicate with your brain. Then you can use the prime mover and be on your way, tearing the universe apart."

"I don't think it will be that violent."

"If you say, great knower of all things spacetime. Now let me see your arm."

I gave him my right one with a slight cringe. "Is this going to hurt?"

"Most definitely," he said. "But don't worry. You'll forget it soon enough."

He took my hand in one of his, but I squeezed my eyes shut the moment I saw the digits in one of his other hands meld into this psycho cross between a syringe and an arc welder. I grit my teeth as the damn thing tortured my arm, even let a string of obscenities fly a few times when more than once it felt like he was filleting my skin. Had I been strong enough, I would've jerked my arm back, but he kept it locked in placed with his hands as he worked.

"Not my best work, but it'll do," he said. "Never could get used to how peculiar the radian and median nerves are on you lot."

I opened my eyes and saw three coins, for lack of a better word, sewn into my forearm. Each one was about the size of my thumbnail and had a spider web of intricate circuitry across its surface. I flexed my hand and stretched my arm. Lightning pain shot through my body at first, but it quickly eased. All that pain vanished instantly when I realized something. "That was me!" I said, jumping up. "Back on the *Vela*! I knew it! She said...oh god..."

"Yes?"

"She was crazy. Or, I was. Or will be."

"An unfortunate potential side effect for your kind, I'm afraid," he said. "That can happen when your memories get squashed."

"Squashed?"

"The human brain is...how can I put this nicely...an entry-level model."

My brow furrowed. "Entry level?"

"It can barely do a billion-billion calculations per second," he said, plopping himself back on his chair. "Not exactly the kind of performance you'd write home to Mother about. Don't even get me started on your recollection capabilities."

"What's wrong with those?"

"I told you, don't get me started. Short of it is, every time you make a jump the artifact is going to have to compact your memories to make enough room for all the calculations your brain is going to have to do. Don't worry too much. They usually come back over time. Before they do, however, your behavior will be erratic."

"How reassuring," I said, rolling my eyes. "You'd think the most technological race ever to exist could create something that didn't have a chance to fry my brain."

Curator laughed. "You're welcome to build a better device if you think you can. Personally, if I were someone careless enough to surf the fabric of spacetime, I'd think temporary amnesia would be a small price to pay."

I gnawed on my bottom lip and nodded to myself a few times, mulling his words over. He was right in that regard. It was a small price to pay. And losing some memories for a bit might not be too bad, especially if I could find a way to control it. Aside from forgetting bad things, I could maybe forget a good joke, that way, when I heard it again, it would be as funny as the first time I'd heard it. Okay, maybe I was stretching things there, but when a girl is about to scramble her synapses, she has to cling on to whatever hope is floating around. And in the end, with Tolby needing my help, it really didn't matter what the side effects were. "Now what?"

"Now we stick a battery in it and get started," he said. He went to the desk and pulled out a cylinder that looked exactly like the one that had been hooked up to the colony ship's reactor. He did something to the device—still not sure what—but in a flash the back end unfolded like beetle wings. In that cavity, he stuck the battery in before closing it up.

Hairs stood up all across my skin as I knew I was speeding to the event horizon of a new and exciting future. "This is going to be awesome."

"Before awesome, let's start simple," he said with a chuckle. "Point the prime mover at the wall and visualize an open door there. When the portal forms, and things are going to go wonky at that point, aim the device where you want the exit and visualize another door. The device will do the rest."

"Got it," I said. "Here goes nothing."

For a mental image, I picked a large oak door with heavy, iron pulls—something straight out of pictures of ancient mansions. My arm tingled as I thought about it and aimed the device at the wall. My vision distorted like everything was being pinched together, but then it snapped back and wavered like the world was on an elastic canvas someone had just let go.

"Don't worry about what you see," Curator said. "It's just the interface learning to talk with your brain, figuring out what you want. The whole process will go faster the more you use it."

His words were easier said than done, but I pressed on. Tiny numbers cropped up on the surface of everything, moving, changing, swimming about. A myriad of symbols appeared alongside them, forming equations that would no doubt take volumes of advanced books devoted to mathematics to understand. Everything tinted a dark green, then yellow, then blue. The smell of raspberries and curry assaulted my nose while I could have sworn something warm and soft was patting my cheeks. Music, faint and light, danced in my ears, while something tangy held on to my tongue. Another half minute of this persisted before a distinct pop echoed in my head and a fully formed portal sprung into being.

"Hot damn," I said, swelling with pride. I turned my attention to a spot on the opposite side of the room and repeated the process. As promised, everything happened much faster, and about ten seconds later, another portal materialized.

Curator pulled out a small blue ball covered in green nubs from his desk and threw it at one of the portals. The ball sailed through the air, entered the portal on my right and popped out the one on my left before hitting the floor and bouncing a few times. "Seems like you've got the knack," he said.

"Oh. My. God!" I shouted. I grinned at Empress like a five-year-old girl before squealing and jumping up and down a half dozen times. "This is the most amazing thing in the world! And I did it! Me!"

"You did it well, I might add," said Curator.

I laughed. I cried. I made another portal since the first had disappeared and sent the ball through. "How long do these last?"

As soon as I spoke those words, the portal shrank into nothing. Other than a brief wobbling of the space around the walls, there was no indication anything had taken place.

"About that long or until you make a new pair," he said. "You can even tunnel to something you can't see, provided you are accurate in how you imagine its location relative to yours."

"I can? Sweet!" I said, still riding high on the awesome feeling I had. "I can't wait to go exploring with this baby."

"Try not to obliterate yourself in the process or bring about another apocalypse."

"Not on my itinerary, don't worry."

With that, we moved on to the really fun stuff: time travel. It turned out that doing that, as well as making pocket universes, was a little trickier, but many of the same principals applied.

Pocket universes are basically little spaces somewhere else where you can store stuff. Nifty huh? To make one, I had to visualize a room, or cave, or whatever, that was surrounded by nothing. After that, I had to pick a number—any number I wanted—the device opened a gateway to a tiny universe outside our own. Then, if I ever wanted to go back to that same tiny universe, I'd just use that number as a reference point—like a street address—and pop on back. It's super handy for transporting things you don't want to carry—like ravenous alien monsters who want to eat you—or for things that you don't know when you'll need to get to them.

The only catch—well, one of the many catches—is that accessing pocket universes created a tremendous drain on the portal device's energy, and after getting to one, you'd have to wait a bit for the artifact to recharge.

Time traveling was very similar, but a touch trickier because on top of imagining where I wanted to be, I had to come up with a good method of when I wanted to be. This was easier said than done.

Ultimately what worked for me was picturing an old-fashioned clock with hands spinning backward until I got to when I wanted. Took me a few tries, but I managed to open a small portal to a quarter hour in the past and gave myself a friendly wave. When it collapsed, my mind felt foggy, like I'd been drinking mimosas for a few hours. I could still remember well enough, but what I recalled about anything and everything was fuzzy. Not to mention, I suddenly felt like I could use a nap, which was apparently the device's way of telling me I'd drained a considerable chunk of its energy.

Oddly enough, jumping spacetime didn't tax the device as much as playing in pocket universes did. Go figure.

We continued, and I got a brief rundown on artifact power levels and recharge rates, stray wormholes caused by inaccurate or low-power device usage (apparently, this can be really bad or really fun), hexa-string-induced quantum blowback (I still have no idea what that is), fractal time limits (something, something, terrible consequences), and rapid mosaic membrane deterioration (pretty sure he made that one up). Seems like a lot of ground to cover, I know, but he zipped through each topic like he was repeating refresher notes from elementary course work at a university.

"I need to get back and get to my sisters," Empress said, tapping my arm. "No matter how and when you save Tolby, be back at our wing fifteen minutes from now. We leave then for the ship."

"Easy enough," I replied. I turned to Curator as I psyched myself up to jump back in time and grab Tolby. "Any other last words of advice?"

"Yes, and this is by far the most important thing I can tell you," Curator said as he caught a ball I'd thrown a minute ago. "Beware the paradox. There's an infinite number of ways the Universe will warn you as you get closer to one, so there's no point in trying to teach them all to you. But as you begin to create one, the fabric of spacetime will push against you more and more, like a white hole. It can be anything from a feeling to a force to a string of bad luck. Some feedback will be benign. Some will not."

"Anything else?"

Curator nodded. "See those three circular patterns I've sewn onto your arm?"

I looked down. They were easy to spot. Each one was about the size of an ancient US quarter. "These?"

"Yes. They're safety discs, the last ones in existence. Each time you near a paradox threshold that would result in either your destruction or the device's, one of those will blow instead—basically to grab your attention and have you reconsider what you're about to do."

"They'll blow, like, take off my arm?"

"Hopefully not," Curator replied. "But I'd be mindful of what the universe is saying regardless, especially if you use them all, because the next paradox backlash will be nothing you'll want to be near."

"Got it," I said. Given how many times I'd heard variations of that warning, you'd think I'd have paid it more heed.

CHAPTER EIGHTEEN

The thing is, if you go back a few minutes in time, it's usually not that big of a deal because there's a lot less you can screw up. Think of it this way: The house you live in is the present time. The front yard—the future—is open, and your backyard—the past—is fenced off. Now, you also have a dog named Paradox. He's allowed in the back, but not the front. As such, the more you wander the infinitely deep backyard, especially as you get farther away from the house where you don't clean up as much, the greater chance you have to step in Paradox's poo.

Turns out the farther you send a portal, the harder it is on the brain, too. When I left Curator's office, I decided to pop back twelve hours. Why? Because twelve reminds me of cupcakes, and man, could I have gone for some cupcakes then, and twelve is certainly better than eleven, which tastes fizzy and sour, and not in a good way.

Anywho, once I jumped back, I spent the next several minutes wandering the halls of the museum, trying to remember why I'd gone as far back as I had, favorite numbers aside. I still remembered I needed to get back to Tolby, but the reason why I'd picked twelve hours before our separation as opposed to one hour—or even less—eluded me.

In my time-warp-induced haze, I recalled Curator reassuring me that given enough time, especially if that time was spent processing things, memory would return as my brain unpacked everything. Course, he did also say that there was always the risk of total deletion to make room in my head, and then something else about another thing that I think was really important, but it's escaping me at the moment, so it couldn't have been that bad, right?

Anyway, I eventually decided I must have jumped back a half a day in order to be sure I'd have my memory back so I could save my bud. So with not much else to do at the moment, I toured the museum.

I soon wandered into the Tentacoiler art exhibit. There I spent a few minutes reading about how the culture grew to settle entire territory disputes by having a competition that decided which elected champion could depict the most realistic night sky using only a needle and paints made from the gland of a nartoad. I was about to go on to their one-dimensional impressionist era when the meeting with the Empress and Curator came flooding back to the forefront of my brain. More importantly, one of the comments Curator had made while I was getting my crash course in all things spacetime.

"The Archives!" I shouted, practically jumping out of my EVA suit. The entire museum might be destroyed along with countless artifacts, but that didn't mean that the information would be forever lost. Curator had mentioned that the entirety of the museum's collection was kept in holographic projection form and stored on scribe cubes that were easily transportable. Did I forget to mention that? Sorry. Memory issues and all. Anyway, that was why I'd gone back so far! I wanted to get to the archives and get a copy of everything that was in the museum!

I bolted out of the Tentacoiler wing, nearly wrecking a petrified amber sculpture in the process. Between heavy breaths, I checked the timer I'd set when I first arrived in the past. I still had about eleven hours before I caught up with the Ratter attack. Though I hoped that should be enough time, I had a nagging feeling it wouldn't since I no longer had my lucky elephant to rub.

I had to run around a little to find a holodisplay of the museum layout and saw that the archives were on the ninety-sixth floor. To get to the nearest turbo lift to take me to it, I ended up going through an exhibit detailing famous explorers of the Milky Way and Andromeda galaxies. I should mention that as best as I could tell, there were probably a thousand more sections to all of these, each dealing with another galaxy, each connected via a web of near-seamless portals, but I didn't have the time to go through them all. It would have been nice to see all my interstellar predecessors.

The few I did see, however, shocked the hell out of me. I mean, when I saw a replica of Pon Yippu, a third-generation human from Mars, triumphantly standing on Triton's surface while gazing at Neptune, that was a no brainer. The display of Commander Kirble from Gliese 581 arguing with his chief engineer about a falling subspace drive was also a gimme (poor guy, never had one expedition that didn't involve at least three critical-system breakdowns). But when I was about a hundred meters from the lift I needed, I saw two crew members of the NTS *Vela* and stopped so fast, so awkwardly, I almost got to first base with the floor.

The first crew member was Navigator Kevyn Hawkness. The display had him holding a Mark II Wel-Yand quad-corder, a handy—but outdated—device that early pioneers of space travel used for data gathering (as you might recall, development of the quad-corder stopped during the third microdrone industry boom). Biographies written on Kevyn always mentioned how young he looked for only being thirty-nine, but I'll be damned if he didn't look a day over twenty. He looked like a kid playing dress-up in his bulky burnt-orange EVA suit, complete with heavy rebreather pack.

To his left stood the famed Captain Jack Hawkness, who looked even more dashing on display than any picture ever did. He stared intently off in the distance and wore a grin that could swoon a thousand, thousand hearts. His broad shoulders were rolled back for perfect posture and the promise that he could take on anything the Universe could throw at him. His vintage Sodak navy-blue coat fit oh-so-lovely over his Olympic body, while his trousers, sporting perfect creases, were tucked and bloused over leather boots so shiny, you could use them to signal for help.

"Why oh why did you have to be born five hundred years before me?" I pined. I know that sounds schoolgirlish, but he was gorgeous. I don't care what anyone says.

I jumped and spun around as a terrible shriek assaulted my ears. From whence I came, Tour Guide came flying toward me, bobbing merrily through the air. His green eye dilated when he neared and he started circling me rapidly.

"Annoyance! You slippery little bugger!" he said. "You're not supposed to be here without a ticket!"

"A ticket?" I said. My initial reaction, however, was replaced by ire the moment I realized something. "Hey, I've got a bone to pick with you about that."

Tour Guide stopped his bobbing and retreated a couple of paces. "Shock. You do? I mean, I'd be happy to hear about any constructive feedback you might wish to offer. There's no need to bring management into all this."

"Management? What management? This place is practically deserted!"

"All the more reason not to bring any in."

"And you tried to sell me a lifetime membership!"

"Calming presence. We are having a sale. It's an excellent value." Tour Guide stopped and rotated a few degrees to the side. "When did you say I tried to sell you tickets again?"

135

"A little less than eleven hours from now."

"Recognition!" he said. "You're Dakota! Should have guessed. You've got that time-surfing aura hanging about you. Hope you haven't blown up too many things yet. No, don't tell me. Wouldn't want you to inadvertently skirt near a paradox and create a black hole or something."

"I'd like to avoid that, too, if possible."

"Have you picked up your membership card yet?"

"No," I said. "You...got distracted last we met."

"Apologizes," he said. He then spat out a small, purple, laminated card from a slot, which I promptly snatched. It had a slew of alien characters on it I couldn't read, as well as three tiny chips that I imagined were part of some sort of verification process—like the credit cards of ancient days. "There you go. This will let you in all the VIP areas."

"Perfect."

"Insider information. Just so you know, I've got a suspicion this museum won't be around much longer. So if I were you, I'd hit as many exhibits as I could," he said.

I balked, unsure how to reply—potential paradoxes and all. "Why do you say that?"

"It's mostly a hunch. I started thinking that when your dream guy and his navigator didn't come back," he said, looking over my shoulder. "Figured the museum must have finally ended before their contract was up."

"You heard that?" I felt my face flush as awkward feelings of being a budding teen resurfaced. That silliness vanished when the implications of what he said dawned on me. "Hang on a minute. These aren't displays?"

"Of course they are. What else would they be?"

"No, I mean they're the real deal? That's really Captain Hawkness and his little brother Kevyn?"

Tour Guide's skin brightened. "Pride. Impressive, yes? I was so elated when they purchased their lifetime family membership, omega level, of course. I mean, you should've seen the replicas we had. Anger. Only accurate to the nanometer. Can you believe that? Hatred. That was the last time we did business with a Horducular merchant. Wishful thinking. It's too bad Oscar wasn't running loose that day. Would've been nice for him to eat that swindler."

"They bought memberships, and you put them in stasis?"

"Two of them did," he said. "The other stuck around, but—embarrassment—there was an...incident...that led to his departure. I really shouldn't say more than that. Guest privacy and all."

I looked back at the pair, marveling at how one of the greatest mysteries of human interstellar exploration had finally been solved. All this time, they were just sitting around, frozen in time, and didn't have a clue that they wouldn't be going back. "You've got to let them go."

"But their service isn't up yet. I could only pro-rate the tickets they bought. Oh, and I wouldn't be able to send them home, either. Paradox and all."

"Are you kidding me?" I said, throwing my hands up. "This place is going to be destroyed in a few days! I think that's a pretty big breach of contract on your end! And I really don't think they'll care about getting pro-rated tickets at that point."

"That's a good point," Tour Guide said. He zipped behind the display and dropped down a meter so he was near the pedestal that they stood upon. A thin wire snaked from his underside and into a tiny port near Captain Hawkness's feet. The air around the two *Vela* crew members shimmered, and a faint buzzing hit my ears. "Tell you what though," Tour Guide said with a chuckle. "Once they pop out, I'm going to go wipe my memory. You can have the honors of bringing them up to speed."

"Me? You're the one that sold them shoddy tickets!"

"Exactly. And from what I remember, your fair captain here isn't the most cordial type."

"If you wipe your memory, you won't remember about the museum being destroyed."

"Not my responsibility. Besides, I'm only a piece of hardware. My existence is no longer needed if the museum is gone."

"This is ridiculous."

Tour Guide didn't say anything else. There was a distinct pop in the air, and the two *Vela* crew members stumbled forward as Tour Guide zipped away posthaste. The two looked equally disoriented, and I bolted to keep them from falling.

Kevyn was the first to get his footing, despite the bulky suit he wore, and the first to say something. "Where are we?"

"You're still in the museum and—"

Jack—hereafter dubbed Nutball—drew a sidearm he had on his hip and pointed it at my head. "Back off, lady. This is our claim."

"Whoa!" I said, hands instantly in the air. "No one is jumping anyone's claim."

"Damn skippy you aren't. We were here first. Now you hop back in your little yellow Mark III Space Hopper and run on home before I turn your head into a pretty pink mist."

I sucked in a breath and tried to sound as non-confrontational as possible. Even though thus far I'd survived a reactor meltdown, my ship getting blasted, and a massive firefight with Ratters, I figured Lady Luck would soon start getting annoyed with me if I kept pestering her. "This might be hard to believe, but you're over five hundred years in the future, and this museum is about to be destroyed."

"Think I was born yesterday, toots? You're not scaring us off."

"No, I think you were born five and a half centuries ago." I shut my eyes and cursed softly, not meaning to sound so snarky.

"I'm getting really sick of your attitude—"

Thank all that is good in the world, because before Nutball could go on, Kevyn put a hand on his arm and got him to lower his weapon as he talked. "What if she's right? She is dressed weird."

Nutball wanted to shoot me. I could see it in his eyes, an unbridled hatred for someone with the audacity to show up on his "dig" and steal his artifacts. Those same eyes, however, had hints of fear—no terror—that I could be telling the truth, terror that he was a half millennia away from everyone and everything he knew. Given that, I guess I can't be too mad he reacted the way he did—eh, I take that back. Yes, I can.

"Let's see what the logs on the *Vela* say," he said, putting his sidearm back in my face. "Then we can decide how much we need her."

They didn't talk much as we went through the museum, me leading the way with them a few steps behind. Nutball, of course, kept his weapon pointed at me the entire time. Figures after all this, I'd save my schoolgirl crush from certain death only to have him bust a coolant coil in his head and take me prisoner. I should've opened a portal at his feet and ejected him into space.

We'd barely stepped two paces into the *Vela* before we stopped. Everything was completely dark, save where our collective three lights swept up and down the scavenged corridor. Kevyn whistled long and slow. Nutball, on the other hand, turned crimson and a couple of veins bulged in his neck.

"What the hell did you do to my ship?" he said. "You better be carrying some damn good insurance."

"I didn't do anything to your stupid ship," I said, my eyes narrowing. "I told you, you're five hundred years in the future. This stupid thing is nothing more than a derelict floating in space."

"Yeah, exactly. You've been getting your dirty little hands on anything of value."

"News flash, Captain. The only thing your ship is good for right now is scrap, and even then, it's not worth the tow." I whipped out my PEN and waved it in front of his stupid eyes. "See this? I've got games on it that use a thousand times more computational power than your entire ship could handle. I don't want this hunk of junk."

Given the escalating confrontation between us, it's probably a good thing Kevyn stepped in. "This isn't helping," he said. "Let's get to the bridge and see what we're dealing with."

"Fine. If she's lying, I get to shoot her."

The trip to the bridge yielded much of the same: occasional pauses by Kevyn to take in how gutted everything was and hot-headed threats by Nutball to remind me where I stood with him.

The *Vela* bridge was egg-shaped and about five meters long. Banks of monitors and computer stations lined the walls and surrounded each of the three crew positions in the center. All of these positions had hack wiring jobs sticking out—the bridge, it seemed, had been the recipient of much of what had been scavenged in the ship. Beyond the flight control stations was an elongated, semi-dome of ultra-plex windows. This screen gave a good view of space as well as the museum exterior looming next to us.

"What's our status?" Nutball asked as Kevyn plopped into one of the seats. "Is Graham up?"

Kevyn went through a series of button pushing, flip switching, and keyboard hammering as he slowly brought the bridge systems to life. The entire ordeal felt like it took forever. I had to admit. It was kind of cute but also sad at the same time because it demonstrated how little luxury those ancient spacefarers had. I could go from a total shutdown to full flight in ten seconds if I had to, and in that time, Kevyn would still be still waiting for the preliminary AI matrix routines to load.

Lights in the ceiling and along the baseboards flickered on, filling the area with much-needed illumination and a faint buzzing in the air. One sparked a second later and blew with a miniature firework display.

"It's out of warranty," Kevyn said with a half grin. "Hope the engines don't do that."

Nutball grunted with even less charm than his usual self. "One thing at a time. When are we?"

Kevyn looked at the dim green display before him. His face paled when he punched up the logs and grew progressively worse with each page he read. Eventually, he straightened and rolled back

GALEN SURLAK-RAMSEY

his shoulders as he tried to take on the role of a seasoned officer faced with any sort of adversity. The ashen face stayed.

"We're five hundred years in the future, just like she said," he replied, slowly swiveling his chair around to face us. "Nathan got sick with an unknown virus. Probably picked it up in the museum somewhere. Since we weren't back yet, our ship's AI wouldn't let Nathan take the *Vela* and leave us stranded. So Nathan ended up leaving on the colony ship. Once he was gone, the AI went into hibernation and let a couple of bots maintain the ship using parts from everywhere to keep things going. It's a tiny miracle the *Vela* is in as good of shape as it is, I'd wager."

"Damn it all. Doesn't that just put me in the bath without my rubber ducky," Nutball said, balling his fists. "What about the rest of our bots?"

"The other two hundred and eight have been cannibalized for parts," Kevyn said after double-checking the logs.

"What's the sitrep around here?"

"Nominal fuel. Plenty in the food stores. Water filtration, operational. Hydroponics looks good, so no air problems. We're not in immediate danger, but we are stranded." Kevyn chuckled before he then added, "Guess that means I don't have to help rebuild Porter's moisture vaporator."

Nutball growled and turned to me. "You. Claim jumper. Where's your ship?"

"Got blasted to pieces right after I got here."

"By who?"

"Pizlow. Artifact collector. We were, or will be I guess, in a race to get here. I win. He gets mad. Goodbye ship."

Nutball arched an eyebrow. "Why are you talking like that?"

My gut tightened. I cursed myself for not bending the truth and then argued a half second more about how to handle the subject. "I'm from about eleven hours in the future. I get here the first time in ten. That's also how I know this place isn't going to be around much longer."

"No shit, eh?" Nutball said, sounding genuinely impressed. "Got a hold of one of those Progenitor spacetime warpers I take it."

I nodded. My hairs on the back of my neck rose, and I tried prepping the device for a portal out of there, but Nutball pointed his weapon at me again and ruined my concentration.

"Why don't you hand that over, and we can still be friends."

I sighed and gave him the device. I then pointed to the interface that was sewn into my arm. "Won't work without one of these stitched in you."

"Yeah, and how'd you get that?"

"The Curator did it for me in the museum. Hurt like hell."

"Well then, let's go pay him a visit. He can do the same for me and send us home."

I kept as straight a face as I could but inwardly prayed the idea I had would work. Well, first I prayed I wasn't about to crack open the galactic cluster since I'd be skirting paradox territory by meddling with the past, and then I prayed everything would work enough to get free of Nutball. "The Curator died just before I freed you. The only way he can help you is in the past."

"And you'd just love to throw us through some wormhole into the nearest star, wouldn't you?"

"At this point, all I want is not to get shot," I said, raising my hands. "You can go home, find the device first, and reap fame and fortune. I'm not really the glory-seeking type, anyway."

"Okay, toots. Sounds like a plan. But you're the first through whatever interdimensional door you open, got it?"

I nodded. What else could I do? When Nutball handed me the portal device, I went to work. I pictured the bridge with a floating calendar in the middle. Slowly, I turned back the pages. Everything wobbled, and something tangy stuck to my tongue while a smoky aroma filled my nose. The months flipped faster, and soon I was watching years roll back faster than I could name them. As we neared the time they originally went into the display, the second day of their arrival at the museum, it felt like I'd slammed face first into a concrete wall.

"Holy shit," I heard Kevyn say.

I held my concentration but knew what the remark was aimed at. I could feel the heat in my nose and blood oozing out of my nostrils. Pushing to those final days ignited a skull-splitting headache. My chest constricted, and breathing became labored. When that last day ticked over, I opened my eyes.

Two strangers stood next to me, though I had the vague notion I should know who they were. One—Nutball—I knew was hostile, but the other I wasn't sure what his role was in all of this. I guess it didn't matter in the end. A couple of meters away from us was a portal into this same bridge, only it was full of electronic life.

"Hot damn, she did it," Nutball said. "We're going to be rich!"

He grabbed me by the back of the neck and started to push me toward the portal. I slowed dramatically, not because I was doing anything, but because it was like he was pushing me up an ever-growing incline with one arm. The Universe was pushing against the paradox.

"Move, damn you!" he said and shoved me hard.

It was enough that I stumbled forward. My arm suddenly erupted in fire—quite literally. Sparks flew from one of the safety discs along with glowing embers of alien tech. The portal twisted immediately in response. I fell to my knees and ended in a coughing fit that put out enough blood that I was sure would earn two points on my frequent donor card.

"What the hell are you trying to pull?" Nutball yelled.

I glanced up to see the view from the portal flutter out of the bridge and down the corridor we took. It jumped to medbay, the cargo hold, and then zipped into the museum. For a couple of seconds, we saw Nutball, Kevyn, and Nathan gawking at the Norphean ragnasaur display at the museum entrance, unaware that we were staring at them from five hundred years in the future.

Nathan turned his head toward us, and the portal fled through the museum like a gazelle running from a lion. It bounded through exhibits, leaped over displays, and plowed through a teal force field before coming to a stop in an arboreal exhibit filled with crimson trees and yellow-purple flora, all of which was smothered in shadow.

The edges of my portal crackled with energy, and the view we had dimmed. "Power is draining," I said between gasps for breath. "It won't hold much longer, and I don't think I can hold it in place."

"Get up and—"

That was all he got out. This beastly monster full of muscle, tentacles, and cybernetic implants charged out of the portal. The damn thing could barely fit in the bridge. Its massive body smashed everything attached in its path, ceiling lights included. In the chaotic darkness, I saw Nutball get slammed to the side and heard Kevyn scream something that was cut off in an instant.

Light flashed from the barrel of Nutball's sidearm. Plasma bolts skipped off the creature's hide and buried themselves into computer banks, starting more than one fire. The shots kept coming, and this nightmarish monster roared so loud it would send a kraken swimming for cover.

I ran out of that bridge as fast as I could. I didn't know where I was going or where I was. I'd barely scrambled out of the room when the shots stopped after an enormous crash. I glanced over my shoulder, and through the open hatch that led back to the bridge, I could see the creature moving in the dark.

The corridor soon passed through a firewall, and I slammed the hatch closed. I wasn't stupid enough to sit there and rest—I'd seen enough horror flicks that showcased cannon fodder doing just that—but as I ran, I did slow from a full panic-induced flight to a controlled sprint. I ran through the ship stores, which had been long since picked clean, down two decks, past the machine shops and bot docking bays, until I finally reached the cargo hold. I made sure I shut every hatch along the way, too.

A dozen shipping crates littered the cargo hold, their lids removed and contents long gone. Some lights flickered on above, giving the entire area much-needed illumination. I guess when Kevyn booted the system, he gave life to the rest of the ship.

I collapsed against the nearest crate and sank to the floor, feeling like my legs were made of rubber and my chest had been slathered with white phosphorous. I replayed the last few minutes over and over in my mind, trying to figure out why the hell I'd let that thing loose and who the two people were who had been with me. They weren't friends, I didn't think, if for no other reason than I didn't feel completely terrible witnessing their death.

My eyelids grew heavy. In the back recesses of my mind, I had the vague notion I had to be somewhere, meet someone. Trying to think of who, what, when, and where gave me a splitting headache, and my stomach turned queasy. I crawled into one of the tipped-over crates and let the shadows blanket me.

I slept deeper than I ever had before and dreamed about spelunking in caverns made of fractals and tiny gnomes giving me a full-sleeve tattoo.

CHAPTER NINETEEN

Born again. No doubt about it. I woke inside my crate of a home feeling sharp as a poltigor's fang. I knew who I was, where I was, and when I was. I crawled out of the shipping container and stretched. A quick check of my timer showed I still had five hours to the Ratter shootout, which was plenty of time to get ready. I was about to slip back to the museum when I saw the network of blue circuits Curator had sewn into me had grown. Not only had the pattern become more complex, but it ran from the tips of my fingers in my right hand, past my shoulder and just under my jaw. I couldn't see that part, obviously, but I could feel it when I probed my neck with my fingers.

I found the entire ordeal natural, as strange as that might sound. Instinct, perhaps Progenitor-induced or tapped into, told me everything was fine. After all, when a butterfly emerges from its pupa, does it wonder how it got its wings? Is it frightened by how much it's changed or does it waste time trying to understand the intricacies of what went on inside the chrysalis? Of course not. All it does is enjoy its new form and new abilities. And that's precisely what I'd been granted: fully functional wings.

No, I wasn't born again. I'd undergone a metamorphosis.

I looked left and picked out a spot in a high corner of the cargo bay, just above a tall rack of storage shelves. As quick and natural as the blink of an eye, I threw up a portal and put its mate on the floor at my feet. I stepped forward, fell through the hole and ended up on top of the shelves. The portal closed behind me at my desire.

"Oh this is going to be fun," I said.

I threw out a dozen more pairs of portals over the next few minutes. I ran through some, jumped through others. I stuck them on the ceiling, on the floor, and everything in between. I let crates fly through the air by dropping them through wormholes and shooting them out a wall. I juggled their momentum and stacked them neatly and quietly throughout the cargo bay. When that got too easy, I challenged myself by seeing what I could make if I treated them like giant building blocks. I made arches, a house, and finally a fort that would be the envy of any kid looking to defend against an army of stuffed animals.

Heat built in my right arm, but I pushed the sensation away as I continued to test my limits. The universe was my playground. While sitting on top of one of two twin towers, a wry grin spread across my face as I decided to up my game. Juggling crates was one thing. Don't get me wrong, sending them through spacetime on a whim had gobs of untapped potential. But could I juggle myself? Could I control my portal slinging when I needed it the most?

There was only one way to find out.

I sucked in a breath, committed the current layout of the cargo bay as best I could to memory, and cannonballed off the ten-meter tower. The ground rushed at me with a vengeance, eager to break every bone I had with its diamond-grip metal surface. I denied such wants with a wormhole. It swallowed me whole and spit me back into the air from the ground like I was on a giant trampoline. At the apex of my trajectory, I got greedy. I decided to try and launch myself back on top of the tower from where I'd started.

I made the entrance portal on the way down to the floor without any trouble. The exit portal, however, left something to be desired. I thought I'd angled it correctly so I'd be gently tossed on top of my target, but the moment I came flying out of the wormhole, I knew I'd aimed low by three meters.

"Oh crap!" I yelled, throwing up another portal a split second before I impacted the stack of cargo crates dead center. My attempt at a save wasn't much of one. Instead of popping out somewhere safe, I shot out of the ceiling. I twisted as I opened another portal in the floor to keep me from turning into a pancake. I didn't put any thought to where it would go, or even should go. All I wanted was to be anywhere else, any when else if need be.

I got the latter.

I sailed out of one of the cargo bay walls and skimmed over the heads of about a dozen Ratters before I slammed into some big guy's chest. It's a good thing he was built like a cephalopod on steroids, because though I'm sure it hurt when we collided, I didn't kill him, not by a long shot.

"Oh, damn," I groaned, rolling on the floor, still not realizing how much trouble I was in.

"Well aren't you the cockroach of the Universe," Pizlow growled.

I craned my head back and left to find Pizlow looming nearby. I didn't recognize him immediately thanks to my temporal-jumping-induced amnesia. I just figured it was some bloke pissed off at how I'd ruined his party in the cargo bay. I did have enough of my wits to realize he was dressed in some hefty, state-of-the-art body armor—a Banshee Mark IV, if I'm not mistaken (and thanks to its mini shield generator, you can practically get run over by a tank and still not be crushed).

"Sorry about crashing your get-together," I said, wincing as I stood. The pain lacing my back and sides nearly caused me to double over. "Anyway, I like to think of myself more as a feline. Nine lives and all."

"You're terrible at landing on your feet," Pizlow said.

Ratters formed a circle around me, and a brutish fellow with fists the size of compact cars and four curved horns protruding from the top of his reptilian face moved toward me like an executioner would a condemned prisoner. "Fast or slow?" he said, pausing less than a pace away.

Pizlow glanced left. "I think we can be cordial for a moment, Veritad," he said, holding up a hand. He then looked at me. "We can be cordial, that is, if you want to tell me what was so vitally important that you barged in on us like this."

"And you've got ten seconds before your stay of execution is lifted," Veritad tacked on with a wicked grin.

"I was going to give her five, but we can do ten," Pizlow said.

My hands shot into the sky. "Hey now, I know we got off on the wrong foot, but I didn't mean to crash into him. I was playing with some portals, it got a little screwy, and it looks like I haphazardly catapulted a few hours into the future. I didn't think anyone would be here, to be honest."

Pizlow raised an eyebrow. "Knock yourself silly?"

I rubbed the back of my head at his comment. "No, I don't think so." I paused and studied the horned, furry behemoth in front of me. I knew I should know him. Somehow. I knew his name, obviously, but was he friend or foe? Competitor? One of the guys that helped me get to the *Vela*? Yeah. That was it. Wasn't it? "We've met, haven't we?"

"You might say that," he said. "Why don't we get back to being friends and tell me all you've been up to? Seems only fair since I've funded your expedition."

"You did?" I snapped to attention. "Oh. Oh! There's this entire museum that the ship is hooked to. The Progenitors built it, and you wouldn't believe all the exhibits that are in there. We're going to be famous till the end of time!"

"Is that a fact?"

"Yeah, and they have the coolest-looking marbles!" I said as I produced the Gorrianian resonance crystal. I guess I should have picked up on the collective gasp by everyone, but I didn't. I simply continued on, putting it on for display so everyone could see. "Spiffy, huh? You'd think this would be a collector's item, how it has that nifty little hum when you put it close to your ear. But the guy I got it from had a sack full."

"A sack full?"

"Yep. Said he had two more bags, too, I think."

"Interesting," Pizlow said with a warm smile. "Can I see it for a moment?"

I handed the crystal over and gave him a teasing point of the finger. "Don't drop it now. This place is such a mess that it would take all week to find it."

Pizlow chuckled. "I wouldn't do that to you. Where did you say the rest were?"

"In the same office where I picked up some multi-dimensional time machine, over by the—" I stopped as gaps in my memory filled in—gaps that involved me and my red space tiger buddy tumbling through the void as my ship got hammered by plasma-capped antimatter shells.

"By the...?" he prompted.

I didn't immediately answer as my mind was reeling at the recent revelation. In hindsight, anything would have been better, especially since the Ratters tightened the circled they'd formed around me.

"Looks like your memory is back since you look like you got brained by a hydrospanner," he said, taking a step forward. "If you enjoy breathing, I suggest you keep giving me info about this place."

"Would you believe me if I said there's a massive beast loose on the ship and it devoured the crew not too long ago?"

"Given the crew has been dead for five hundred years, no," he replied. "Even if there were such a thing, we have more than enough firepower to deal with it."

"Well, it was worth a shot."

"Not particularly. My patience is wearing thin. Tell me about your arm."

Yeah right. Like that was going to happen. There was no doubt he'd make a beeline for Curator and get an interface installed ASAP. There was no telling what he'd do with that power, especially since he'd also get his hands on all those resonance crystals. Okay, there was no telling what I'd do with that power and money either, but at least I was trying to behave with it. "Well, there's this room near the basement that leads into a giant vault."

"And?"

"You need a key to get in, which I might have lost in the Uktar safari exhibit when a diapod tried to mate with Tolby and ended up running off with our pack when it got its heart broke."

Okay. That sounded stupid once it left my mouth, but during the microsecond I cooked it up, it sounded plausible.

Pizlow looked over my head and gave a short nod. "Veritad. Rip her legs off."

Driven by a hundred percent pure instinct, I dropped a portal at my feet. The fiery-red wormhole sucked me in and spit me out with a vengeance onto the cargo bay floor, three hours into the past. Before it closed, Pizlow and one of the Ratters dove through after me.

I still don't know what memories I had to sacrifice to make such a jump, but they weren't the ones that told me who this raging hulk of fur and horn was who was coming after me.

I vaulted over a large, open crate and plopped another portal open. I aimed the exit of this one at one of the exits to the cargo bay. Once I rolled out of the wormhole, I made a mad scramble for the hatch.

Three strides into the run I felt my gut tighten and my face warm. The air felt heavy and quickly grew thick like molasses, and immediately I knew the Universe was giving me a harsh warning. No one had to tell me what the sensation meant, even though Curator had warned me about paradoxes. It was all instinct, like when your brain knows that the pain signal your body sends is bad. But did I listen? No. Of course not. I had to get out of there. I didn't even listen when another safety disc shot out a jet of flame from my arm.

A pace away from the exit, I saw the grav tile in the hall collapse. Chunks of metal panels tore from the ceiling and walls and slammed into the broken tile before the entire thing exploded in a magnificent fireball.

I managed to pivot and leap to the side as the fireball shot into the cargo bay. Flames kissed my cheek and singed my hair while pieces of metal cut through my thigh and shoulder.

I thudded hard into the wall and heard the Ratter chasing me howl. Twisting around and ready to dodge a hail of bullets, I saw the pitiful creature clutching the side of its face with both paws while a wicked piece of metal jutted out of its skull.

"Impressive," Pizlow said.

He brought up his sidearm as I dropped another portal at my feet. I came out behind some cargo containers on the far side of the bay right as his shots zipped through the air I'd been in only moments ago.

"Most impressive."

I kept low and tried to get a view of the other exits to the bay. I figured if I could see them, I could drop a portal and be gone, assuming the universe didn't give me some paradox backlash again.

"Are you still here?" he said, amusement in his voice. "Or did you flee to some other time?"

Of course, I didn't answer. As goddess-like as I felt twisting spacetime to my will, I figured my divinity would come to an abrupt halt if he managed to kill me—something that was an inevitability if he kept getting shots off at my head.

I dared a peek and saw Pizlow facing the other direction. I considered dropping a crate on his head via wormhole, but I could see the faint flicker of shield around him, and as I said before, you could drive a tank over him with that thing on and still not crush him. As such, I kept still and hoped he'd go away.

He didn't. Instead, he tilted his head up and kept his nose high in the air for a moment before dropping it. "Still here," he said. I couldn't see his face, but his gloat was more than enough to picture how he must be enjoying this cat and mouse game. "Stay here if you like. I'm going to go check out this museum of mine, and if I run into your feline friend, I bet he'll look nice mounted on my wall."

Pizlow's mention of Tolby boiled my blood. God, how I wanted to open a portal at his feet and toss him onto that broken grav tile, but that would be over too quickly. No, I wanted him to rot in a cell for the rest of eternity.

"Hey!" I shouted, coming out from my hiding spot. "I got something for you."

Pizlow turned as if he hadn't a care in the world, but before he could say or do anything, I opened a portal at his feet, and the pocket universe on the other side swallowed him whole.

CHAPTER TWENTY

It figures that even with the ability to go anywhere and any when I pleased, I could still manage to be running late to something important, like hightailing it back to Tolby. In my defense, however, it's not as if xenoarchaeology has a lot of hard deadlines and early-bird-gets-the-worm moments. It's not like a dead culture is going to rise from the grave and up and disappear on you because you slept in a few extra hours. And let's also be honest, how many fedora-wearing diggers had to deal with constant life-or-death scenarios when chasing down some holy relic?

Of course, the memory loss I incurred after pocketing Pizlow didn't help things at all. Once he was gone, I went back to the museum and took a leisurely stroll through one of the more unique wings, "The Most Disastrous Technological Blunders of the PicaPoca Galaxy." Fascinating, horrifying, and at times, hilarious exhibits.

For example, a company decided to go live with its newest marketing technology before thoroughly testing it. Said technology was supposed to order everything you would need or want without you having to do anything to make shopping even more of a breeze.

Well, apparently there was a glitch, which ended up sending the king of the Midsan Empire a basket of dead fish, four bottle caps, and a jigsaw puzzle. Weird delivery for everyone else, but he saw it as a bad omen from the gods and immediately ordered all his servants to shave their heads and dye their skin green. This wouldn't have been so bad if the next day he didn't get a surprise visit by an ambassador from a neighboring country who thought the king believed he was the bad omen, and ultimately, they fought a century-long war over it all. Said company did, however, offer an apology and an extra month of their exclusive delivery service as "fair" compensation for the mix-up.

I was right at the tail end of that story when I remembered Tolby and all the bad stuff that was about to happen. Without finding out who won the war, I bolted out of that area and raced to the nearest turbo lift. The lift itself was a couple of meters in diameter with a semi-circular window that gave excellent views of the museum as it descended the forty floors to the lobby. It makes me sad to think about all the stops I wanted to make. Aside from exhibits devoted to countless species and their varied existences (pretty sure I saw one that apparently worshipped the pogo stick, that would have been fun), I passed two desert biomes, the entrance to an oceanic wing, and three arboreal wings, one of which was filled with orange treehouses decorated with wild plumes, and four consecutive floors dedicated to fun parks. I had half a mind that when I snatched Tolby, we should blow back in time a few extra weeks to grab some much-needed R&R.

When I reached the entrance floor, I bolted out of the lift so fast I'd give Hermes a run for his money. Flying through the Hall of Precious Gems, I heard a loud explosion echo from up ahead that was quickly followed by sounds of a lopsided firefight. And if by some stroke of luck I manage to stay alive through all this, please god let me remember to "save" some of the pieces from that place. I could set up my family for ten generations on the outer rim or put a down payment on a nice two-bedroom condo in Orlando, Florida, with a sack full of those.

When I left that hall, I paused for a second to check the directory map at a T-junction and then hooked left. This took me through a gallery depicting the origins of all life in the Universe. From what I could gather in the half minute I spent sprinting through it all, a couple of gods (or extra-dimensional beings, whatever you want to call them) were having a bakeoff and one knocked some extra charm quarks into the batter of this universe they were cooking up and voila, out we came.

After a right turn, I barreled into a gift shop that gave an excellent view of the unfolding action in the Welcome Center via the exit on the opposite side. I saw myself and Tolby taking cover behind thick pillars, popping shots off as best we could. I figured I had to wait until Old Me left before I could grab Tolby due to potential paradox backlash, so I took cover behind a rack of plushies. Funny how universal a plush doll is, isn't it? I wonder if they ever had one of Mister Cyber Squid. Not sure if it would give me nightmares after all of this or if it would prove therapeutic.

With muscle and mind ready to spring into action, I watched the firefight unfold. Even though I knew I'd lived through it not that long ago, the entire ordeal felt like I was watching an action-packed movie. I did cringe when a blast tore a chunk of stone near Old Me's head, and when the grenade came sailing through the air, I reflexively shouted out a warning to myself.

"Look out!"

Tried, I should say. The moment I drew in air to fuel my words, I sucked some spit down the wrong pipe and ended in a coughing fit. By the time I recovered, Old Me had run off down the side hall, leaving Tolby to fend for himself.

I didn't wait to see what would happen at that point. I formed a portal next to me and created its mate right behind my furry buddy. I reached over and yanked him by the elbow, instantly closing the wormhole the microsecond he was through.

Tolby twisted in my grip as we stumbled backward. I lost my footing, which I think is the only thing that saved my life because his weapon zipped around faster than his eyes and out came a shot that nearly took my head off.

"How did you do that?" he said, stumbling over his words.

I pushed myself up with one hand while the other held my forehead in a vain attempt to soothe a newly born headache. "Oh, I don't think I was supposed to do that so soon," I moaned. "Remind me I need more time to rest after surfing time."

Tolby jerked his head to the side, like an angry bee had tried to kamikaze into his ear. "Planck's end! What did you do to your arm?"

I looked to my right and found myself drawn in by the fractal overlay of circuitry that covered my arm. I knew the answer. It was right on the tip of my tongue, waiting to springboard out the moment my brain got around to remembering what everything was all about.

"I got it..." I tapped my head a few times, but to no avail. Then I saw a plushie that looked a lot like Curator, and it all came flooding back. "Tolby! I remember!" I said, grabbing his paw. "I could write a book on everything that's happened thus far. That girl we saw before. That was me!"

"I figured that part out already," he said, eyeing me with concern. He glanced around the midfloor display we were hiding behind. "It's not going to take them much longer before they realize I'm not there anymore."

A smile larger than a starliner grew on my face. "Oh, we're going all right, but when we get there, you've got to help me remember, okay?"

"What are you talking about? Remember what?"

"Everything. Anything."

"I'm not going to like this, am I?"

I shook my head and laughed. "No, you're going to love me from here to the end of the Universe and back."

With that, I dumped a portal at our feet and threw us out five hours into the past.

A paw squeezed my hand. Claws dug in my skin. I straightened and rubbed my eyes, realizing that I'd been staring at this gargantuan skeleton for far too long without blinking.

"Dakota?" this huge furry guy next to me said. "You okay?"

"Oh. My. God. You are the most adorable giant teddy bear I've ever seen in my life!" I said, bouncing on my toes. "And look at your spiffy spacesuit, too! That has to be the cutest thing ever."

Paws gripped the sides of my face almost as hard as fear gripped the tiger's face. "Dakota," he said. "Please tell me you know who I am."

"Did I buy my ship from your dad?"

"No, I—" His eyes narrowed, and then he shoved me in the chest with both paws. "I hate you. That should be a punch in the face."

"Oh, come on," I said, laughter bursting out of me. "That was funny."

"No, it wasn't." His eyes still shot daggers at me.

My throat tightened. Maybe I'd gone too far. "I didn't mean to scare you that bad. Forgive me?"

"Yeah. I guess. So that bit about your brain getting scrambled was all a big setup?" His eyes widened, and he was on me in a flash. "You're bleeding. Bad."

I thought about what he said, and that's when I realized pressure was mounting behind my eyes and warm, sticky blood was coming out of my nose. I wiped my face with the back of my hand, and it came back crimson. I coughed, too, and ended up spitting up just as much blood on the gift shop floor. "It does that...sometimes..." I said, trying to sound a lot more confident than I was feeling. "It's normal."

"No, Dakota. Bleeding out of your head is not normal. It's probably as far away from normal as you can get, minus turning into a talking star or your feet changing into a scoop of ice cream."

"I meant it's normal when I use this and go to a different time," I said, holding up my right arm. "My memory also gets...compressed...I think it was called...by this time traveler guy. Or maybe he invented it?"

"Who?"

"A doctor?" I shook my head, trying to push through the fog I'd wandered in. Thankfully, the name snapped to mind after a few moments of me muttering to myself. "Curator! It was the curator of the museum."

"Is that what I'm going to love?" Tolby asked, looking perturbed as he picked through the selection of plushies on the rack next to us. "I mean, don't get me wrong, if this were a normal dig you had us on, I'd be thrilled to be here, but on the chance that your memory has been jarred too much, let me fill you in on the particulars of what's going on. Our ship is destroyed. Pizlow has a battleship full of Ratters parked outside, and they're currently trying to kill us. Then, to top things off, you're gushing blood out of your head and now you're telling me your brain is tilapia."

"I think you mean tapioca. Tilapia is a fish. Tapioca is the pudding."

Tolby gave a half snarl. "You know what I mean, so you'll understand how getting a Q&A session with the museum's curator isn't high on the list of my priorities, unless you can somehow wormhole us home."

I wrapped my arms around him and squeezed before holding up successive fingers for each upcoming point. "First, they're not currently trying to kill us. They will try and kill us in about five hours. I'll be back to my unfoggy self in about half that time. Second, there are archives we can go to and get a copy of everything here to take home."

"That's something," Tolby said, looking more relaxed. "Hope they aren't in book form."

I shrugged. "Can't remember that part. But I'm pretty sure Curator said taking what we wanted would be as easy as playing a kid's game—or something like that."

"How long have you been traveling for?"

I shrugged again. Though I didn't have an answer, I was still feeling upbeat and divine. "No idea. Still fuzzy on the details, but not that long, I don't think. Why? Do I look old?"

"No, but I was wondering if I should dare to hope that you found us a way home."

My mouth twisted to the side. I had found a way home, hadn't I? Or come up with a plan? With the power of Progenitor tech literally at my fingertips, we could probably commandeer Pizlow's ship without trouble.

"You look like that might be a yes."

"I get the feeling that I came across something, or I came up with something. For some reason hijacking Pizlow's ship seems good."

"I'm assuming you have something a little better than strolling into a cruiser sporting antimatter cannons, waltzing by a crew of several hundred Ratters and who knows what else, all armed to the teeth, and flying us home."

My gut tightened. When he put it like that, my idea might have needed some work. Still, I knew leaving the museum and my Progenitor arm were linked. "I think I came up with something better than that," I said. "It'll come to me. We've got time."

"Are you sure?"

"Yes to both."

Tolby nervously patted his sides as he glanced around the gift shop. "We should get moving," he said. "But if this marvelous plan of yours doesn't materialize in a couple of hours, I say we scour the museum for something else. Maybe they've got a working ship somewhere. Or at the very least, we can go back to this Curator of yours and maybe he can tell us what you should already know."

CHAPTER TWENTY-ONE

The archives were on the ninety-sixth floor. We had to go through a portion of the museum dealing with religious worship surrounding black holes and then duck through the Hall of Time, which focused on all forms of time travel—attempted and successful—before we'd reach our destination. Sadly, I still couldn't even recall what I couldn't recall, and thus, signs of danger and paradox backlash went unheeded.

"Check this guy out," I said, admiring the display of a dashing guy in a black, 5th century PHS business suit, standing inside a library of books (yes, actual books). His face was chiseled with equal parts determination and worry, and his eyes looked like they'd seen a thousand years. "Such a cutie."

Tolby barely gave him a second glance. "If you say. What do you make of the blue box in the back?"

"That's how he gets around," I said.

"It's rather small," Tolby replied as he moved on to the next display. "Still, looks cozier than what this mouse and gerbil are running around in."

My eyes glanced to the display behind Tolby. There stood the figures of a white mouse wearing an eye patch, darting out of a grandfather clock with his companion in tow. Said companion was a pudgy little guy wearing a blue suit and a terrified look upon his face. "I think the other one is a hamster."

"Close enough," Tolby replied. "For the record, as far as time machines go, these aren't very sleek looking. You'd think they'd look better."

"I guess when you're hopping around all of eternity, aesthetics takes a backseat."

"Too bad this place went belly up," he said. "You could've had your own figure here."

"I get the feeling that if this place was still in business, things would be a lot different."

My stomach rumbled, and I reached into my pocket and pulled out a Kilgore's Mega Bar—a delicious treat I'd discovered when we'd passed through a food court not long ago and found that snacks were being kept in a stasis vending machine. I eagerly tore off the wrapper and took a bite. The crispy cookie crunch with a delicious, chocolate-caramel-like coating was heavenly. "I should've grabbed more," I said, sad I was halfway through the bar. "These are delicious. I don't care how fast it goes to my thighs."

Tolby gave me an icky face. "I can't believe you like that."

"I can't believe you don't. All it needs is a nice root beer to wash it down."

Tolby scanned the area. "Is any of this sparking any new memories?"

"No, sorry," I said, wiping my mouth before tossing the wrapper on the floor.

Tolby grunted. "How terrible."

"I think a little bit of litter is the least of this museum's worries," I said, my face giving a slight scowl. "Besides, do you see a trash can?"

"Not you. That." Tolby pointed a single claw off to the side where half a set of pants lay in tatters. "Someone tossed a display."

I cocked my head and turned. Sure enough, off to the side, there was a ruined exhibit piece. I approached it slowly. It didn't take long to realize that the pants on the floor were vintage, first-century AHS, and likely part of an EVA suit. I could tell by the caraflax fabric for the outer shell that always had a distinct orange to it. When I noticed the deep brown stains along a portion of the leg, I grimaced.

"This could be bad," I said, willing myself to pick it up. As I feared, the other side was stained even more. "This could be really, really bad."

Tolby sidled up next to me. "Is that blood?"

"I hope not, but I don't think these were sitting under a leaky engine block, either." I studied the floor. It was composed of black-and-brown swirling marble. I couldn't see any stains on it, but given the texture, I couldn't be sure there weren't spatters of blood elsewhere without carefully inspecting every square meter. "Maybe we should get moving and leave the mystery to someone else."

Tolby checked his sidearm. "Did you find anyone else in here while you were hopping about?"

My brow furrowed. "Curator, but you knew that. Some others, too, I think?"

"Friend or foe?"

"The Ratters were foe, but those were the ones with Pizlow." I sighed heavily and shook my head in frustration. "I'm still alive though, right? And no worse for wear. They couldn't have been too bad, if they were, that is."

"True. Let's go."

We pushed through the rest of the Hall of Time. There were a few displays that had fallen over here and there, and one that—aside from a handful of larger chunks—had been pulverized into a fine powder as if a mountain giant had taken up tap dancing and used the display for shoes. I told myself it had happened eons before we got here, and I'd almost managed to convince myself that was true when I spotted part of an electrical board nearby shorting out, sending tiny sparks into the air and signaling it was in fact in its final throes of life.

I didn't point it out to Tolby, figuring he might opt to insist we leave the area posthaste and find a way out before we got the archives. And since we were this close to them, this close to having the most monumental find in all of history at our fingertips, to having a near infinite number of stories and cultures and technology to learn about, I couldn't bear doing anything that might take that away from me.

As we pressed on, there was a faint, slow and rhythmic sound that reminded me of an antique train engine expelling steam. I probably would've given it more thought, but by the time I really took note of it, we'd made a few turns and ended up at a door thrice my size that was set in a large arch. Running up the right side of the arch were a few rectangular protrusions, like the ones Empress had used to get us into Curator's office. Above that arch was a holographic projector that flickered to life. It cycled through a few symbols before it finally popped something up we could both read: Museum Archives.

"How do you suppose we get in?" Tolby said after trying to push open the door and it not moving one iota.

"Hoping this will do it," I said, pulling out the purple museum membership card.

I waved it in front of one of the rectangular boxes. A happy series of beeps followed, and the door slid away. I grinned at Tolby and ran inside with all the restraint of a little kid getting permission to buy anything in a candy store.

The hall beyond the door rose a few meters before ending at the outer edge of a spacious, circular room. Said room was about a hundred meters across with a domed ceiling that was easily twenty stories tall. Soft but ample light came from ornate sconces along the wall as well as from small orbs that floated in the air. Stretching

165

from floor to ceiling at regular intervals were black columns laced with fractal circuitry identical to what was on my arm. At the center of the room was a navy-blue, doughnut-shaped desk that had a lip an arm's length above my head.

We approached the desk, and the floor raised in sections to create a set of stairs. Once we reached the top, another hologram flickered to life. White symbols floated a few centimeters above the desk. They twitched, scrambled, then cycled through dozens of forms, like someone rapidly changing channels, before they displayed the following:

Master of Records. Ring Bell for Service.

"Bell?" Tolby said with an amused grunt. "This guy must really like throwbacks."

"Wonder where said bell is?" I said, noting the rest of the desk was bare. "Or if he's even around anymore."

Tolby put his paws on the sides of his mouth and called out. "Hellooooo?"

"Probably got axed with the rest of the cuts. Looks like we're on our own."

"Ding! Ding! Ding!" Tolby shouted, patting the air about service-bell height above the desk. "Can we get some help here?"

I cocked my head to the side and grinned. "Really?"

"Worth a shot."

Tolby barely got the words out before a deep, rushed voice filled the archives. No, it wasn't a voice, it was three, all speaking together in a major triad so they were perfectly harmonious. "Hang on! Hung on! Will hang on and stay, yes? We came, coming, will be there soon!"

I looked up and saw a spidery monstrosity descending upon us from one of the columns. Ten legs supported a bulky, metal-plated body from which three heads sprouted. Seven mechanical eyes—similar to those on Tour Guide, only larger—on each head fixated on Tolby and me while a trio of owl-like beaks chirped at us. Had I not been petrified with fright, I'm sure I would've bolted.

Only when the thing plopped down behind the desk did I realize that Tolby had crouched slightly and his claws were out.

"Calmed, settle, you ought to relax in this portion of fabric," it said, snaking a thick leg behind us. "What has the Master of Records done, do, might help you with sometime in this approximate when?"

"Hello. I'm Dakota, and this is Tolby," I said uneasily. "Could you say that again? I'm not sure what you meant."

The Master of Records leaned uncomfortably close. His middle head took up almost my entire field of view. His eyes, each the size of a fist, made me feel like he was absorbing every detail about me, right down to the quark. As mind-blowingly technologically advanced as he clearly was, I couldn't help but knock him down a few pegs on the IQ chart when he took my request literally and spoke at a snail's pace. "Calmed, settle, you ought to relax in this portion of fabric. What has the Master of Records done, do, might help you with sometime in the when?"

"Why are you talking like that?"

"It was, is, and will be difficult to speak to primates trapped in single points of present time," he replied with amusement. "Imagine, if you could, how hard it is for me to hear you well as you lack multi-dimensional timeslip interaction."

"I'd suspected as much," I said, wondering if I should even bother asking him to clarify anything ever again.

"Good!" he said. "You've been, are, and will be more clever than I'd assumed. So, to returned again to my question: what might I help you with in this approximate when?"

"We want to browse the museum archives," Tolby said.

"Ah, yes! That is the most common reason for you to have, had, or will come," he replied. "If you hold or will hold omega memberships, you can search to your hearts' content for free. I have archive copy cubes in this desk you may use."

"Yeah, about that," I said. "We don't exactly have that membership, per se..."

"That was, is, and will be too bad," he replied. "Correction will be needed on your part."

"Could we look for a bit?" I said. "We won't take it for long, I promise."

"Took, take, taking?" All twenty-one of Master of Records' eyes closed as he chuckled. "Such things haven't been, are not, nor will be free in this space of when, nor any when for that matter."

"You're saying we need to buy one?" Tolby said, his face looking as strained as my brain felt in keeping up with the conversation.

"Buying is and was a primitive descriptor of our possible transaction." Master of Records eased back and squatted behind the desk. "A mutually agreeable compensation should be reached as copying the archives has and will take effort on my part to create since you are without membership."

"I'll gladly give you all the money I have," I said. "Though I'm afraid it's not much—especially for what I'm sure you guys are used to."

The Master of Records laughed so loud and deep I could feel the vibration running through the floor. "Money? You take me for a species still and once clamoring to be a paltry million years old?"

"Ah, no," I said with a blush. At the moment I paused, I heard Tolby snicker and shot him a look of playful annoyance. "I'm not sure what you'd want is all, but I can't express to you how much I'd appreciate getting a copy."

"You'll appreciate it greatly, I've not doubted. Tell me in this when, from zero to a thousand, how appreciative would you be if you obtained a copy of the archives?"

"A thousand, thousands!" I said, laughing. When Master of Records didn't reply, or even move. I recomposed myself with an awkward throat clearing. "I mean, I'd rate my appreciation at one thousand, for certain."

"One thousand?" he said, perking. He gently tapped my head with the tip of a leg. "Such lies, no, no. Mistakes I should have say.

You will appreciate other things more, like your life and your friend's. But since losing them has not happened yet for you, you aren't sure. Understandable."

"I would like us both to stay alive. This is true."

"I would also like us to stay alive," said Tolby.

Master of Records gently swayed side to side. "Ah, there we go. I think I've adapted to your reference point in this when."

"You are a bit easier to understand," I said with a nod.

"Wonderful. Now, back to our transaction. Perhaps a better estimation for you is nine hundred? It is a lovely number, yes? A total of four two hundred and twenty fives."

I cringed at Master of Records's heavy emphasis of the number four. "I prefer to think of it as three, three hundreds."

"Your loss."

"I guess. How does this relate to us getting a copy of the archives?"

The giant spider-beast-robot used a leg to open an enormous drawer behind him. From it, he plucked what looked like a big cake stand—sans cake of course—that held three figures on it. All three looked ghastly. One reminded me of a decaying elephant that had been propped up like a scarecrow. Another looked like a malnourished turkey with an elongated neck and a humanoid head that was gnawing on its own innards, and the third was simply an old, dead tree with expansive arms and a creep factor that rivaled any horror writer's imagination.

"I hope this doesn't have anything to do with summoning the apocalypse or sacrificing my soul to a trio of maleficent deities." I chuckled.

"Nonsense," Master of Records replied. "This is a Jorgun's Run board, and it will be famed throughout your galaxy for the skill required to play with excellence."

"I like games," I said, relaxing slightly. I looked closer and noticed each piece was sitting in the middle of a hexagon with a different shade of light grey. "You want to play, I take it?"

If his beaks could smile, I'm sure they would have, given the excitement in his voice. "I haven't played in some fifteen thousand years, going by your vector in spacetime. To play a challenging game again would give me a satisfaction of four one hundred and fifties."

"You mean, if we play you a game, you'll give us a copy of the archives?"

"Correction. If you provide me with a challenge, I'll give you a copy."

Tolby nudged me with an elbow. "In other words, don't suck."

"Right," I said, sucking in a breath. "How long does a game take? Few minutes? I only ask because we've got some time constraints."

Master of Records scooted the board so it was centered between us. "We can play fast, if wishing. The concept is simple. You win by doing one of the followed: capturing the twenty Provinces of ether, escaping off the board with any of your ninety-two harbingers—similar to escaping with the king in your ancestor's game of Hnefatafl—or by building five temples to the deity of your choice. Each of your twelve-hundred armies will have unique traits, so you should learn those first before we continue."

I looked to Tolby for some input, but the confusion on his face dwarfed my own. Feeling like I was about to ask a stupid question, I pointed to the decaying elephant. "What's this guy?"

"Your bishop of hallowed songs," Master of Records replied. "A powerful piece you should protect."

"Okay," I said. "Where are the armies? And temples?"

Master of Records tilted his head up slightly so he was staring at an empty space about a half meter above the board. "These are your armies. They watch your sacred spots where I will try and erect temples." His gaze shifted to more empty space on the right, and he continued. "And these are your harbingers who sit upon dark tiles of imprisonment."

"I'm still not following," I said. "Sorry."

"One of these is a harbinger."

"Still not seeing it."

Master of Records's eyes narrowed, and his beaks rapidly clacked together. "Oh...damn..." he said, easing back. "I forgot. You're a vintage species."

"Vintage?"

"Yes," he said. "In my excitement, I missed you were a mere human, not an advanced descendant of future years."

"Hey, I'm not a mere anything!" I said. I raised my Progenitor-infused arm. "I can surf time with the best of them."

"Despite that, your brain can barely process three dimensions." Master of Records chuckled as he pushed the gameboard to the side. Even though the guy was as alien to me as anyone could possibly get, I swear I saw pity in his eyes. "I suppose I could make a three-dimensional projection of the seven-dimensional board space, but that will take several hours and put my happiness index at a smaller amount."

"We need to be gone in several hours," Tolby said.

"Need or want?"

"Need to if we want to stay alive," Tolby said. "Some unfriendly competitors are coming."

"And the museum is going to be destroyed," I tacked on.

"And the museum is going to be destroyed," Tolby repeated. He took a half step away from me. "What do you mean the museum is going to be destroyed?"

"It's going to be destroyed," I repeated hesitantly. I looked around the archive room, trying to figure out what had sparked that memory and if anything else around would help me fill in the gaps. "It just came to me. Curator was watching these screens showing futures where the museum was destroyed in all manner of ways. Implosion. Explosion. Unchecked warzones. Gravitational collapse. Pretty spectacular stuff, honestly. He said it wouldn't be much longer now."

Tolby spun me around so I faced him, and he grabbed me by the shoulders. "That's a pretty damn big thing to forget!" he shouted. "We need to find a way out of here ASAP."

"I know, but it's not that bad."

"The entire museum exploding while we're stuck in it is the very definition of bad!"

I eased his paws off my body as I explained things best I could without sounding condescending. "I have a way out of here, remember? We've got time."

"You say that," he said. "Maybe you forgot that you don't."

I shook my head. "No, I do. It'll come to me. I promise." I checked my timer. "Another hour, tops, which leaves us with plenty to get to wherever."

Tolby turned to Master of Records, who hadn't said or moved at all since our mini-altercation. "Why are you so blasé? Or is this exploding museum only news to me?"

"My presence is not tied to this insignificant portion of spacetime. I exist across seven dimensions and twenty-eight universes in the multiverse. You are like fish in an aquarium, and what you see of me here is like a fingertip dipped in water."

"Which means what when this place is destroyed?" I asked.

"I will remove my finger from the water before that happens."

Tolby pulled my hand. "Let's go. We don't have the luxury of hopping around the multiverse."

Despite the wisdom of his words, I wasn't about to leave without an archive cube. We were one stupid game away from having the entire universe's history in the palm of our hands, and a little thing like the museum's armageddon wasn't going to stop me from getting it. "You want a challenging game in exchange for a copy of the archives, right?" I said to Master of Records. "Since I can't play the one you offered, maybe we could do a different one? Something we both know?"

"I'm aware of all the simple games you humans play," he said. "Such predictable pursuits aren't entertaining enough to meet my needs."

"What if we played something with dice? Backgammon? Flutter wing? Risk?" I asked, hoping the random factor would sway his mind. "Or maybe a card game where you have to read your opponent like poker?"

"I'm afraid we're at an impasse. Random chance leaves little room for skill and reading humans is far too easy for me," Master of Records replied. There was a touch of disappointment in his melodic voice, but apparently there wasn't enough sympathy for him to simply give me the archives. "I've charged everyone for my services. It would be unfair to others not to do the same for you. You are free to browse what we have until you need to go or the museum ceases to exist. At that point, I suppose, you will be forced to stop reading."

"But if the museum's gone, so are your archives!" I protested. "Don't you want to save them?"

Master of Records chuckled. "I keep backups offsite, of course. Besides, with the Progenitors gone and my service to them paid in full once the museum closes for good, I think I'll take up another hobby."

"Please," I said, dropping to my knees and clasping my hands in front for added effect. "I need one. How about two truths and a lie?"

"As I've said, too easy for me."

"Come on," I begged. "I bet you'll find me harder than you think. Here's one you can practice on: I've got an apartment on Mars. My favorite drink is orange juice, and I had two cats growing up."

"Your favorite drink is not orange juice," he said without a second's hesitation.

I grunted, and my face soured. "That was a warm-up. My mom teaches dance classes. I'd rather be in my jammies than an LBD, and my brother Logan tripped me when we were little and I busted open my chin."

"The last one's a lie. We're done."

"If we've got time, we'll come later, Dakota," Tolby said, giving me a nudge.

"No," I replied, shaking my head. His words gave me a fantastic idea. "I can do this. I lost on purpose, feeding you false information."

"I'm tired of this," Master of Records said as his eyes tinted a slight shade of red.

"All the marbles on this last one," I said.

"Then we up the stakes. You win, you get a cube. I win, I infect you with the Juxipode plague."

"And now we're finished," Tolby said, pulling me along.

I slipped out of his grasp and squared off with the Master of Records. Before Tolby could make a second attempt, I offered my left arm as an injection site for whatever epidemic-causing needle he had and met the challenge. "My name is Dakota. Before today, I've never been drunk, and you've got archive cubes in your desk."

CHAPTER TWENTY-TWO

Tolby cursed. Loudly. More than once. I lost track after a dozen, to be honest. Though I mostly kept my eyes locked on Master of Records to continue issuing my challenge to him, I couldn't help but throw a glance at my tiger buddy when he started stomping around.

"Well, which one is the lie?" I said, my voice ironclad.

Master of Records eased back and crouched as if he were about to pounce on some unfortunate prey. All twenty-one eyes cycled rapidly through the spectrum of colors while his plentiful beaks nipped at the air like he was plucking unseen snacks that flew by. "Not possible," he said. "Your affect says you're not lying and lying at this exact moment of when."

"Is that a fancy way of saying you resign?"

Master of Records drummed his feet on the floor, sending strong enough shockwaves up my legs that my lower half tingled. "Tricky, tricky, tricky," he said. "What do I know about you? Do you treat me like a fool? Or a better?"

I said nothing and concentrated with every fiber of my being not to show any expression whatsoever as he continued.

"Of your three offerings, only one I am unsure of, so clearly the lie is the second choice," he said. "But only a fool would take the obvious bait, and since I know what is in my desk, you might call yourself Dakota, but that is not your name. However, I see respect in your eyes for all that I am, and you know I am no fool. You would count on it, like all the others who've played such deadly games, from kidnappers to pirates, so I can obviously determine your second statement is the lie."

"Is that what you're going with, then?"

Master of Records tapped the floor some more. "Hardly. As a primitive species, your methods of communication leave much to want, thus you've learned not to trust others. So, you wouldn't trust me acting as I should, so I can clearly pick the first."

I sighed, making sure I exaggerated it as much as I could before topping it off with a look of pity. "We all know where this monologue of yours goes. You're not getting anything from me. Make a decision or admit defeat."

Master of Records closed the distance between us. He brought his head so close to mine that I could have leaned a hair forward and kissed him. "You're cheating," he said. "They're all truths."

I swallowed, even though I didn't mean to. "Is that your answer?"

"Yes."

I dropped my arm and smiled. "I win. There aren't any archive cubes in your desk."

Master of Records jumped back and roared. "Lies! No, truths! No!" He spun around, and I raced to the edge of the desk to see what happened next. A tentacle sprouted from his chest and pressed against a portion of the desk on the other side of me. A panel popped out a few centimeters before sliding to the side and revealing an empty cabinet inside.

My legs tensed and my hand found Tolby's paw. I hoped Master of Records would be a good sport about losing, but if he wasn't, I had to be ready to catapult us through a wormhole to safety. Okay, maybe the safety part was hopeful thinking.

"Where are the cubes?" Tolby whispered.

Master of Records turned around. He didn't squash me, but I wasn't expecting the deep laughter that bellowed from all of his mouths. "Clever, clever," he said. "I've underestimated your resourcefulness, but only because I erred in thinking you basic."

I bowed. Apparently, my gamble on future actions had paid off.

"Put them back, and you can take your prize and go," he said.

A portal opened inside the cabinet and out spilled a dozen grey cubes, each about the size of a softball.

"Will someone please tell me what's going on?" Tolby said. "Is this more of your time-hopping shenanigans?"

"Something like that," I said, rubbing the top of his furry head. "I'll explain—well, show you—but once I do, you've got to be patient with me again."

"Again?"

"Yeah, my brain is going to be mushy soon."

"Don't you dare forget anything else! We're in enough trouble as it is!"

"Too late," I said, pointing to the archive cubes in the cabinet. "I'm already going to do it." At that point, I tuned out Tolby's further objections and threw up a portal that started right in front of me in the now and ended inside the cabinet fifteen minutes ago. Quickly, I reached in and scooped out each archive cube. Once I had them at my feet, I moved the exit to inside the cabinet a few minutes prior and kicked all but one through.

"Well earned," Master of Records said.

"Oh, hello," I said to the giant spider-robot guy with three heads. "We're looking for the archives. Are we in the right place?"

Tolby grabbed my hand and whipped me around. "I hate you," he said. "I want you to know that. And if you get us killed because you willingly scrubbed your brain with a cheese grater, I'm going to make it my mission to exact my revenge in the next life, and the one after that, too."

"I wouldn't do that," I said, laughing. "You worry too much, Logan."

Tolby growled. "I'm not your brother."

"How can you say that after all these years?"

"We're not even the same species!"

"Probably why Mom likes me best." I gave him a playful punch in the side. "I still love ya though."

Tolby batted me on the cheek, hard. "Snap out of it!" he said. "This entire place is going to blow up, and I'm not in the mood to play stupid games whether you can help it or not."

"I never hit you, even when you deserved it being a little hellion that always tried to pick fights with me," I said, eyes watering. "And even when you were a total brat, I still stood up for you when you needed it most."

"I'm not the bad guy here!"

"Says the one who just hit me," I said. "When you feel like apologizing for being an ass, you can help me find the archives."

"We're in the archives!"

"We are?" I said. The unexpected boon made the sting on my cheek vanish. I glanced around, and once I saw the archive cube sitting on the floor, I scooped it up. "Awesome sauce! I told you this would work out. I did say that, right? Let's go find the food court and get some grub to celebrate. I'm famished."

"You've really gone and mucked things up, haven't you?" he said.

"I don't see how," I replied, feeling frumpy. "Hey, you're supposed to be apologizing to me."

"No, I'm going to go find us a way home before we both die. But if that's not possible, I hope your memory comes back enough so you can realize what you've done and be swamped with guilt."

With that, Tolby stormed out of the archives.

* * *

Incoming tangent, I know, but it's relevant. I promise. Anyone who knows anything about warp cores will always tell you that proper maintenance is vital if want your displacement drive to operate efficiently and if you value having your atomic structure remain intact as you zip around the galaxy. Of course, when your parents buy you your first spaceship, you aren't always paying attention to basic advice such as:

Remember to check the radiation seals from time to time, Dakota.

Make sure you rotate subspace grabbers every ten thousand light-years, Dakota.

Clean your ejection ports once a month or else you risk blockage, Dakota.

The last one is super important. I found that out three months after I was given free rein to pop over to any system I could afford the fuel to. As I prepped my core for a jump back home, some four hundred light-years away, a klaxon blasted in my ears and a dire warning about impending reactor meltdown filled my ship's HUD.

"No. No. No," I said over and over again, staring stupidly at the screen. After the third skipped beat of my heart, I realized if I wanted to live, I had to do something. Anything. So I flipped up the safety to the emergency egress system, hammered the button, and pulled the cord for all I was worth.

The cockpit immediately sealed itself off as solid-fuel rockets hurled me away from the rest of my ship as the cockpit broke away. The G's slammed me into my seat so hard I was sure my brain was driving into my stomach. By the time the rockets let off, the bulk of my ship was a tiny dot on my scanner. Said bulk never blew up, by the way. I found out why after I was rescued and paid a hefty sum to get my ship into drydock.

Because I'd been less than stellar in cleaning the port (i.e. never), I hadn't noticed a tiny gap that crud was getting slammed into. That crud managed to short out a sensor, which after an unfortunate cascade of other little problems, led to a false disaster warning.

Even though I came out of the ordeal unscathed—though poorer—and even though technically I wasn't ever in real danger, I'd never been so terrified in my entire life. In fact, as I stared at that bright, angry warning screen, certain I was about to ride the Fission Express, I knew in that stark moment of terror that if by some stroke of luck I survived, nothing would ever scare me that badly again.

Holy snort was I ever wrong.

I became acutely aware of that fact when I caught up to Tolby on the other side of the Hall of Time exhibit, and he stood petrified, eyes fixated on what was about forty meters down the hall.

This...creature, for lack of a better word, was staring us down with seven eyes set in a squid-like head. Five tentacles hung from under those eyes, one of which tightly clutched the remains of a first-century AHS EVA suit. An array of cybernetic implants poked out from pink leathery skin, and the damn thing stood on powerful legs that were nearly as thick as I am tall. Worst of all, it didn't take an alien mind reader to know he was looking at us like a snack and that he was responsible for wrecking the *Vela*'s bridge.

"Please tell me he likes carrots," Tolby said.

"I don't think so."

Before I could say more, the monster roared and charged. Reflexively, I opened a portal. I didn't know to where or to when, and I imagine because my brain had yet to congeal, I opened it up thirty meters away and on the museum ceiling. The wormhole looked sickly, if a wormhole could, that is with ill-defined edges and this red, mostly transparent film that covered it. I couldn't tell where it led to, but I did see a table drop out and smash to the floor. The raining furniture was more than enough for the creature to pause in front of it and then shoot a tentacle into the great unknown.

Well, mostly unknown. Wherever the portal led to, it was a place of utter chaos as I heard shouts and screams of all kinds. Not that that's too surprising. I mean, what would you do if you were having a lovely chat around a table and all of a sudden that thing popped up next to you?

"Dakota! Move!" Tolby said, yanking my hand.

His order snapped me out of my transfixion, and we darted into the exhibit across the hall. It was the start of a musical wing that dealt with cultures that combined performance pieces with olfactory input. I only took note of this—no pun intended—because every ten meters or so, a new piece of music filled my ears along with the most peculiar smells (I have no idea who thought mixing something jazz-like and rotten blueberries was a good idea).

We were about halfway through when the creature took up the chase. He came careening into the exhibit, smashing to the side. In the mad scramble, my feet found something other than the floor and down I went, taking Tolby out with me. We both crashed against the wall, and as I rolled over, it was painfully obvious we were both about to get a good look at that thing's dental work.

The monster lunged at the two of us. As he flew through the air, tentacles eager to wrap around our bodies, those all-too-familiar alien formulas raced through my mind and filled my vision. A wormhole opened between him and us, and in the creature went. I saw him tumble down a dark tunnel before sleep overtook me.

When I regained consciousness, I lay sprawled out on the same musical wing where I'd banished Mister Cyber Squid. The air was filled with 3rd century PHS neo bubblegum pop music and held notes of lavender that tantalized my nose. Tolby paced nearby, though he didn't see me rouse.

I pushed myself up and whimpered as muscles along my side and shoulder spasmed. "Hot damn that hurts," I said, clearing my eyes. "Are you okay?"

Tolby bolted over to me. "Are you just saying that or do you actually remember what's going on?"

"Oscar attacked us, I think?"

"Oscar?"

"That monster with all the tentacles."

"Why are you calling him Oscar? Pretty sure Tour Guide called him Eddie."

I shrugged as I got to my feet. "Oscar is as good as Eddie."

"Well, if we're making up names for him regardless of what he's called, I think Mister Cyber Squid is better," Tolby said. "And yes, he attacked us, but you threw him into a wormhole before passing out."

"For how long?"

"Four hours," he said. "We're practically back when we started."

"When?" I bit my lip, desperately trying to get to memories I knew were right there under the fog in my mind.

"The Ratters?" he prompted. "The firefight?"

"The Ratters? Oh! Oh god, yes!" I laughed and hugged my tiger buddy as tight as I could. "Tolby, you're never going to believe what I found!"

"It better not be Mister Cyber Squid's older brother."

I let go and grinned. "No. I found Kibnali. A whole bunch of them!"

"Not funny," he said, face stern and eyes hard.

"I swear!"

"They're dead, Dakota. Every last one," he said. "Aside from me, the Kibnali are extinct."

I shook my head and laughed, even though he didn't share my joy. "No, they're not. I met the Empress. Or an empress. And her handmaidens, too. The Progenitors snatched them right before your world was destroyed. On my life, Tolby, they're alive and waiting for us!"

I could see the truth of my words sink into his head. His head tilted, but he didn't smile. "You're serious, aren't you?"

"As flying through a supernova!"

"You found the last of my race and didn't think it was important enough to tell me?"

I probably shouldn't have chuckled, but I did. To my defense, it was because I was nervous and confused as to why he wasn't as excited as I was. "If I could remember anything past my name, I would have! Look, yell at me later, but that's not the end of it. They've got a ship we can use to get off this place!"

"They have a ship, too?" he yelled. "We went back in time, nearly got killed for a stupid little cube, and now we've got to deal with the Ratters again when we could've left anytime we wanted?"

"No! It's not like that!" I said. "We can't see them until after the Ratter attack."

Tolby crossed his arms. "Why?"

"Too risky due to paradox backlash," I explained.

"A what, what?"

"Paradox backlash," I said. "See, they helped me when we got split up, so if we leave with them before that, that changes things."

"So?"

"So I might not have made it to Curator's office without them, and then, well, bad stuff could happen as the Universe tries to correct all that."

"And you know this how?"

"That Curator guy explained a lot, but some of this is instinctual now, kind of like when you're hungry. No one has to tell you what the feeling means. You just know you need food or you'll die."

"Or maybe you're wrong. Maybe we could've left and in the new future you would've made it some other way."

"Please, let's argue about this later. Hate me later, if you want," I said. "But we've got to catch up to them before we get left behind."

"Fine," he said. "But no more damn portals. Got it? You're going to wipe your memory so bad one of these times it's going to be the end of both of us."

"You got it."

CHAPTER TWENTY-THREE

We never did catch up to them, the other Kibnali that is. We were on our way back when...oh god, that hurts. Would whoever is scrubbing my brain with a cactus please stop? I swear, trying to piece together some of these memories is worse than having rats gnaw off fingers.

I remember we were a dozen floors away, maybe two. Tolby and I had come out a turbo lift and run right into a group of a couple of dozen Ratters. One had a bazooka, was it? Or a pack of mechanoid wolves with teeth the size of daggers? Gah, that doesn't sound right.

I do remember being pinned behind an exhibit dealing with counter-espionage and lie detecting as plasma bolts ripped through everything all around. Tolby, taking cover about fifteen meters away at the entrance of a side hall, kept his shots accurate enough so the little vermin didn't overrun us.

At least, until a Ratter the size of a polar bear came barreling down the hall, sporting a rotary phase cannon.

"Tolby! He's going to vaporize us!"

"Not if he's without a head," Tolby snarled. My bud peeked around the corner to pop off a few shots, but instead of taking the Ratter out, he took a hit to the shoulder. Tolby immediate recoiled and grabbed his wounded shoulder, dropping his sidearm in the process.

It's funny how facing certain doom can inspire you to greatness. Or madness.

Realizing we couldn't even crack open an egg before they were going to crack open our skulls, I gave them a better target—a juicier, easier one. I shut my eyes and tried to form a portal near the Ratters with its opening next to me, only a few minutes into the past. I could feel the backlash building in my mind as a paradox grew near—namely, the Ratters having a clear shot at the back of Old Me, before I had a chance to open this wormhole.

The air grew cold around me, and Tolby's cries filled my ears. "Dakota! What the dark void are you doing?"

"Making a banana split!" I shouted as my mind quickly approached tapioca status. "It'll be yummy. You'll see!"

"You're making another portal, aren't you?" he shot back. "Damnit, Dakota, your brain can't take all this!"

I guess he was right on that since I still can't remember all that happened. I do know that a split second later, the giant Ratter spun and shrieked with excitement as the wormhole I'd wanted sprang into existence. Six other Ratters turned and shot wildly at the portal and at Old Me. Thanks to the pushback from spacetime and the universe abhorring a paradox, their shots bent away from the wormhole.

Grinning, I kept the portal open as long as I could. My mind fogged. The taste of cotton candy filled my mouth, and I began humming along to Beethoven's Fifth Symphony as it played mightily in my head.

That symphony was silenced as a huge explosion ripped through the portal, incinerating half the attacking Ratters and closing the wormhole. I reeled back while the museum spun around me. Tolby yelled, roared, and then something hit me in the back of the head and down I went.

With a moan, I rolled over to see Veritad, that brute I'd met in the cargo bay earlier, standing over me. In one hand, he gripped a baton crackling with energy, and in the other, he casually held a pistol at his side.

"Cookies? For me?" I said, feeling so light-headed the line between reality and dreams had long disappeared. "Why sure, back up the truck..."

The rest of the scene gave way to darkness.

I'm sure a lot happened after I came to, but I'm not sure what.

My first solid memory after getting dropped by Veritad was realizing I was strapped to an interrogation chair with two guys named Drugar and Lucun next to me. They were muscle-bound goons similar to Veritad, and they were currently trying to pump me for info.

Correction, they weren't pumping me for info. They'd grown weary of listening to me ramble, something I was keenly aware of when Drugar slammed a fist practically the size of a compact car onto the steel table in front of me, causing everyone—Lucun included—to jump. Drugar leaned his dragonish face so close to mine that the tips of his four horns rested against my forehead.

"We're not interested in your life story, little girl," he said with a growl. "Tell us where Pizlow and the resonance crystal are."

Bile rose in my throat as his breath hit me. I swear a full septic tank that's stewed for a hundred years would easily be more bearable. That said, I didn't think it was wise to offer him a breath mint or a toothbrush—even if his dentist would appreciate it. Meatheads did go to the dentist, didn't they?

I got smacked on the side of the head before I could continue the thought, which spurred a reply out of me. "You said to tell you everything," I replied with a wavering voice and hands trembling.

"That's all I'm doing, I swear. My memories are fragmented so all I can do is say what comes to me."

"Fragmented? Right. Sounds like you're stalling to me."

I could feel my face drain of what color it had left. "I'm not stalling. Trust me."

"The last people I trust are the ones who tell me to trust them," he said with a snort. He then glanced over to his twin steroid-popping buddy, who was currently tinkering with the power supply that ultimately led to the torture chair I was in. "Get that damn thing fixed yet?"

"Almost," Lucun replied. "Give me ten minutes, tops, to swap out the transformer and put it back together. Then we'll see if she's telling the truth."

At that, Drugar showed off triple rows of razor teeth. "Sounds like you've got some time left. Tell me about this device of yours."

Sweat dripped from my forehead into my eyes, and I tried to rub them on my shoulder. I guess Drugar took that as me trying to buy more time because he dug his claws into my left arm and drew blood. I yelped in pain and blurted out an answer. "It's a Progenitor artifact."

"You said that already," he replied. "Tell me more about it."

"It turns people's brains into goo," Tolby interjected with disgust. Like me, he was lashed to a chair and was beaten up pretty badly. Blood caked his fur, and it looked like at least one tooth was cracked. That beaten look, however, paled in comparison to the hateful glare he cast upon me.

"What do you mean it turns people's brains into goo?" Drugar said.

"What I mean is that the artifact is too much for her pea-sized brain to handle," Tolby spat. "Every time she uses it, it screws her up, and she forgets everything."

Drugar chuckled with amusement. "You seem bitter about it."

"You might say that," Tolby said.

"What would you say?"

"I'd say she deserves to die alone and have her name wiped from history for getting us into this mess, but that's still probably too good for the likes of her."

My heart had never known so much pain in that very second. I'd have gladly died a thousand deaths than have been responsible for the sudden change in Tolby's attitude toward me. Tears rolled down my cheeks, and I wracked my brain trying to figure out what I'd done, but my memories were fleeting, and I couldn't piece anything together.

"What happened between you two?" Drugar said, throwing me an amused glance. "Steal his catnip?"

"I have no idea," I replied. "My memories are wiped—that's the price of using the artifact and why I can't tell you where Pizlow is. Not yet, at least."

Drugar dug his claw into my skin where my shoulder met my neck. Blood seeped from the wound and further stained my shirt. "Stalling is pointless and painful. No one is coming to save you."

"I know. You have no idea how much I'm aware of that fact."

"Sounds like you need a reminder."

I shook my head and rattled off as much as I could about the portal device, where I got it, and how it worked, but I'm afraid it was such a jumbled mess that none of it was very helpful. At the very least, my spilling of info was shamefully cowardly enough that Drugar didn't think I was hiding anything and let me talk right up until a low hum emanated from the generator that Lucun was working on.

"Is it ready?" Drugar asked.

"It's ready," Lucun replied.

Drugar grinned and placed a silver band over my head like a crown. Only, it was nothing that royalty would wear since it was designed to accurately scan brains to determine when the truth was being told. After all, there's not a lot of fun in ruling over the peasants when they know you're full of it. Unless of course, you've got the army from hell to enforce your will regardless of what people think. To my dismay, however, the only army I had ever had were some plastic soldiers I'd played with as a kid. They weren't very frightening, and they only did so much damage when stepped on with bare feet. And they were eight thousand light-years away and boxed up in an attic. So, they were out.

"What color are your eyes?" asked Drugar, cutting into my thoughts.

"Brown," I replied without hesitation.

"Where did you meet Tolby? And lie this time."

I balked, but when my captor gave the wound on my neck a twin for company, I answered with a grimace. "We met after I beat a street magician twelve times in a row in three-cup monte."

Electricity raced through my body. I thrashed against my restraints, but they held fast. A faint smell of cooked flesh wafted through the air, and I slumped in the wooden chair.

"That never gets old," Drugar said with a glint in his eye. "Now tell me another lie, but you pick what it is."

"I love you," I said, breathless.

Again, the shocks came. When they finished, I fell limp in the chair.

Drugar leaned back and laughed. "How sweet of you."

"Looks like it's working," Lucun said as he checked a computer display nearby. "All the readouts are solid."

"Solid enough to know when she's omitting the truth, too?"

Lucun nodded. "We'll know something is up. It'll fry her just the same."

Drugar then stuck his face in mine and slowly enunciated each syllable in his next question. "Do I need to hear everything that happened?"

"If you want me to remember all the details so you can operate that thing, yes," I replied weakly.

"Why?"

"Because after being knocked silly and shocked a few times, I'm not sure how else to make sure I don't miss anything important," I said. I then nodded as best I could toward the portal device. "The power cell is still recharging, anyway. You might as well hear me out."

"How much longer?" he asked.

"Not long," I replied, wishing to God that it was otherwise. "Should be full in another ten minutes."

"I can't use it until then at all?"

I thought about flat out saying no, since that was mostly the truth, but I didn't want to risk another blast of a thousand volts. So I ended up shaking my head as I explained. "You can, but it needs to be at full capacity if you're going to bend spacetime enough to reach the pocket universe Pizlow is in. You'll be rolling the dice with anything less. That's not a roll you want to lose."

"What happens if you shoot before its ready?"

Tolby shuddered and wiggled in his seat. "Bad things."

"Be specific."

"If you're lucky, you get a destabilized portal that will make a bit of a mess."

"And if you're not?"

"Every molecule in your body will explode at the speed of light."

"Total protonic reversal, huh?" Drugar said, sounding impressed. "How'd you find that out?"

"There was a training video, for lack of a better word, that Dakota watched," Tolby explained. "It was one of a few examples of things not to do."

Drugar still looked skeptical, so I figured I should chime in. "What happens is about as pretty as a quantum detonator exploding inside a septic tank."

"What's it say?" Drugar said, looking to Lucun.

"Says she's telling the truth," his cohort replied.

"Of course I am," I grumbled.

Drugar smacked me on the back of the head. "Mind your mouth and tell us the rest while we wait for this thing to charge."

CHAPTER TWENTY-FOUR

I'd barely talked for five minutes before Veritad stormed into the interrogation room, nostrils flaring. I never thought the guy was particularly smart, maybe a dozen points away from breaking a hundred on an IQ test, which meant he was probably twice as smart as Drugar and Lucun combined. This also meant he was probably four times as dangerous, too.

"She's lying," he said.

"I'm not—" was all I managed to get out before Veritad was in my face with a dagger as big as my forearm pressed against my neck.

"Don't play games with me, little girl," he growled.

Drugar glanced to Lucun, who checked the monitor before shrugging.

"How do you know?" Drugar asked.

"I went back and checked around the museum where we caught them," Veritad replied, digging the point of his blade into my neck. "Turns out there's an exhibit a few rooms away that not only showcases this lie detector but also describes how to beat it."

My eyes widened in terror, and I shook my head while speaking as fast as I could. "I had no idea that exhibit even existed."

"She's still telling the truth," Lucun said.

"Of course the device says she is, you brainless warp worm," Veritad growled. "I just told you she knows how to beat it."

Drugar, thankfully, decided to ask questions instead of have my head. "Then why did it shock her?"

"Why do you think? She did it on purpose to throw you off and stall for time, stupid," Veritad replied.

"Time won't save her," Drugar said. "She knows that."

"No, but whatever she's waiting for will," Veritad replied. He grabbed me by the hand and squeezed hard enough that it was a small miracle my bones weren't crushed. The pain, however, was more than enough to make me scream. "Bring Pizlow back."

"I can't," I said with a whimper. "If I try and open the tunnel before there's enough power, it'll lock on to the first spacetime portal it can find."

"Which means what?" Drugar said, putting a hand on Veritad's shoulder.

"Which means who knows what's on the other side," I replied.

Veritad shrugged his comrade off. "I won't ask again."

"I'm not even sure where Pizlow is! There are infinite pocket universes! I can't pick one at random and hope it's his! It'll be a disaster!"

To my surprise, Tolby groaned loudly. "Chop her stupid head off, already. I'm tired of her whining, and I'd like to enjoy my last few moments alive without her."

My heart skipped a beat at his comment, and twice more when Veritad chuckled. At that point, as I still had no escape plan and apparently no best friend either, I gave in. "Okay," I said. "I'll take possible death over certain death. Undo the restraints on my wrists."

Veritad laughed as he picked up the artifact. "How stupid do you think I am? You think I'm going to let you touch this when I know you're lying to us?"

I muttered a string of obscenities under my breath. I guess I was too hopeful for that one. I bit my lower lip and tried to remember the coordinates I'd haphazardly picked when I'd tossed Pizlow down the wormhole, which was a lot harder than you would think because I wasn't paying a lot of attention when I had. I was pretty sure I'd ended up picking nine hundred something. Nine forty, was it? For the life of me, I couldn't get those memories to work so I picked a combination of the best numbers I knew, ones that made me feel warm, safe, and tasted like fine wine: Nine, three, seven. Once they were firmly seated in my head, I prayed wherever this wormhole led wouldn't result in all of us having front row seats to an event horizon. At least I'd get to taste a lovely merlot one last time if we did.

"Here goes," I said, shutting my eyes and making the mental connection to the portal device as I'd always done. The entire process took only a second, but it sucked the energy out of me— something I'd later come to realize as the device trying to warn me that it was operating under hazardous conditions. Still, what choice did I have? They weren't listening.

"Is it ready?" Veritad asked, looking the device over.

I nodded as my gut tightened. "Yeah. Just point and shoot."

With one hand, Veritad aimed the device, and with the other, he wrapped his fingers around my neck. "If Pizlow isn't on the other side, I'm crushing your throat. Understand?"

"Yes," I said, swallowing hard.

"Good," he said before pulling the trigger.

The wall shimmered before a glowing red oval appeared that stretched from floor to ceiling. Initially, it reflected our room in a tinted light. After a few heartbeats, however, the image distorted. There was a loud crack, and the scene of a random floor in some random spot in the museum took its place.

Abruptly, like our room had been turned on its side, everyone slid toward the open portal.

At that point, there was a lot of yelling and hysterics. Mostly from our captors, but I'm not ashamed to say I was screaming, too. I had enough wits at least to kick against the floor as hard as I could to push myself to the side and avoid side-falling through the portal.

Everyone else did the same, more or less, and the only thing that fell through into whatever lay beyond was the table.

Brute bodies piled on the wall, narrowly missing both the portal and me. Lucun crashed into Veritad with enough force that I'm pretty sure he cracked a few ribs. Tolby tumbled into both an instant later, but since he was still restrained in his own torture chair, he couldn't do anything when Lucun shoved him off.

"Shut that portal down!" Drugar bellowed. He tried to push himself up off the wall, but ended up slamming into it once again.

Despite the chaos and danger, I couldn't help but smile at their powerless state. It felt good to see those bastards get a little bit of karma served up hot and fresh. That smile faded, however, the moment a gigantic tentacle shot out of the portal and groped the room with all the delicacy of a rabid bull in a china shop.

"What the hell is that?"

"Kill it!"

"Look out!"

I wasn't sure who said what, but a shriek came from Veritad when the tentacle coiled around his chest, slammed him into the wall twice, and then yanked him through the portal a nanosecond before it closed.

Spacetime, no longer having an acute, local identity crisis, returned to normal and everyone in the room fell to the floor.

Drugar was first to his feet. He was holding his dagger and was shakily pointing it to where the portal once was. "What was that?"

"That would be Mister Cyber Squid," Tolby said, upside down and face pressed against the floor.

"Oscar," I corrected.

"Mister Cyber Squid!"

"I'm the one who nearly got killed saving you from him, so I get to name it!" I shot back.

"And you only had to do that because you didn't listen to me! I said we had to leave, but no, you wanted to run around the archives right where that damn thing was!"

"AND THAT'S..." I stopped and slumped against my restraints. "Okay. Yeah. I ran us to the archives."

Drugar seized the back of my chair and hoisted me upright. He grabbed me by the hair and yanked my head back. "You knew that would happen."

"I had no idea where that portal would go," I pleaded. "I told him that. I told all of you that. The device needs a full charge to reach a pocket universe! I can't change that!"

Drugar's grip tightened, and some of my hair tore free from my scalp. Before any more damage could be done, Lucun pulled his shoulder. "Scan said she was telling the truth the whole time," he said. "Veritad was wrong."

Drugar looked at his cohort out of the corner of his narrowed eyes. "So?"

"We still need her to get Pizlow and the treasure."

"Unless you want to chance meeting Osca—Mr. Cyber Squid—again," I dared to say.

Drugar held his grip for a few more seconds before releasing. "Fine," he said. "Hook her back up to the machine, but if it beeps funny at all, I'm ripping out her heart."

Less than a minute later, Lucun had it set up again and gave Drugar the green to work me over. I barely noticed when he did, however, because a new memory crystallized in my mind. A memory I loathed sharing.

"You're thinking about something," Drugar growled. "Out with it."

"It's nothing—" I said, purely out of reflex. Sadly, the machine still considered it a lie and let me have it.

"Would you like to correct that statement?" Drugar said with a dark chuckle.

Slumped in the chair and ready to die, I nodded. "I know a few of the coordinates to Pizlow."

"A few?"

"Yeah," I said. "I think there are a couple more I can't quite think of."

Drugar grunted. "That's a start. What about the power levels? Is there enough juice to reach him?"

"The portal device will take a few more minutes to recharge after that last portal," I said. "Maybe ten."

"Ten it is," Drugar said.

Time ticked on, and the room grew unnervingly silent. This made all the screams in my head about all the nasty things that were going to take place that much worse. With only a few minutes left until the device was fully recharged, Lucun cleared his throat and spoke with hesitation.

"I had a thought," he said. "What if Veritad was right? What if she's playing us and getting us killed one by one?"

Drugar snorted. "You're the one that argued against that first."

"I know," he said. "But sometimes I've got to think things through, you know. Make sure what I'm knowing is right and proper. That's why I always win my fights."

"I'm not trying to get anyone killed," I said. "Veritad made me do that. You saw. Everyone saw."

"Maybe that's your game," Drugar said coming over to me. "We might not have a lot to work with when it comes to you, but I promise it'll take a long time before you die if we break each one of your bones. In fact—" He cut himself off and grinned like the devil before walking over to the comm on the wall and hitting a few buttons. When the call was answered, he said, "Go ahead and pick up Miss Dakota's brother once you arrive. If you don't hear back from us in a few hours, fillet him nice and slow."

"No!" I shouted, surging in my seat. "He's not a part to any of this!"

"He is now," Drugar said. "And if we don't come out on top, he's going to have his parts all over the galaxy."

An ugly cry burst forth, one that was anything but dignified and fueled by feelings of being helpless and powerless. "I don't remember where Pizlow is. I'd tell you if I did."

"I'll make a deal with you," Drugar said, leaning close to my face so once again his rancid breath assaulted my nose. "I won't break any of your fingers until that thing recharges. If you don't remember by then, anything goes. And if you make me wait much longer after your fingers are gone, you're going to find out what your best friend's eye tastes like."

"Ex-best friend," Tolby corrected.

"Shut it," Lucun said, striking Tolby in the cheek.

Tolby growled. "I've got a better deal for the two of you."

"Let me guess, let you go, and you won't kill us?" Drugar said with a laugh. "I've heard that one a few times now."

"No," Tolby said. "I'll tell you the code, and you let me go. I don't care what you do to her."

CHAPTER TWENTY-FIVE

Drugar flew across the room, dagger in hand. He dug the tip into Tolby's arm, but he didn't flinch. "You've known all this time and never said a word?"

"I wanted to make sure I was in a good position to negotiate before I played my hand," Tolby said, never breaking eye contact.

Drugar glanced to Lucun, who checked the monitors. "He's telling the truth. He knows."

"Then you're going to tell us right quick," Drugar said, "or you're going to get to taste your own eyeballs, and once I'm done with them, you'll get to eat hers, too."

"I'll eat hers right now," Tolby said, never blinking.

"Tolby, please," I said, managing to stop my ugly cry long enough to get some words out. "I don't know what I did to make you hate me, but I'm sorry. I never would do anything to hurt you."

"Shut up," he said. "The adults are talking."

"No, you're the one that's going to talk," Drugar said as he slipped the blade into Tolby's arm and gave it a twist. "Now tell me the code."

"Not until you let me go," Tolby said without a flinch.

Drugar snorted, and the tone in his voice carried a sizeable amount of respect. "Impressive, but I doubt you can do this all day."

"I don't have to," Tolby said. "This entire place is going to blow soon."

"You're lying," Drugar said.

"No, he ain't," Lucun said.

Tolby grinned and nodded slowly. "That's right. I'm not. Tell them how, Dakota."

At first, I didn't know what he was talking about, but then memories of Curator's office crystallized in my mind, and I let out a gasp as I remembered all the destruction I'd watched on those screens. I relayed what I saw as quickly and with as much detail as I could.

Drugar threw a glance to Lucun once I was finished. "Still telling the truth?"

"Yeah. The museum is getting nuked for sure."

Drugar stretched his arm and hit the comm button once more. A squeak of acknowledgment came from whoever was on the other end before he spoke. "Start a continuous scan of the museum for any irregularities and put the crew on notice. We might be leaving in a hurry."

Lucun's eyes went wide. "We're leaving the loot?"

"Loot is no good if we're not around to enjoy it," he said. He then went back to the comm. "Tell the boys inside to stuff our cargo hold. Let 'em grab anything and everything they want as long as they stay away from the reactor. Anyone goes near there, and I'll personally debone them for the next week. Understood?"

There was an excitement of Ratter chatter that I couldn't follow before Drugar cut the line and redirected his attention to Tolby. "I take it your bargaining then is you saved our lives, so we save yours."

"Something like that," Tolby said. "You get the treasure out of it, too."

"You've got a lot of gusto to think that's going to work."

"Perhaps," Tolby said. "But I've known mercenaries for my whole life. So I understand what you're doing here isn't personal, but you understand that me saving you is. So if we have a deal, I go home. You get money, and you get to feel good about doing the honorable thing."

"He's got a point," Lucun said. "If we get that crystal, who cares what happens to them, right?"

Drugar crossed his arms and thought for a moment before grunting. "Okay. We'll stick you in a pod preprogrammed to go to whatever dump of a planet you want."

"Oh, thank god," I said, exhaling with relief. "Just send us to Mars."

Drugar laughed. "You're not going anywhere. He's the one who warned us about the explosion. He's giving us the code. So he goes free, and you're going out the airlock."

"But—"

A backhand by Drugar ended my protest. "Out with it," he then said to Tolby. "On my word, when Pizlow gets here, I'll let you go."

Tolby shook his head. "No. Restraints first. Then you get the code."

"So you can attack us and escape?"

"I've no intentions of attacking you," Tolby said. "All I want to do is get the hell out of here."

"He's still telling the truth," Lucun said.

"And we're rapidly approaching the end of the museum," Tolby added.

Drugar dropped a hand on my shoulder as he pulled his pistol and pointed it at Tolby. "So, Dakota," he said. "How would you like Tolby's deal? All you have to do is give me the code before he does, and you're the one who goes home."

Was he serious? I didn't know, but even if he was, there was no way in hell I was leaving Tolby. I wouldn't let him go to his grave thinking he was anything but the world to me. Before I could answer, Tolby did.

"All right," he said. "It's eight, thirty-one, nineteen, seventy-seven."

"You're sure?" Drugar said.

"Absolutely," Tolby said. "She kept singing the numbers over and over to try and remember them for later. Guess that part didn't work."

Lucun smiled and gave a nod. "He's telling the truth. One hundred percent."

"And a deal's a deal, right?" Tolby asked.

"A deal's a deal," Drugar replied.

My mouth dried as all eyes focused on me. I know other people have their life flash before their eyes when facing death, but mine didn't. I felt numb and lost in a nightmare. I didn't even have the energy to try and make sense of Tolby's betrayal. All I could do was muster an apology to my best friend, even if he still hated me.

"Tolby, I'm sorry for whatever I did. I love you more than anyone else, and you've helped me out of more pickles than I ever deserved," I said. "Whenever you get home and back with your family, I hope you live a long, happy life, and maybe somewhere in that life you'll be able to forgive me."

Drugar snorted. "Touching. Now bring back Pizlow."

I sucked in a breath of air and shut my eyes. My brain danced with the interface as fractals swarmed my mind and warmth spread down my neck and into my arm. Numbers took shape. Pizlow's numbers.

Eight. Thirty-one. Nineteen. Seventy-seven.

"There," I said, opening my eyes. "It's set. All you need to do is point at the wall and shoot."

"It's about damn time," Drugar said as he squeezed the trigger.

A perfectly formed wormhole sprung to life and stretched from floor to ceiling. Through its glass-like opening, I could see a shadowy tunnel on the other side. It wasn't a dirty, mountain tunnel, nor a created one built out of metals or bricks, but rather it looked as if it was burrowing through a heavy, dark fabric that was slowly swelling and contracting. Deep within, almost imperceptible, was a large something moving, a shadow within a shadow.

"He's down there," I said.

"Looks like you weren't completely useless," Drugar said before waving to Pizlow and calling out to him. "Pizlow! Over here!"

The shadow turned and charged. Before anyone could react, Mister Cyber Squid squeezed out of the portal, gripping Pizlow's limp, goo-covered body in his tentacles. A light-blue energy field encased him, but despite the protection the shield offered, he still looked lifeless.

I instantly threw myself backward, toppling my chair. I hit the ground with a thud and flopped over, hoping that would make me a less appealing lunch. Several screams, a roar, and two reports of a sidearm rang through the air before Tolby was in my face, undoing my restraints in a flash.

"But...how?" I stammered.

"I'll tell you later! Now let's go!" he said, yanking me to my feet.

Mister Cyber Squid thrashed about, nearly flattening each of us into a wall. As we ran for the door, a bloody fight between him, Drugar, and Lucun raged on, though it was more one-sided than a Wanyani saber cat batting a pair of pod mice for fun.

Along the way out, I grabbed the portal device and the Gorrianian resonance crystal that happened to roll nearby, and Tolby had enough wits to snatch the archive cube and a small bag near the door.

We bolted down a long corridor and stopped at the end where a locked fire door blocked our way. I tried to use it, but the stubborn thing was so uncooperative it didn't even light up.

"I don't have my PEN," I said. "Can you do anything?"

Tolby brandished the bag he'd grabbed and took the handy device out. "You mean this PEN?"

I squeezed him tight. "You're amazing."

"I know," he said as he went to work on the control box. "Next time pay more attention to where they put our stuff."

"I'd rather there not be a next time if it's up to me."

"Good call."

"So you don't hate me?"

Tolby paused long enough to look me in the eyes and give a reassuring smile. "Never," he said. "But I needed them thinking I did so I could get free."

"You really scared me," I said. "Bad."

"I know. I'm sorry."

I shook my head and forced the memory away. I still had another question, though. "Did you know they both were in the same pocket universe?"

"Yeah, you kept laughing about it when you sent Mister Cyber Squid away before your brain went to mush," he said with a chuckle. "Thank the Great One you couldn't remember that tidbit when they were questioning you."

A roar blasted down the corridor and I spun on my heels. Mister Cyber Squid whipped his head, launching the pulverized body of Drugar into the air. The brute got about halfway to us before hitting the ground and rolling, leaving a bloody mess along the way.

"Work faster, Tolby," I said, eyes fixated on Mister Cyber Squid.

"I know!"

"I mean it!"

"I know!"

I glanced at the portal device. Tunneling through to the pocket universe had drained the power supply, but it had changed a little since that time. I could clearly see that the hologram had hints of orange to the red display. Then again, maybe that was wishful thinking on my part.

"You know," I said with a nervous laugh. "It's a good thing fatty over there can't squeeze through the door."

"Agreed."

Fatty, however, wasn't content with my assessment. He rammed his head and half a shoulder through the door, and slowed only a few heartbeats before his body contorted like an octopus squeezing through a tube before he pushed toward us, tentacles leading the way.

My eyes widened tenfold. "Tolby, you've got about thirty seconds before we're going to be able to study Oscar's dental work."

Tolby growled in frustration. "This isn't going to happen. Security is too tight."

"I don't care! Make it happen!"

Tolby glanced over his shoulder, and his jaw dropped. "Use the portal device."

I checked the display and wished I were religious, because if I were, maybe some god out there would listen to my frantic prayer and recharge the battery. "It's not ready."

"It's ready enough, Dakota! Just do it!"

"We could end up anywhere!"

"Which for me right now is a thousand times more preferable than getting a guided tour of that thing's digestive system!"

I swallowed hard and conceded the point. I figured popping a portal to the hall on the other side of the door wouldn't take too much energy, and so I aimed the portal device and fired. A wormhole sprang into existence, not even a meter in diameter. Its edge looked blurry. Bright arcs of electricity danced around it. What lay beyond was nothing but a swirl of color, rough texture, and flashes of light.

Before I could question the wisdom of my decision, I grabbed Tolby by the arm and dove through.

CHAPTER TWENTY-SIX

Blinding light and a crack of thunder assaulted my senses. My world spun like I'd been caught in a tumbler. A hard floor rushed up to say hi and knocked the wind out of me. A split second later, Tolby landed on my back. Thank god he had the wherewithal to partially catch himself so he didn't break my spine.

Still, he hurt like hell when he hit.

"Oh god, get off," I moaned. I tried to push him away, but I was too weak. My vision was shadowy, and my stomach churned. I barely turned my head to the side in time before throwing up.

Tolby staggered to his feet. "Let's not do that again. I can only get sick so many times before I lose my will to live."

"Where are we?" I asked as I pushed myself up and wiped my mouth with the back of my hand.

"Fifty says this is the museum power core."

"Oh, good."

"No. It's bad. It's very, very bad."

Tolby's words chilled me to the core. I rubbed my eyes to clear them, and once my surroundings came into focus, I gasped. We were inside a circular room that had a massive, cylindrical body standing on end at the very center. There were a dozen portals equally spaced around it from which gouts of plasma flowed toward the center. Above all of that was the wormhole we had come through, and tendrils of blue and yellow stretched from its edges toward the reactor.

"We're the ones who destroy the reactor," I said, my voice barely a whisper.

"Well let's not do that," Tolby said.

"I don't know how!"

Plasma from one of the tubes leaped toward the portal's tendrils, slamming into the force barrier that was responsible for containing it. The barrier glowed orange and held, but part of the plasma kept trying to break through and the wisps of energy from the portal above kept growing.

The force barrier then flickered, and a gout of plasma shot through and melted a chunk out of the ceiling. As fast as it broke free, the barrier appeared again, but this time, it had a deep blue color to it.

"Now I'm no expert in Progenitor engineering, but I'm going to say that can't be good," I said, backing away.

"And I'm going to say we're officially on borrowed time," Tolby said.

Curator's voice, calm and soothing, filled the air. "Attention. Emergency containment procedures are now in effect. The museum is scheduled for complete destruction in twenty-seven minutes. We thank you for your patronage throughout the ages and hope you enjoyed the exhibits."

"Twenty-seven minutes!" I shrieked. "That's how long we have?"

"Last minute items can be found at the gift shop for eighty percent off. All sales are final."

"I don't care about your stupid gift shop!"

"Museum members are encouraged to return to the sector in twenty-eight minutes to welcome Tatius IX to its new home.

Members are also encouraged to update their star charts with the blue giant's new location."

Tolby yanked me toward the exit. "Come on. We've got to get to my kin and whatever ship they have ready for us."

Another wild jet of plasma ripped through the barrier, cutting nearby consoles, ceiling, walls and floor like they were made of tissue. I dove to the side, managing to tackle Tolby in the process. Heat flashed across the back of my neck, and Tolby's eyes had such fear to them, I would've sworn he was looking at a ghost.

"What?" I asked, blowing out a nervous puff of air. "We're alive."

"And you've got a new haircut."

I took to my feet and brushed a hand against my now half-shaved head. "Damn it. It took me forever to grow this out."

"It doesn't look too bad."

"Gee, thanks. Let's get out of there."

"Music to my ears," Tolby said.

We bolted out the door and down a short hall to where a lift was stationed. I hammered the call button, and right as the elevator arrived, more plasma shot between us. It blasted the lift doors and vaporized everything. Sparks shot from the control panel, and with its death, so died my hopes of a quick getaway.

"Any other lifts nearby?"

"I don't know," I said, feeling like the universe was against us at every turn. But as Tolby started toward one of the other halls, I grabbed him by the shoulder as the most amazing idea came to me. "Hang on a sec!"

"What?"

Feeling equally awesome and clever, I whipped out the archive cube and flew through the menus, searching for the layout to the museum. It didn't take long to find, and within moments, I had our location pinpointed as well as where the Kibnali wing was in relation to us.

"That's a long walk," Tolby said, grimacing at the map.

"Walking is so yesterday," I said, aiming the portal device at the wall and squeezing the trigger.

A wormhole opened, but it did little to comfort either of us as the view it offered was a dark, fuzzy scene that flipped every few seconds, like someone was playing with the remote and trying to get through a slew of channels with bad reception.

"I'm not too sure about this one," Tolby said, eyeing the portal like he would a hungry megalodon who enjoyed snacking on large felines.

I rubbed my temples since an unseen bear trap had clamped down on my skull. "I hope so," I said. "Not sure if I have the energy to make another one for a few more minutes. It needs to recharge."

"Yeah, well, I don't think going through that can end well," Tolby replied.

My best bud's poignant fact soured my stomach worse than the riding a teacup ride for three hours with a crippling case of the Forivian flu.

"We're going to have to chance it," I said as I clipped the artifact to my belt. "There's no other choice."

Tolby backed up. "No way. We could come out inside out with our brains turned into scrambled eggs. And I don't mean figuratively. Literally, scrambled eggs."

"It's better than sticking around here." I tried to grab him, but he kept away.

"There's got to be another lift."

"We've got to get to the Kibnali now!" I said. "We'll never make it to them or their ship if we run."

"We'll never make it to them if we're turned into pancakes, either!"

A clap of thunder sent me staggering. Past Tolby, I caught sight of lightning bolts arcing around the reactor room. Without a second thought, I threw myself through the distorted portal, and Tolby followed right on my heels.

CHAPTER TWENTY-SEVEN

I sailed out of the portal and into a face full of leaves and branches. Thankfully, those branches weren't the thick, unyielding kind, so I didn't end up breaking my nose in two places along with my jaw and skull. However, because they were the thin, bendy kind, the supple ones often found closer to the tops of trees as opposed to the bottom, I quickly realized I was several dozen meters above the ground and in dire straits.

I cursed and yelled as I bounced off tree limbs, wildly flailing to try and grab on anything I could to slow my descent. My shoulders, back, and thighs turned three shades of purple before I finally came to a stop—upside down no less.

"Oh, thank goodness," I said, panting. After a silent prayer of gratitude for not turning into a pancake, I pulled myself up on the branch I was on and looked for Tolby. "Hey! Where are you?"

"I'm coming. I'm coming."

I found my furry copilot using his claws to easily scurry down the tree trunk. I wish I could say I wasn't jealous, but of course, I was. So I stuck out my tongue. "Cheater."

"I don't know if you should buy a lotto ticket or never step outside of the house again," he said.

"Why's that?"

"You're either incredibly lucky for surviving that fall or incredibly cursed for diving through a portal thirty meters off the ground."

I chuckled as I worked my way down the tree in a more controlled fashion. "This is a prime example of why I make you rub the plastic elephant."

"Except you don't have that anymore."

"All the more reason why we need a new one ASAP. Where the hell are we, anyway, and why are we dropping through trees?"

"By the Planck," Tolby muttered. "You've done it again, haven't you? And you didn't even time hop this go around."

"Done what?"

"Turned your brain to mush," he said, dropping to the ground and giving the area a look.

"Okay," I said, "not sure what that's about, but are you going to tell me where we are?"

"The Kibnali exhibit, if you were accurate with that last wormhole. If not, I have no idea."

"Kibnali exhibit," I softly repeated. The name was familiar, and when Tolby arched his brow and pointed to himself, gaps in my memory filled. "Kibnali! Yeah, you're one of their members, right?"

Tolby sighed and shook his head. "Close enough."

"That's not it?"

"I am Kibnali. We're a species. Not a book club."

"Right. I knew that." I tried a sheepish smile, but the anxiety in my buddy's face barely eased the tension between us. "I'm forgetting something important, aren't I?"

"Yeah, lots."

"Sorry."

"At this point, I know you can't help it, but you owe me. All you need to know is we're in a space museum that's about to blow, and if we don't get to the other Kibnali and get on board whatever ship they've got stowed away somewhere, we're going to die."

I cringed. "Where are they?"

"Their temple, I imagine. I can only go by the story you told."

"When?"

Tolby groaned as his eyes rolled and his paws formed fists. "Forget about that. Focus on the now. Does any of this look familiar?"

I shook my head, but a second later, I realized it was a premature response. Somehow the forest had earned a special spot in my mind, but it was more a vague feeling than anything else, like trying to remember the details of a dream an hour after you wake up. But then I spied a worn footpath about a dozen meters away, and I could feel my face light up. "I know that path."

Tolby looked over his shoulder. "You sure?"

"No."

He shrugged and laughed. "Good enough. Lead the way."

We moved at a good clip, and traveling was uneventful, save for the frequent earthquakes and low, distant rumbles. Okay, so maybe not that uneventful, but that's all relative, you know? We weren't being chased by Mister Cyber Squid, after all. Anyway, we kept going until we came to a fork in the path. There, I walked tight circles, like a hound trying to find a scent, as my brain tried to work out which way to go.

It didn't take long.

"This way!" I said when a nearby split in a tree sparked my memory. I grabbed Tolby's arm and pulled. "Come on!"

We bolted down the trail for a few hundred meters. When we curved around a massive boulder, I jumped to the side, nearly taking Tolby out in the process. Ahead a pair of Ratter bodies with gaping wounds across their chests lay at the base of stairs leading up to a temple.

"What if there's more?" I whispered.

"Doubtful," Tolby replied. "This fight happened a while ago."

"Did they lose?"

Tolby chuckled and stood from his crouched position. "Those two definitely did."

"That's a good sign for us, right?" I said. "I mean, that means the other Kibnali are still alive."

"I would think, but they should have sentries out this close to the temple," Tolby said with a flutter in his voice. His lips curled into a snarl. "I can't believe this is going to be destroyed. This is probably the last Kibnali temple in existence."

My gut tightened, and I could feel my eyes water. As much as I loved the idea of seeing everything in the museum, and as much as I loathed the loss of it all, what was being lost now was far more meaningful for Tolby than for me. I was losing the chance at learning history. Tolby was actually losing his history. "I'm sorry," I said. "We'll build a new one when we're out of here. Ten times bigger and better."

"Will we?" he asked, sounding hopeful and doubtful at the same time.

I didn't know how to respond, and my lips pressed together as I thought about it. His concern was infectious, and my muscles in my neck and back tightened. I don't think he doubted the sincerity of my promise, only how realistic it was. What if the other Kibnali had been forced out of the temple and we were now left behind? Or worse, what if Empress and the others had been killed? What could he and I possibly rebuild, especially since we needed them to escape alive?

A deep rumble throughout the museum spurred us into action. We took the stairs two and three at a time and raced through the stone archway and into the courtyard.

More Ratter bodies littered the grounds.

Seeing them, I slowed to a trot. "This is still good, right?"

Tolby's face hardened with determination. "Yes. They were clearly ambushed. I doubt they took more than a few steps before dying."

"Remind me to never get on your bad side," I said.

"Don't try and attack us and that won't be a problem."

I peeled my eyes off the Ratter bodies and looked at the temple. Its heavy double doors were shut in the main archway, as was the single door on a balcony above.

"Whatever happened here, looks like it stayed outside," I said.

"Agreed. Let's get inside."

We hurried to the temple doors. I tried to push them open, but they held fast, because seriously, why would anything be easy for us at this point? So I tried again and again, each time more forceful than the last. Tremors ran through the ground, and at that point, on the verge of panic, I rammed the door with my shoulder.

It's a tiny miracle I didn't dislocate it given how hard I hit.

"Oh, that hurt," I said, easing off the door.

"When has turning you into a battering ram ever worked?" Tolby said.

"I took out a castle my brother made with blocks when we were little," I replied. "That might be my last successful fortress assault."

"How's the head? Can you tunnel us back in time? Maybe get us here before the attack?"

I concentrated as best I could. The landscape dissolved into swirls and smears of color, like an abstract oil painting, and something scratched the inside of my skull. A clock formed in my mind's eye and started to spin backward, but only for a moment. That scratching changed into a tearing, and pain ripped through my head so intensely that I dropped to my knees with blood oozing from my nose.

Tolby grabbed me under my arms and helped me rise. "All right, that's out. We'll find another way inside."

From a safety standpoint, that was probably the best choice. But I wasn't ready to give up, especially since the museum was on the short track to total destruction. "It's only a meter to the other side, right? I mean, how thick can those doors be?"

"What are you planning on doing?"

"Simple portal," I said. "It's not as taxing as a timey-wimey one."

"Yeah, but can you even make one in the state you're in?"

I shrugged. "I don't know. We'll see."

I shut my eyes and tried to imagine what the first few paces of the temple looked like beyond the doors, how the stone floor felt underfoot, and how the light from the outside struck the walls—basically everything I could imagine doing to convey to the artifact where I wanted this blind portal to be created.

Pressure intensified in my head, but it was exponentially more bearable than my previous attempt. A few heartbeats later, the pressure vanished, and a portal leading into the temple opened at the door as perfect as any other I'd pulled off before. To say I was glowing with pride would be the understatement of the century.

"Hurry!" Tolby said, pulling my hand.

We entered, and thankfully, the inside of the temple was unscathed from any fighting. Hope filled my soul at that thought, but that uplifting feeling crashed the moment we stepped foot in the main hall and realized no Kibnali were there waiting for us.

"Your Most High?" Tolby called out as he rushed to the center of the room.

I glanced at all the alcoves as Tolby checked behind the altar, but neither one of us turned up anything. Before total despair could kill us, I spied a tablet lying in the middle of a side table, its lit screen beckoning me over.

"Hey! I got something!" I yelled, darting to it.

Tolby was at my side in a flash. "What is it?"

"Tablet with a note," I replied, picking it up. "Went to seize the *Revenant* as planned. See you there."

"The *Revenant*? As in, Pizlow's *Revenant*? We were just there!" Tolby shouted, throwing up his paws in frustration. "How do you forget that was their plan?"

"They didn't tell me!"

"Or you forgot!" Tolby said with a groan. "Damnit, Dakota. You really screwed this up!"

"I didn't forget! I swear they didn't tell me!"

"Why wouldn't they?"

I shook my head and offered the only explanation that I could think of. "They must have found a way to take over the ship and were worried Pizlow would find out. I mean, they seemed to know what was going to happen to me when I first met them. I guess they knew about us getting captured, too."

"That...actually makes sense," Tolby said with a grunt. The aggression in his affect softened. "Sorry. I want out of here, and we're so close."

I smiled and squeezed his arm. "Me too."

"So how do we get on the *Revenant*? Can you portal us there?"

"If I could see it, probably, but we'd have to be close." My voice trailed. "I mean, look how big the museum is and I screwed up that jump. If I mess up getting us into the *Revenant*, I'll open a portal into space. I'm not exactly dressed for that, you know?"

Tolby nervously tapped his foot and drummed his claws on the table. "Escape pods on the *Vela*," he said. "We'll get out on those, and they can pick us up."

"And if they can't?"

"You're going to have to either warp us inside or back in time, otherwise we're going to be star food."

I gave a nervous snicker. "Yeah. I don't think I'd trust this to hop spacetime anytime soon, so no pressure, right?"

CHAPTER TWENTY-EIGHT

With ten minutes left, per Curator's countdown, we ran into the museum entrance. Despite my aching sides and runaway heart, we kept up our mad dash until we reached the escape pods. I had to use the portal device to hop us beyond a couple of broken hatches, which thankfully went well, but it did mean I used up some precious power that might be needed later on for a time hop.

When we got to the lift that led to the pods, I mashed the button down with an open palm. The lift descended with a slow whine, and as it went, I glanced to Tolby. "I really wish I had my elephant to give a lucky rub."

"As long as we're wishing, I wish your ship was still intact."

"That too."

The lift came to a stop, and we ran out. The hall we found ourselves staring down was long, but unlike the others on the *Vela*, this one was in pristine condition. No panels were missing from the walls, nor grates pulled from the floors. Protective covers still shielded junction boxes and power relays, and for a second, I wondered if somehow we'd been mystically transported to another ship.

"What the hell do you make of this?" I asked.

"Ship AI probably prioritizes this area for maintenance above all others," Tolby said.

"Good point."

A tremor ran through the ship, along with a groan of twisting metal.

"That's our cue to leave," I said. "We can't have much time left."

"I think we're on so much borrowed time right now it'll take ten lives to pay it all back," Tolby said with a nervous laugh.

We moved on, and the hall bent ninety degrees before entering a stretch that ran farther than my light could reach. On either side of the corridor we were in were hatches spaced at twenty-meter intervals.

"Thank goodness," I said, running over to the nearest one and working the control panel as fast as I could, which sadly, wasn't fast at all. Though it flickered to life in a few seconds, it was sluggish to my input. Then, to my utmost horror, the readout came back with three red words that seared into my mind:

Pod One: Offline

Refusing to believe it, I continued trying to get it to open, but my attempts proved futile. Finally, I gave in. "This one's gone."

Tolby, who was looking at the hatch on the opposite side shuttered. "Pod two is down as well."

I growled and set my jaw, but neither improved our luck.

As we continued down the hall, pods three through ten all showed the same inability to do anything. So I did the only sensible thing. I punched the wall. That didn't change anything, but it was successful at giving me a new ache to think about.

"Hey!" Tolby said. "Tell me that one up there is open."

I looked up from my throbbing hand. Forty meters away, a faint blue light spilled into the hall. Ecstatic, I sprinted forward as if a single breath of hesitation or spoken word would cause it to disappear.

As I neared, my heart's tempo grew faster. The hatch was open, and thus, the pod had to be online. It just had to. Who the hell leaves an open hatch to a busted pod, right? No one. Not even sick, twisted psychos are that depraved. Or so I told myself.

Within a few paces of the hatch, I slowed drastically when I saw splatters of white goo all along the floor and wall. I'm not an expert in vintage ship design, but I did know enough to realize that goo was incredibly out of place.

"That can't be good," I said.

Tolby stopped along with me and then bowed while extending his paw. "Ladies first."

"You're the big, tough guy," I said. "You should be protecting me."

The ship rumbled again, reminding us both that we had no time for friendly banter. I trotted up to the hatch and peeked around the corner. Given our recent luck, I half expected to see a nightmarish creature with fangs like daggers and acid for blood to be lurking inside, waiting to pounce.

There was no monster beyond the hatch and airlock, but there was a thoroughly smashed repair droid.

"It's just a robot corpse," I said as I headed inside.

"I hope whatever destroyed it isn't around anymore," Tolby replied. "That thing looks like it was tough."

"No kidding," I said with a nod. "I know it's a little late to ask, but do you know how to fly this thing?"

"Yes, because unlike you, I read up on the *Vela* and her operating systems before we got here," Tolby said with a grin as he hopped in the pilot seat.

"That's why I keep you around," I said, hopping in the navigator's seat.

"I thought it was because of my handsome ruggedness."

"That too."

As Tolby began the launch sequence, I hit the remote to close the airlock behind us. The moment it sealed, Tolby groaned. "This can't be happening."

"What are you talking about?"

"We can't launch."

"What do you mean we can't launch?" I said, eyes wide and voice cracking. "The whole purpose of this pod is to launch, and launch immediately without any troubles, ever."

Tolby pointed to the only one of four screens in front of him that was lit. "Ignition batteries are drained. There's not enough juice in them to restart the reactor."

"We have to leave, Tolby!"

"I know."

"We don't have time for dead batteries!"

"I know, Dakota, but I can't magically make them recharge!"

I twisted in the seat, looking for something—anything—to help us escape. "Can we charge them?"

Tolby shrugged. "Maybe, but that'll take a hell of a lot more time than we have now."

"How much time?"

"No idea," Tolby replied. "A few days? A few months? We have to find a way to do it first. It's not like you can hook anything up to a dark energy battery and have it not explode in your face."

His words were poison to what hope I had, and I was going to be damned if I was going to let that hope die. "Okay. We go back and make time."

"You can't change what's here now," Tolby said. "The Universe abhors a paradox, remember?"

"Then we find another way off that's not this pod," I countered. "We stay here, our odds are zero. At least we'll have a chance anywhere else."

The lifeboat rocked. Klaxons blared throughout the *Vela*. Tolby, face full of worry, sucked in an anxious breath through his teeth before replying. "I hope you know what you're doing."

"So do I," I replied.

I shut my eyes and tried to make the mental calculations I needed, but all I could think about was the paradox alarm blaring in my mental ear, and how I had no idea if we could safely jump back five seconds let alone five hours or five days. Granted, I wasn't out of safety discs, but I couldn't shake the feeling jumping back in time would end with me being vaporized by a paradox backlash big enough to shatter a star.

An explosion from outside split the rear hatch in two. Large chunks of twisted metal wrecked the cabin, while two more fist-sized pieces of shrapnel embedded themselves in the pilot's control panel, nearly shredding both of us in the process.

Reflexively, I ripped open a portal to the past without a second thought as to where or when we'd wind up.

Immediately, I dropped into the bridge of the *Vela*. There were enough lights still working since Mister Cyber Squid had gone on a rampage to show me that all the controls were smashed beyond repair, and there was also more than enough light for me to see Kevyn's broken body smeared against the far wall.

"Sorry you ended like that," I said with a cringe. I then turned and headed for the exit. "Let's go, Tolby. We've still got to get to the *Revenant*. Or was it away from it?"

Tolby didn't answer, and the reason why only came to me when I made a quick, panicked scan of the area. He wasn't there at all. He'd been left behind.

But left where?

We'd come from...the museum was it? Was he still in the gift shop? Or the Pets Across the Galaxy wing? No, that didn't seem right.

I shut my eyes and tried to find those elusive memories as to where I'd last seen him. But try as I might, all I got for my efforts was an acute case of vertigo that forced me to lean against broken consoles, lest I smooch the floor.

"Freeze, or I'll blow your head off!"

APOCALYPSE, HOW?

My eyes snapped open, and I saw Veritad standing in the middle of a side hatch, rifle shouldered, and Ratters stacked behind him. Though my mind still swam in a thick fog, I thankfully had enough clarity left to know I shouldn't talk to any of them, and if I tried, I'd likely end up as a Dakota-skin rug somewhere. As such, I dropped another portal at my feet and popped out down the corridor opposite my would-be captors.

The moment my feet touched the deck, I ran. The unexpected jump in my position, no doubt, was the only thing that saved me because though Veritad snapped off a few shots, all they did was bore deep holes in the hull.

I raced through the *Vela*, taking turns, ladders, and halls at random. I didn't have any idea where I was going. All I knew was I had to lose my pursuers and find Tolby at all costs.

Despite the quickness in my step, the Ratters kept right on my tail. What hatches I closed behind me only slowed them for a couple of seconds. After I sealed yet another firewall, I made a couple of quick right turns and ducked into the ventral communication blister—thus running straight into Old Me and Old Tolby.

"Oh, crap," I said, feeling my arm tingle and realizing I was a hair's breadth away from wiping out the galaxy.

"Crap?" Old Me replied.

In the not-so-far-away distance, I heard the rapid approach of Ratters, and so, I did the only thing that made sense. I shot myself.

CHAPTER TWENTY-NINE

I tumbled out of my portal, and a few moments after that, Old Me and her Tolby fell out as well. When Old Me hit the ground, she puked on the floor, and though she was the one doing it, I swear I could taste the bile in my throat.

Old Tolby groaned and staggered, trying to get to his feet. "I'm going to be sick," he moaned.

"I already was."

My head spun worse than a teacup ride with afterburners. The encounter took on a surreal nature as my mind struggled with the immensely different—yet same—viewpoint of what was now taking place. Does that make sense? If yes, you understand this time-hopping stuff better than I do. If not, then welcome to my world.

Anyway, having to literally live through this event once again in a different body belonging to the same person put me in an acute identity crisis. Trust me, it doesn't take but a half second of actually seeing Old You, remembering what you said, knowing what you're going to say, and not knowing who you are in all of it, to make you go bonkers. Worse, each time I went to speak, my head felt like it was on the verge of collapse, and I had to check more than once to make sure my arm wasn't on fire.

Old Me kept asking questions, kept talking, and no matter what I said or did, she wouldn't stop. All I wanted was for the encounter to end. Why the hell wouldn't she listen to me? Couldn't listen, maybe? On and on she went, not understanding what I was trying to tell myself, yet here I am, trying to explain, and I can't even say what it was I said.

Finally, after one last exchange between the two of us, the pain in my head and arm grew too much to bear. I wrapped my arms around my midsection and felt my face go scarlet before screaming, "Get out!"

Old Me and Old Tolby left right after, thankfully. I sank into a chair, and over the next few minutes, my unseen torturer slowed his work and then stopped altogether. A few minutes after that, bits of my memory returned. Not much, but enough to remember how I got there, and where I'd left Tolby—my Tolby.

I leaped up and ran as fast as I could to the escape pods. I nearly tripped a couple of times along the way in dark corridors littered with debris and had to sneak a touch as well to dodge a group of Ratters. When I finally reached the pods, I entered the one we had in the future and steadied myself to open the wormhole.

I briefly considered waiting a little so my memory would come back some more, but I felt that could be as big of a mistake as not waiting due to the Ratters looting the place. So I gave myself a little prep time instead with a small countdown.

"On three, Dakota," I said to myself, hoping I wouldn't chicken out. "One...two...three."

The wormhole to the future opened without a hitch. I jumped through, grabbed Tolby's shoulder, and yanked him back from whence I'd come before the portal closed. We tumbled to the floor, completely tangled.

"I don't know where you went, but for a split second, you scared the hell out of me," Tolby said, laughing and freeing his leg from under my back.

I let out a sigh of relief, and a smile crept over my face now that I had my best friend back. But back from where? My mouth twisted to the side and my brow furrowed as I tried to answer that question.

"What?"

"I don't know where we came from," I said. "Is that bad?"

"Normally, yes," he said. "But you've been forgetting and remembering a lot lately."

"Oh," I replied. Butterflies took to my stomach as a general sense of unease grabbed ahold of me. "I don't think we should be here."

"You mean the museum?"

"No," I replied, shaking my head. "Something else. Or someone else."

Tolby pressed for more details, but I tuned him out, trying to remember what was so wrong about this place. Or was it this time? That seemed to resonate with me more.

I heard the muffled sounds of screeching Ratters, and since the hatch was closed, they had to be nearby on account of how thick the door was. This proved true when one of the Ratters stuck his ugly face in the viewport and his beady eyes found mine.

I sprang into action out of pure instinct and panic. I grabbed on to Tolby and opened another wormhole and carried us through.

The trip through spacetime was over in a heartbeat, but I felt a thousand years old when I smacked into the cold, steel floor of the escape pod. Non-slip diamond plate left a painful mark in my cheek, but at least the pattern was symmetrical.

"Martian babes on a stick," I said, pushing myself up and wincing as I touched the side of my face. "How much have I had to drink?"

"Not a drop. That was us hurling through one of your portals," someone replied.

I twisted to find a huge furry space tiger staring back at me with predatory eyes. My jaw dropped, and the alien smiled, flashing sharp teeth that could saw through a rebar.

"Get the hell away from me!" I yelled, leaping away and into the back of the pilot's seat.

"Whoa! It's me, Tolby," the massive feline said, paws up defensively. "I'm not going to hurt you."

"That's right, you're not!" I whipped out my PEN and gave it a quizzical look before pointing it at Tolby's head. "This right here is a screaming cicada. It'll take an elephant-sized chunk out of a tank, so imagine what it'll do to your head."

Tolby's arms dropped, and his head tilted to the side with a pitiful look. "That's a PEN, Dakota. You're not blowing a hole through anything," he said. "And you're holding it backward."

"What? No, I'm not." I fumbled with the device, trying to figure out if what the furball had said was true. I was going to feel pretty stupid if that were the case but felt pretty confident that it was not.

In a flash, Tolby snatched the PEN from my hands. I flipped over the pilot seat in response and used it as a shield against the superweapon.

"Look, I know you don't know what's going on, but I had to take that from you because I didn't want you frying anything around here we might need," Tolby said. "I'm only trying to help."

Unsure how trustworthy he was, I glanced around the escape pod for clues. It looked familiar, but I wasn't sure why. My stomach turned to knots, and my breathing accelerated as I tried to get a handle on the situation. "What's going on?"

For the next half hour, Tolby gave me a synopsis of what had happened to us, starting from our investigation of the crash site on DD-3123. When he got caught up to the here and now, he tacked on one final thought. "It seems as if each time you do your time travel trick, you lose your memory more and more."

"I do?"

Tolby nodded. "Yes."

"How do you know?"

"Because we're best friends," he said. "I figured you would've inferred that from the story."

"Now you've gone too far. I mean, you were stretching things with this time travel nonsense, but now I'm best friends with a big kitty? I'm such a dog person." That comment struck such a chord in me I couldn't help but laugh. It took me a few seconds to recompose myself, but once I did, I realized that I had a palm full of blood and that blood had come out of my nose. "Oh damn. That can't be good."

Tolby eased forward with a pillow sheet from a nearby bunk. "Yeah, that happens, too."

I took the sheet and pressed it against my nose, grimacing as I did. The threads turned scarlet and then burgundy before I pulled it away. I touched my upper lip and noted it was still sticky, but at least what was coming out was now a slow trickle.

"I need to get to medbay," I said. "Dad's medibot can patch me up quick."

Tolby straightened like he'd been rapped on the knuckles by a Sister Superior. "This isn't your dad's ship."

"Sure as hell isn't mine," I said with a huff. "I mean, size aside, I'd never be caught dead in a POS like this. And that's saying a lot, because I'm hardly flying a Lamberari."

"I didn't say it was yours, either. Like I told you, it's a derelict. We found it not long ago."

"Oh. Guess I missed that part."

Tolby leaned against the wall with a sigh. "The time warping is hurting your short-term memory, too, it seems."

"For how long?"

"Don't know. It's always come back, eventually, but until it does, you'll have to trust me on a few things. Okay?"

"Maybe I shouldn't trust you, and when I remember everything, I'll know why," I said, sticking out my tongue. I tilted my head as the playful act toward the giant feline felt familiar, in a good way, and thus I decided to entertain his little theory. "If we're such best friends, what's my favorite drink?"

"Root beer," he replied without hesitation.

I crossed my arms over my chest and gave a smug grin. "Ha! Not even close."

Tolby grunted and pushed by me to go to the control panel. "You can tell me how wrong I am when you're feeling yourself," he said. "Right now, I've got to get us back to the other Kibnali so we can go home."

The exit hatch to the escape pod swished open as he worked the buttons. I spun around as a Pademar Series VII engineering droid lumbered into the lifeboat. It stood almost two meters high on a pair of supple limbs and looked pieced together from at least nine different robots. Two sets of worn arms hung off the torso, each one sporting four joints below the shoulder that allowed it to reach tricky spots needing repair.

The bot stared at me with four purple eyes, but only one of those wasn't sporting at least one crack. I guess it was in dire need of repair, too.

"You are not authorized to be here," it said. "Surrender, and your purging will be painless."

Hairs rose on the back of my neck, and the last thing I wanted was to pick a fight with this guy. Even repair bots were known to be deadly and aggressive when the situation called for it. Not to mention, it's a lot easier to cut apart flesh and bone that it is a bulkhead, and that thing could chop them up all day. "Our mistake. We were just leaving."

"Ship is off limits. No exceptions."

Tolby jumped to my side and pointed the PEN at the robot. "Back off! This is a screaming cicada, and it'll punch a hole through this entire ship if I want, so imagine what it'll do to your head."

"That's an 'an elephant-sized chunk out of a tank,'" I whispered with a half grin.

The repair bot hesitated. "Scanning for verification."

Tolby nudged me with his hip and whispered. "Get us out of here."

"With what? My good looks?" I whispered back.

"Use your portal thingy!"

"What portal thingy?"

Tolby groaned. "The portal thingy Curator gave you! Come on, Dakota, I just told you all about this!"

"Scan complete," the bot said. "Power inside device lacks the capacity to meet the claim."

At that point, I wished Tolby had a screaming cicada, but that wish disappeared quickly. Pins and needles crept up my spine and the back of my skull, and I realized some long-forgotten part of me was now waking. A portal opened beneath the robot's feet, and it tumbled through the floor and flew out of the ceiling, only to come crashing onto the deck, head first.

"Oh my god! Do I do that?" I yelled in delight.

"Yeah, now do it again!"

The droid twisted and tried to right itself, but feeling like a vengeful goddess, I repeated the process again and again, each time being easier and more natural than the last. After I gave it a dozen more awkward drops, its movements became sporadic, and thick white fluid leaked from several of its joints. On the nineteenth drop, the head snapped off in a shower of sparks and electrical pops. The mechanical body thrashed around for a few seconds, then it went limp.

"That was really cool," I said, admiring my handiwork. "When have I been able to do all that?"

"One sec and I'll tell you," Tolby said, getting back in the pilot seat. It took him a minute to power on the main console, but once it came up, the date and time were displayed on the bottom right. "You've been doing that since tomorrow."

"Come again?"

"Again?" Tolby said with a tired sigh. "Fine. Here's the super-fast version." For the next five minutes, he recapped our adventure, and once done, he held his paws together and rested his chin on them. "Please tell me this is starting to stick in your brain."

"Sort of," I replied. "I feel like you're telling me about a dream I had a long time ago."

"Good enough," he said with a chuckle. "Come on. Maybe Empress will jog the rest of your memory. If not, I'm going to put a leash on you so you don't wander off. No offense."

I grinned playfully. "Ruff!"

CHAPTER THIRTY

We zipped through the museum, and the entire way, energy surged through my body as I could barely contain my excitement. I couldn't wait to see what these other Kibnali would be like. At first, I had a vague recollection of meeting Empress and the others, more of a sense of wonderment and awe, but as we passed through countless exhibits, images of my time with them formed. By the time we passed through the musical wing of the Second Martian Empire, I could remember practically everything about them and everything else, including a few things I wished had stayed forgotten.

A few meters from the entrance to the Kibnali wing, Tolby pulled on my arm and we stopped. He fidgeted with a horn made of bone that had been wrapped in leather and carved with intricate hunting scenes across its entire body. It was a piece from a nearby exhibit that he had picked up not even ten minutes ago, and other than looking immensely cool—and something I wanted to give a good blow to out of curiosity on how it sounded—its significance to Tolby was lost on me. That said, I did suspect that wouldn't be the case for much longer.

"What's wrong?" I asked.

"I've been trying to come up with a better idea on how to meet them," he said, eyes locked on the horn he had in hand. "But I've got nothing."

"What are you on about?"

Tolby looked at me with worried eyes. "The Kibnali aren't the most hospitable species when it comes to first contact. We're more of a conquer-and-enslave-first-and-ask-questions-probably-never kind of group."

"Things...change," I said. "I know you guys saw a lot of war before, but look at us, we're best friends, and you didn't try and kill me when we first met."

Tolby balked.

"You did?"

"You were running right at me."

"Yeah, because I had a Hannan terror beast on my tail, which you promptly shot when I tripped." I paused as the reality of my words seeped into my brain. "Oh my god, you were aiming at me!"

"Sorry! I didn't know you then!"

"You were going to kill me, and I didn't even do anything!" I said.

Tolby sighed and muttered to himself. "I said I was sorry. I shouldn't have said anything."

"You're damn right you shouldn't have said anything. What kind of BFF shoots his best buddy?" I said with a huff. "Forget it. Don't answer. I don't want to think about it. But for the record, when I met your Kibnali before, or later, or later before... Whatever... You know what happened? Nothing. They were very pleasant and definitely didn't try to blow my head off."

"That's because they'd already met you, remember? That meeting was a first for you, not them. Trust me on this, Dakota. They're not going to be your friends this time around, and Kibnali have been known to tear arms out of sockets if they feel sufficiently insulted or threatened."

I grimaced and instinctively clutched both of my shoulders, as over the course of my lifetime, I'd grown rather fond of them. True, a lot of people out there prefer the synthetic lifestyle, but I've always been a fan of natural beauty. Besides, swapping flesh arms for cyber arms, or even no arms, does require a half-decent surgibot to prevent bleeding out, and I was reasonably sure that wouldn't be afforded to me by an irate Empress.

"Hang on a second," I said as a more pleasant thought dawned on me. "Everything must go well right now because otherwise they wouldn't have been nice to me in the future, right?"

Tolby chewed on my words for a few moments, but when he replied, his voice lacked the enthusiasm I was hoping for. "You sure about that?"

"Of course. How could this not have gone well?"

"Maybe later they think you're someone else."

"Both Empress and Yseri used my name," I countered, smiling and feeling good about myself. I mean, how do you beat that logic? I would've been a great lawyer. With that, I pressed my case to its logical conclusion. "Since they're going to see me tomorrow, I don't think there's a big chance at a mix-up. Besides, how else would they know me if we didn't get along?"

Tolby shrugged. "No idea. Maybe they felt bad for you. Maybe in the previous timeline, you did make it, but not this one. I don't think either of us dying before we get to the *Vela* tomorrow is going to create a paradox at this point. It just means the future timeline will be a little different."

"Me losing my arms is more than a little different."

"Still not enough to rip the galaxy apart though, I'd wager."

I grumbled as I mulled his thoughts over. He did have a point, and the way he was hammering on about it made me think I was going to detest whatever it was he was balking at discussing. "Okay, maybe you're onto something," I capitulated with a heavy sigh. "How do I need to go in there? I'm assuming there's some royal protocol you want me to adhere to?"

Tolby cringed. "Not exactly."

"Then what?"

"I need you to get down on all fours and crawl into the temple, all while wearing this pack," he said, holding out a backpack he'd nabbed not too long ago. I'd thought it was simply for storing loot, but apparently that wasn't the case.

"Look, I am not going in there like some stupid pack animal, not to mention, I don't want my knees ruined."

"Think of it more like a majestic elephant bringing a prince's effects along as they return home to his people."

I snorted. "That's supposed to make it any better?"

"Look, the safest way for you to be introduced is as my *Chetarin*," he said. "Anything else and there's no telling what they'll think, especially if you're toting around Progenitor tech. For all we know, they'll think you've turned me into a cyber puppet, and you're about to exterminate each one of them."

I growled as I tried to wrap my head around such a nonsensical request. What kind of species runs around blasting anything that's not carrying goods? Apparently, the large furry kind that's bent on galactic conquest. "If you're pulling one on me, I'll never forgive you."

"I'm not. I swear."

"I mean it."

"Dakota, look at me," he said. "I'm not lying. It probably won't last more than ten or twenty minutes, tops. They only need to be sure you're subservient to me, and then we're good."

"I can't believe I'm doing this," I said, sliding the pack on before easing down to my hands and knees. "We don't speak of this ever again. Yes?"

"On my honor," he said, furry paw over his heart.

With that, we eased around the corner and into the first part of the Kibnali exhibit. The backpack weighed considerably more than I had expected, and I quickly grew miffed that he hadn't stuffed it with pillows. I wasn't sure what he had put in there, but lead bricks would've been easier to carry. The weight of the pack constantly shifted on my body thanks to an ill fill, and that shifting did a number on my spine. More than once I wondered how many discs were going to be out of place when this was all over, but that pain was secondary to the ordeal my knees were going through. Since they weren't padded, the floor was hard marble, and the hall stretched for a long, long way, they were taking more of a punishment than a sinner cast into the seventh circle of hell.

"This isn't going to work," I finally said. "That temple is still a good three or four hundred meters away, and this is killing my joints."

"Shh," he said. "Don't talk."

"I'm going to buck this pack in a second if you don't come up with something else."

Tolby sighed. "Fine. This is probably close enough."

Tolby raised a foot and placed it on my shoulder while bringing the horn to his lips. After taking in a lungful of air, he blew. A powerful, resonating sound came out that lasted a good ten seconds. Once it was over, Tolby used the horn to sound off three more times, equally strong, but progressively shorter and lower in pitch. At the end of the third time, he blew one last time, issuing another ten-second blast, but this time it was a full octave above. Once the final note faded away, Tolby used the leather strap to sling the horn over his shoulder.

"Here we go," he said, not looking down.

I dared a glance over my shoulder. With his one foot still forward on me, he looked as if he were a statue of a conquering war hero on display in a local park. Despite his strong stance, I could see hints of nervousness in his eyes. Was he anxious because he was finally going to reunite with others of his kin, those he thought had been long extinct? Or were the Kibnali that hell-bent on domination and conflict that even in my embarrassing state, they would decide to shoot first and ask questions never? After all, it'd been what, five hundred years since the last time anyone was around the museum? God, even if they didn't feel threatened by me, maybe they'd just need to get their killing fix in, like some crazed junkie who was struggling in the worst part of a dry spell.

"How much longer?" I whispered.

"They should be here soon," Tolby replied. "I'll give another announcement in a few if they don't come, but that was the official call of the Guard for House Yari I blew."

To my relief, I didn't have to wait for a second blast. Down the hall, two Kibnali dressed in battle armor stepped out of the archway leading to the temple exhibit. Despite the distance and the fact that both were wearing full helmets, I could tell they were startled by our presence due to their hesitation. The Kibnali exchanged words and a flurry of gestures before rapidly approaching, hands resting on the hilts of their swords.

"Steady," Tolby whispered.

I tucked my head, thinking it a good idea that the Kibnali didn't see me whisper back. "No kidding."

The two arrived in moments, and in perfect unison, they took an aggressive stance, right leg trailing behind the left, each bent and ready to launch them forward or backward as the situation demanded, all the while both pairs of hands staying poised to unsheathe their swords.

The slightly shorter of the two spoke with a strong, cautious tone. "Who is this being who walks among us? What instrument are you of the Empress?"

"My name is Tol'Beahn. Second born to Undun and Rajap of the House Yari, captain of the royal guard, veteran of every Yari campaign since the Suroh Heresy," Tolby answered. "I have come to rejoin my kin."

As impressive as his title and brief bio was, the Kibnali didn't rush to embrace him. Instead, another question came. "Where have you been when our need was greatest, Tol'Beahn, second born to Undun and Rajap of the House Yari?"

"I am ashamed that I did not fall with my brothers and sisters during our Final Act of Defiance," he replied, sorrow saturating his tone. "I shall give my story to Empress, and if it is her will, I will move on from this world to the next so my disgrace affronts her no longer."

There was a brief pause in the exchange, and my heart hammered against my ribcage, and a lump strangled my throat. I mean, it was nerve-wracking enough I was facing down these giant tigers for the first time, but my best buddy wasn't really going to commit some backward-ass ritual suicide, was he? This was Tolby, after all. My well-adjusted, laidback space tiger who hated fighting and war and everything that went along with it—recent events notwithstanding.

The Kibnali removed their helmets and dropped them to the floor. Their swords followed suit immediately after. Confused, I dared to raise my head for a better view right as the two Kibnali females launched themselves over me. Their combined force on impact was more than enough to knock Tolby off his feet and send all three crashing to the ground.

I was up in a flash, scooping up one of the swords. "Leave him—"

My sentence never finished. The two Kibnali had Tolby pinned on the ground, but they weren't assaulting him, at least, not with blows. Instead, they were pawing all over his furry body and showering his face and neck with a tongue bath that would put any overly zealous Labrador to shame. As they ravished his body, the amount of force Tolby exerted in stopping them wouldn't even register in the micronewtons.

A sigh drew my attention away from the gratuitous make-out scene. Next to me I saw Empress, casually leaning on a spear. The Kibnali glanced at me and smiled. "Kids these days."

I straightened at the unexpected comment and ended up fidgeting, unsure what to do given how Tolby's prior instruction contrasted with Empress's casual attitude. Feeling increasingly awkward, I thrust an open hand to the matriarch. "I'm Dakota, by the way."

"We know," she replied. "We've been expecting you."

"You have? Again? Oh, wait, let me guess. Curator told you?"

"He did," Empress said. "He's told us a lot of things over the centuries, most important of which the two of you would be coming, and you'd have a ship for us to leave on."

"Mine's destroyed, or will be shortly," I said. "I won't arrive here until tomorrow. Time travel and all. But this other guy Pizlow is coming—he's the one who destroys my ship—and Tolby is sure that we can sneak aboard and steal his shuttle to escape."

"You can only take his shuttle?" Empress asked with a clear tone of disappointment. "Are you so weak you can't commandeer his entire ship?"

"It's pretty big and has a crew numbering in the hundreds. Are you suggesting we can win against those odds?"

"Yes, but not without a high chance of losses," she replied with reluctance. "Perhaps my eagerness to meet Tolby has clouded my judgment, and perhaps we should be content with this shuttle for now. Can it take us to other worlds?"

I nodded. "Easily, but there's not a lot of room in it, so pack light."

Empress smiled at the momentary brevity. "We'll make do. We always have." She then looked over to Tolby and the handmaidens who were currently eyeing third base. "It's time to move."

None of the three lovers made any indication of hearing her request, so Empress growled and tapped the butt of her spear sharply on the marble floor.

Both handmaidens jumped to their feet with Tolby following suit. "Apologies, Empress," the three said in semi-unison.

"You can make kits once our preparations are done," Empress replied without a hint of scolding. "For now, however, we must ready our assault."

"Yes, Empress," they said. "We are your fang and claw."

Empress turned and began walking. I was a step behind, and Tolby and the handmaidens followed right after. Despite Empress's demands, it wasn't long before Tolby was once again properly distracted by his new love interests, and so I dared a question. "Empress, I'm curious about something. Tolby seemed to insinuate the three of you might have...how do I put this...been more cautious in meeting me."

"You want to know if you had to come in like a donkey."

My skin warmed. "Yeah."

Empress grinned. "If he hadn't, and had Curator not told us who you were, your pretty little head would have made a nice trophy over my fireplace. Though one day it still might."

CHAPTER THIRTY-ONE

Twenty minutes later, we were seated at a stone table inside the Kibnali temple. Tolby sat across from me with the two handmaidens, the trio having recently returned from their third "repopulate the species" exercise. I should be thankful that at least they had the decency to duck into another room, but since they were louder than a slew of horny alley cats, they might as well have stayed put. In that time, however, I'd managed to get the archive cube working, and I was hopeful we could use it to get back home alive and in one piece.

I was hopeful we could use it, that was, if Tolby would stop making out for five seconds.

"Hey! Snap out of it!" I yelled as I slammed an open palm onto the table.

Tolby, Jainon, and Yseri jumped. "Sorry," he said. "What were you saying?"

I frowned as he eased back into the girls' embrace and readopted his playboy mood. Under normal circumstances, I wouldn't have blamed him for indulging his physical needs, especially since it had been how long since he'd seen another of his species? But we were still stuck inside a museum that had less than a day before being permanently demolished, and we were still sans ship.

"I was saying," I said, clearing my throat. "I got the archive cube to bring up the schematics to Pizlow's ship. It works a lot like the old T-800 consoles, so just wave, pinch, poke what you want more info on. You can even bring up a holographic keyboard by touching the area at the bottom."

"Oh, good," he replied, feeding Yseri a piece of bitter fruit.

"That means it's your turn to find us an entry point, preferably before tomorrow rolls around and you three are playing kissy face inside of a star."

"Right," he said as he reluctantly pulled free of his lovers. He leaned across the table and scooted the archive cube closer to get a better look at the hologram it was displaying. His first attempt at interfacing with it resulted in a total schematic shutdown. After a few curses, he managed to bring the ship layout for the *Revenant* back up and get used to the controls. Initially, the cube only showed a broad cutaway with bits of text scattered across the bottom, but once Tolby got the hang of the controls, he quickly cycled through decks and ship components in rapid fire.

"Looking at all this, the shuttle is still the way to go," Tolby said. "Especially with Mister Cyber Squid eating everyone. There's only one problem."

"What's that?"

"Assuming we can override the hangar doors and launch, the *Revenant*'s shuttle is too slow out the gate. A single hit from its cannons will turn the shuttle to scrap."

My face soured as much as my stomach. "Ugh. Can we disable the guns?"

"I think so." Tolby shifted the display and pointed to a small room in the midsection of the ship. "The *Revenant* has a GORAS damage-control system, which is pretty good but not without its problems. If you can portal us in over here, there's a cluster relay I can sabotage that will make the system think the containment fields for the antimatter rounds are too unstable to use."

"How long will that last?"

"Normally only a minute or two, tops, before the system readjusts," Tolby replied. "But if we're going in at the same time Mister Cyber Squid is tearing up the place, we'll probably get five or ten minutes since the system will take a lot longer to verify the damage isn't real."

"Not sure if I'd qualify that as a lot longer," I said with a frown.

Yseri leaned forward, the glow on her face giving way to a look eager for a fight. "We'll only need half that."

"Or we'll get torn in half," Jainon chimed in with a grin. "And you're short enough as it is."

"This is no time for levity."

"With you, there's never time."

"Let's keep our focus," Empress said as she joined us at the table. "Did I hear correctly that we have a plan?"

"It's a something," I said before giving her a recap. "One thing I'm wondering, however, is where do we wait to strike? Here or on the *Vela*?"

"The museum is large, and it's not likely the Ratters will find us before we have to leave," the Empress said after a moment's thought. "But it's probably even more unlikely that they'll be searching the *Vela* once they learn of this place."

"My vote is inside this airlock," Tolby said, bringing up the *Vela*'s schematics on the cube and pointing to his proposed launch point. "It's the best place to start to get to our target in the *Revenant*."

I drummed my fingers on the table to get rid of the nervous energy building. It turned out to not be enough, so my right leg bounced along to help. "It's close to the cargo bay, which is where they were searching before."

"Which means they'll probably have searched it already and there would be no reason to look again," he said.

"My vote is still somewhere else," I replied. "That's too close for comfort."

Yseri studied the schematics. "If they're looking for salvage or treasure, they're likely to be everywhere. It would be best if we could come up with something that didn't involve a lot of speculation."

"I'm not sure how to do that," Tolby said. "We won't have time for proper reconnaissance."

Jainon pulled away from Tolby, and for the first time since I'd met her, she looked deadly serious, and all previous traits of lightness were gone. "There is one way. We can consult the divine."

"Who?" asked Yseri as she, too, pulled from Tolby. "Taiso? Hisoshim?"

I glanced at Tolby, who gave me the answers without me having to ask. "The messenger god and god of war and peace, respectively."

Jainon's tail flipped in front of her and she played with it a moment before answering. "Nashir."

"You would appeal to the Most High for something so trivial?" Empress said, eyes wide. "We cannot. The risk is far too great."

"This is hardly trivial, Empress," Jainon countered. "Our very species will rise or fall based on this one act. We must know where to stage our attack. If we choose poorly, we will all die, as will our legacy."

"And if your request for knowledge is seen as superfluous, you'll be struck dead," Empress said, her voice sharp and unyielding. "The gods do not show favor for those who refuse to help themselves. Where then will we be with only one suitable mother instead of two?"

"Better one mother than none," Jainon said.

Empress narrowed her eyes, and the words that she then spoke were quiet, even, and unyielding. "I will not allow such reckless behavior."

For a moment, Jainon wilted under Empress's words, but after a moment, her tail tucked behind her as she stood, tall, proud, and determined. "I am the High Priestess. I am outside of law and caste when it comes to matters of the divine. I shall consult Nashir, and he will direct us, if for no other reason than he would not want his cherished creation to become extinct."

Empress went to counter, but Yseri spoke first. She put a paw on her sister's and said, "Then seek out Hisoshim if you must. You won't be the first High Priestess who has tried to speak to the Most High only to fall dead mid-ritual. At least Hisoshim has a fondness for battle and may grant your request on that alone."

Jainon looked to her sister for a few moments in silence, and during that time, I realized how incredibly tense I was. I had no idea the specifics of what was about to take place, but there was no doubt to the seriousness of it all. That said, for the life of me, I couldn't understand how a ritual would turn deadly unless it involved drinking sea snake venom or playing hot potato with a thermal detonator.

"Hisoshim it will be," Jainon said, breaking the silence.

She said no more and quickly left the table and the room. Not even a half minute later, she came out of a storeroom with a wooden box inlaid with pinkish metal and a large black gem set squarely on the middle of the lid.

She placed the box on the table and opened it before taking a single step back. Without any words between any of the Kibnali, Yseri and Empress took out brushes and jars from within the box and began painting Jainon's face, inscribing it with symbols that had no meaning for me. The High Priestess kept her eyes closed throughout the mini-ceremony.

When they finished, Jainon opened her eyes and plucked one of six miniature, crystal decanters from the box. She chanted softly before taking the stop out of the decanter and downing the glowing neon-yellow liquid inside.

"For the sake of the Empire, I call," Jainon said, her voice weak. "For the sake of the Empire, I go."

Her body went rigid, and her eyes rolled back in her head. Yseri folded her claws together and rested her chin on top of them as she anxiously kept her gaze on Jainon. Empress, too, looked ill at ease, for her ears flattened, and her tail flipped back and forth. Even Tolby looked worried. His brow dropped, and his jaw clenched.

So many questions ran through me. Had she taken psychedelics? Was she inducing a low-oxygen state via some weird paralysis that gave hallucinations? Either would explain both the communing with a god and the danger of the ritual. I mean, she wasn't really talking to some mystical, all-powerful being, right? I wanted to ask all that and more, but figured now was not the time, so I made a mental note to dig into these religious customs later.

Jainon gasped. She fell to her knees and managed to catch herself before fully hitting the floor. "Tolby's plan," she said, panting. "We use Tolby's plan."

Relief washed over Empress and Yseri, and the two dashed to her side and helped her up. "You spoke to Hisoshim?" the matriarch asked.

Jainon nodded, but her face was filled not with elation, but terror. "We're not all getting out alive."

Empress froze. "He said that?"

"He did," she replied.

"Will any of us?"

Jainon's gaze drifted down, and it took her a moment to respond as if she were trying to recall a distant memory. "He said of all who try at least one must die."

I frowned. Why did the gods always want death? I mean, seriously. Why couldn't we get one that was just like, "Hey, drop me a thank-you note, and we're good." Or even better, one who wanted chocolate. Maybe it comes with the job, some divine policy

245

that says death is the only acceptable payment for such things. I certainly didn't say any of this, but I sure as hell was thinking it.

Empress broke the silence, addressing us all. "If that's the price we pay to rebirth the Empire, so be it."

"What now?" I dared ask while silently praying either this prophecy was a total farce or that at least Tolby and I weren't included in the "at least one must die" part.

Empress turned toward me and spoke. "Now we take care of a couple more things that must be done before we go."

"Like?"

"First, we must meet your earlier selves as the future demands."

I closed my eyes and cursed. I'd forgotten about that after all the one-of-us-is-going-to-die talk from before. "Yeah, I guess that's probably important. What's the other thing?"

"We must make sure you are worthy of joining us in our exodus."

CHAPTER THIRTY-TWO

A shiver ran down my spine. I stood inside the temple forest with trees that felt thousands of years old. They had gnarled limbs and scarred bark that had no doubt weathered all that the eons had thrown at them and more. A few paces away were the Empress's two handmaidens, dressed in bone-white armor, each holding a small torch while softly singing a haunting melody. My bare feet shifted uneasily on the damp forest floor as the chorus's tempo picked up.

Empress approached and stretched her arms toward the heavens. "Who is this outsider who walks among us?" she said, fiery eyes locking on mine. "What instrument of the Empress will you be?"

Following the instructions that Tolby gave me as best I could remember, I knelt. "My purpose was set by the Great One when time was born," I said as I extended both hands, palms up, in order to receive all that would come my way. "May I find it, wield it, and be wielded by it in a manner that brings glory to the righteous and death to my adversary."

I stumbled over the last half of the recital, but Empress said nothing, much to my appreciation. Tolby had warned me—indeed, so had the two handmaidens—that failing to perform the sacred ceremony could be held as nothing short of blasphemous and cost the sinner limb if not life. I was fond of both.

"May the Great One, whose voice now speaks through me, ring true in your heart and guide you to where you must be," said Empress.

"My spirit is ready, and my mind is clear," I replied without losing a beat, though I wasn't certain of either. Holes still plagued my memory, and I feared all that time-hopping was going to end up doing me in when I couldn't remember something important.

The handmaidens ceased their song and began a steady, sharp rhythm on drums almost half their size. The energetic beats filled my ears, and my heart quickened. There was something almost magical about the cadence, and I felt my blood warm and my body grow eager for a fight.

Tolby lit a smelter behind Empress. The incense within its belly burned brightly and let loose thin, aromatic wisps of smoke that held top notes of citrus and a core that reminded me of my dad's spice rack. Tolby then presented Empress with a barbed spear that had a dark garnet shaft and an ink-black head.

Empress gently took the weapon and placed it in my hands. "In your service to me, one day you are at a handmaiden's command, who gives you her spear to signify you act on her authority. She then orders you to remove a peasant from his home. The handmaiden insists that there are details she cannot provide that justify the eviction, but you suspect she wants the land for herself. Do you give the spear back and refuse the order, or do you keep the weapon and carry out the handmaiden's will?"

I did my best to control the mounting tremor in my arms. I knew there would be questions to answer, but I had hoped they'd have obvious answers. I shut my eyes to weed out distraction and made the story come alive by focusing on the spear's weight. Time and again I asked myself what the Kibnali would do, for this was their ritual, but I had no inkling which way any of them would answer, Tolby included. But then I quickly realized what others would do was not the point. Thus, I answered by offering the spear back to Empress. "My spirit would not agree with such action."

Empress said nothing, which in a way was worse than if she'd expressed displeasure. At least then I'd have an inkling as to what she expected of me.

The Kibnali matriarch placed the weapon aside and put a spyglass and a heavy iron key in my hands. "All your life you've wanted to explore the unknown, and now you've been offered the chance to captain a ship that will explore a new galaxy where signs of intelligent life have been detected. Before you launch, your brother falls seriously ill and trusts only you to run his store while he regains his strength. Do you resign your commission to come to your brother's aid, or do you politely decline his request and follow your heart to sail the stars, knowing he can afford to hire a manager to help in your stead?"

I raised my head and studied the two objects in my hand. My eyes settled on the spyglass. Logan would understand, I knew, but more important, Logan wouldn't ever place me in such a predicament, especially if he had the means to support himself. I was going to answer as such, but then it dawned on me that Empress was asking something else. She only wanted to know one thing: would I follow the call of my spirit over the call of my kin?

The time I spent making that decision spanned two heartbeats. Being honest with myself, I had only one real answer. I placed the spyglass in front of my knees and gave back the key. "If my brother's life is not in danger, I must follow my heart, whether he understands or not."

Heavy blows rained on the drums, and the voices who were once silent sprang back to life. Given the fierceness and seriousness of the ceremony, I felt caught on a tripwire, as if one wrong move would cause the Kibnali to explode into a frenzy.

Even Empress, who moved with deliberate form, had bloodlust in her eyes. She placed a slender, long-barreled pistol into my open palms and spoke once more. "I have charged you with tracking down and killing a spy who has killed two of your friends. After many years, you find him at the edge of the Empire where he works at an understaffed hospital and has saved the young kits of many Kibnali colonists. When you apprehend him, he offers no resistance but convinces you that he is no longer the man he once was. Do you execute the former spy, upholding your oaths to me and justice, or do you let him live, knowing the spirit of the law is what matters, and his life has new purpose serving the Empire?"

My body tensed even further, and my mouth dried. How could either be right? Did I kill someone who was no longer my enemy out of pure vengeance at the cost of young lives? Did I spare his life and deliberately disobey the Empress and fail at bringing a murderer to justice? What if that spy had killed Tolby? Could I even have the patience not to shoot the spy dead right then and there? Probably not.

When I realized time had passed far longer than everyone was comfortable with, I spit out the first answer that came to mind. "I don't know."

"You must answer," said the Empress.

I tried to force myself to choose. I really did. But I reversed myself three times in two seconds before finally making my commitment. "That is my answer. I don't know what I would do."

The drums went silent.

CHAPTER THIRTY-THREE

To my surprise and relief, Empress nodded with a smile. "Sometimes the best answer is the profession of not having one," she said. "It is good to know your limits, for it is the foolish warrior who thinks he has none. From this day forth we will be kin, not in blood, but in ceremony."

"As is your will," I replied. Though we were near the end of the ritual and all had gone well thus far, I knew I couldn't relax yet. There was still one more small part.

"Your blood shall seal this covenant," Empress said. With a single claw, Empress reached over and began carving an ancient set of symbols into both of my cheeks. When she finished, she cauterized the wounds with a chemically laced cloth given to her by Tolby. "Do you, Dakota Adams, swear upon the souls of your ancestors, upon your very fabric of nature and being, that you will forever uphold the Code of the Kibnali in all that you say and do?"

I hadn't been prepped for this last part, and so I hesitated. I was being sworn to what code now? Forever? I didn't have a clue as to what that entailed or could be in terms of consequence, but I also realized I didn't have time for a lecture. The only thing I did know from Tolby was that to swear about the souls of one's ancestors was the most serious and binding oath a Kibnali could make. So, of course, I agreed, because, well...I wanted to go home and didn't want to be left behind. "I do so swear, on all who made me and all that I am, I shall be your fang and claw."

Empress lifted my chin with a single claw and looked at me with approval. "Rise, Dakota, first-degree initiate of the Kibnali Guard, jumper of space and time."

I took to my feet and exhaled sharply. The sides of my face burned, and I longed for ice to cool them, but that wasn't an option. Instead, I cleared my eyes and tried to ignore the fire in my cheeks. "Thank you, Empress. I won't let you down."

Tolby came over and gave me a one-armed hug. "Knew you'd do fine. How much longer till we arrive?"

I checked the timer. "None. I think we're about to have an extended spacewalk courtesy of Pizlow."

"Then we move without delay," said Empress. "Get dressed and do whatever you need to get ready. We will go meet your earlier self, and once that's taken care of, we'll board your enemy's ship and take his shuttle."

Empress and the other Kibnali hurried off, leaving Tolby and me alone. As I grabbed the EVA suit Empress had brought from the museum earlier, I turned to Tolby, wondering if he had the same itch I did. "Are you at all curious to go see ourselves? I mean, we know where we'll be in a few. We could sneak a peek."

"No," Tolby said as he crossed his arms over his chest. "I think we've skirted disaster enough when it comes to playing with time. Let's focus on getting out of here."

I wiggled into my EVA pants and sighed. "You're probably right. What do we do in the meantime?"

"Exactly what Empress said. We sit tight and get ready to steal a shuttle."

The next thirty minutes flew, as I was a ball of nervous energy. I never wanted to get used to going to battle. I wasn't a space princess leading an intergalactic rebellion. I was just a girl who wanted to find lost alien treasures and get home. And get rich and famous in the process, too, but that's always a given.

After running through the fortieth potential disaster scenario in my head, Empress and her handmaidens returned, sporting weapons of fallen Ratters.

"Take," she said, handing me a pistol. "I thought this would be easier for you to wield at the same time as your portal gun than a rifle."

"Much easier, I'm sure," I replied. The moment the weapon touched my hands, I felt better about our odds, especially as the power pack was reading almost a full charge. I still clung to the hope that I wouldn't need to fire it at all, but I knew that was a pipe dream at best.

Yseri gave Tolby a plasma rifle, and he flipped it around a couple of times before resting it over his right shoulder. I knew he could always look the part of a complete badass, even if he had the patience of a saint for the most part, but now with that weapon and a hardened expression on his face, he looked ready and able to rip through a thousand Ratters without breaking a sweat.

"How long till Mister Cyber Squid crashes our interrogation?" he asked.

"A little under an hour," I replied, checking the time and then setting a timer on my HUD.

Yseri, holding a pistol in one hand and resting the other on the hilt of her sword, nodded in the general direction of the museum entrance. "We should go now. There's no telling how long it might take us to get to our staging point unseen."

After universal agreement and Empress giving the formal order to go, the five of us made for the *Vela*. The trip through the museum was quiet, and to my surprise, nearly uneventful. Only twice did we run into Ratters, but they were so preoccupied chasing down the best places for loot and fighting among themselves about who gets what, we managed to pass by unseen and without the need of portals.

As predicted earlier, the *Vela* was even easier to move around unseen. Our group ran into no one else, something I was thankful for. Once inside the airlock we planned to launch our assault from, I finally managed to relax.

All Kibnali around me were bathed in soft, red lighting and looked like death machines in their armored EVA suits. They each had large packs on their backs, stuffed with invaluable items they didn't want to be lost forever, historical recordings, religious artifacts, personal effects and the like.

As we stood, the Kibnali's fierce eyes stayed locked on the exit hatch, and none of my feline companions had offered any conversation since they had closed the inner hatch a minute ago. I didn't know what each one of them was thinking, only that it involved mentally rehearsing all the different ways to disembowel a Ratter. Even my best buddy, Tolby, had the look of a vicious killer, painting him as a total stranger to me. Was it the fact that he was reunited with his kin that made such a shift in his behavior? Or was he simply reverting to old ways because that was what was necessary for survival? I didn't know. Maybe both.

After spending almost all the time we had until launch in silence, I had to speak in an effort to combat my nerves, especially when I started to dwell on Jainon's earlier prophecy about how badly this could end up. "Well, this is weird."

Everyone but Tolby ignored the comment. "What's that?"

"Never thought I'd be in the middle of a cutting-out party of deadly, furry space marines who are seconds away from a boarding attempt."

Tolby regained some of his liveliness when he replied. "But bending spacetime has always been something you knew you'd master."

I chuckled. "You know what I mean. Besides, this feels more dangerous."

"Let's hope not," Tolby said. "We've cheated Death enough, don't you think?"

"Quiet," ordered Empress. When we hushed and straightened like grade-schoolers caught whispering during a test, she asked a single question. "What is your duty?"

The Kibnali answered in swift chorus. "To serve your will."

"And what is my will?"

"That we should spread amongst the stars."

"And now that opportunity is at hand," said Empress. "These Ratters have assaulted our home because they do not fear us. Before this day is done, before the approaching star swallows them whole, their fear of us will be second to none."

"We will carry your will like a torch and burn away the darkness that impedes us."

Empress smiled, and the red lighting made her razor teeth even more sinister. "To battle, to glory, to our destiny."

In unison, each of the furry warriors popped a small, brown wafer into their mouth—a potent synthetic drug that supposedly heightened reflexes and perception tenfold. I say supposedly because I was also told due to my singular heart and slight body mass, said drug would cause me to drop dead, so I was keen on taking their word for it when it came to what the drug could do without trying to experience it for myself.

Within seconds, the eyes of all the Kibnali narrowed, and their breathing rapidly increased. They lowered their faceplates, and I tensed in anticipation of all that was about to come. My mouth felt like it was filled with cotton. Even swallowing became difficult as thoughts of our last spacewalk flooded my mind. Funny, wasn't it, that both arriving and ending at the *Vela* involved swimming in the void, and both involved a fight that I had never thought I'd have to have.

"On my mark," the Empress said, putting a paw on the outer-hatch lever and interrupting my musings. "Three...two...one...Mark."

The Empress pulled the lever, and the hatch swung open. The Kibnali raced out of the *Vela* as if there were a prize for beating the escaping air. My brain kicked into gear, and I followed suit. Once I cleared the ship, I could easily see the *Revenant* nearby. The umbilical that stretched from it to the *Vela* was almost a hundred meters away.

It was too far for me to see details with just the naked eye, but utilizing the visual enhancement to my HUD, I got a better look. There were a few Ratters moving from one ship to the other, which alone didn't mean much, but when I spied three sentry bots making their way down the umbilical as well, I smiled. Those had to be the second group of reinforcements Drugar had sent during my interrogation with him.

I flew to the airlock where we intended to breach the ship, but I misjudged my speed and came in hotter than I intended, hitting the ship's hull with a dull thump. I cursed to myself and hoped no one saw me kiss metal.

"Want to ring the doorbell next time?" Tolby said as he came up next to me.

"No, but there's something I want to say before things get crazy—you know, just in case."

Tolby put a hand on my shoulder. "We'll be fine."

"This is important."

"Love you, too."

I smiled warmly. "No, that's not it. I was going to say that I want you to remember that if I die, I want a Viking funeral."

"I'll keep that in mind."

The words had barely left his mouth before Yseri pointed to the *Revenant*'s umbilical. Ratters raced through it away from the *Vela*, weapons drawn. A pair of sentry bots followed, and when they were completely through, the umbilical started to retract. "I believe that means your monster has arrived," Yseri said.

"Agreed," Empress replied. "Dakota, drop us in."

I held my breath and prepped my mind to open the wormhole we needed. The image of what I wanted, a portal on the outer hull of the ship extending about five meters in, crystallized without hesitation. The wormhole formed flawlessly a heartbeat later, giving a perfect view of the *Revenant*'s interior halls.

Tolby punched through the portal first, followed by Empress, Jainon and Yseri. When they were clear, I flew through as well. The moment I crossed the portal's threshold, artificial gravity pulled me down and slammed me into the floor, not even a half pace from the others.

Alarms blared and fire doors both in front and behind slammed down.

"Damn, that tripped the decompression sensors," I said.

A calm, feminine voice came from unseen speakers. "Breach in atmospheric integrity detected, deck one," it added. "Cause unknown."

"And they'll be here soon," I added. "Still, could've been a worse announcement, yes?"

"Warning: Quarantine procedures failing. Structural integrity compromised. Unknown ravenous alien drastically shortening crew lifespan on deck three."

"And it's worse," Tolby said as he took to his feet and helped the others up. "Work your magic and get us through that door before Mister Cyber Squid finds his way down here."

"On it," I said. I bolted for the nearest fire door. In no time, I tunneled through with a wormhole, but when it opened, instead of a short stretch of hall that ran to the hangar greeting me, it was a pair of Ratters, each sporting plasma rifles in hand and shocked looks upon their faces.

Before I could react, Tolby snapped off two shots from behind. The first caught the lead Ratter in the throat, killing him instantly. The second took the other Ratter high in the chest, which caused him to stumble, but not drop. A dozen shots slammed into him an instant later from the other Kibnali, and the poor thing fell to the ground in a smoldering heap.

"Holy snort that was fast," I said, amazed at the Kibnali's effectiveness while also feeling embarrassed at how much I'd locked up. I shuddered to think what would've happened if it were only me running around there.

"My two-week-old kits have faster reflexes," Empress said, looking at her kill. "They're a disgrace to their species."

Yseri's brow dropped as she looked at me. "If you survive, I'd suggest you train more for combat."

"Point taken, but honestly, this isn't something I plan on doing a lot of," I said as I snatched the power packs from the Ratters and tossed one to Tolby. The extra charges for my sidearm were comforting, but my mind still flipped back to the first firefight I'd been in. "Here's to hoping we don't need the extras, eh?"

"I don't think that will be the case," replied Tolby.

The five of us sped deeper into the *Revenant*. In less than thirty seconds, we reached the cluster relay Tolby needed to hack. It was tucked away in a small room crowded with machinery. We ran into a single Ratter there, and the wretched thing didn't even get a squeak out before Tolby pounced on the creature and ripped out its throat.

"Watch the halls while I make the hack," he said as he let the bloody body fall to the floor.

"Man, I did not need to see that," I said, cringing.

"Needs and wants seldom line up," Tolby replied with remorse. At that point, he went to work, and the rest of us set up to cover him from any Ratters wandering by.

About a minute later, the voice of the female announcer returned, and it delivered her usual, cheery news. "Warning. Internal lifeform sensors damaged. Unknown ravenous alien no longer being tracked. Last seen headed midship."

"Tolby, can you hurry things up?" I asked.

"I'm trying."

"Because I'm pretty sure we're midship."

"I know, Dakota," he grumbled as he used his PEN in a mad flurry on the relay's circuitry. "Sabotaging a system isn't as easy as it looks. It's not point-and-shoot, you know."

He was right, and I'm sure my added worry wasn't helping. So I took to biting my lower lip to keep from saying anything else. How I wished I could be more like Empress and her handmaidens. Their utter faith that Tolby would pull through was admirable. It was like the idea of failure wasn't even an option their imagination could fathom.

"Holy baby furries of the Great One," Tolby said, punching the wall next to him. "I got it."

"Guns down?" Empress asked.

"Yes. We've got five minutes. Maybe ten if Mister Cyber Squid keeps wrecking the place."

"I don't think that will be a problem," I said as we took off through the *Revenant* once more. Our race was a short, but tense, fifty meters to the shuttle bay, and to my delight, we didn't cross paths with any other Ratters by the time we reached the hatch leading to the hangar.

"We're going to make it, aren't we?" I said, smiling and welcoming the taste of freedom we were about to get.

Tolby slid to a halt next to me. He gripped his rifle with one hand, while the other was poised to open the door. "Ready?"

I shook my head and laughed. "Yep."

Tolby grinned and bowed slightly. "After you, then."

"After us," Yseri corrected, pulling Tolby back. "As the only male Kibnali who still draws breath, your life is greater than any other at this point."

The handmaiden hit the orange control panel, and the door slid open with a pressurized hiss. Immediately, she slipped through, and I followed, while the other Kibnali brought up the rear. The hangar was three decks high. On either side were diamond-plate stairs that led to a control station that hung overhead. Directly in front of us was the *Revenant*'s crescent-shaped shuttle, resting about twenty meters away on tricycle landing gear with a ramp extending from its belly.

I approached the shuttle's loading ramp with caution, while everyone else fanned out to either side.

"That is the most beautiful thing I've ever seen," I said, noticing that the twin micro-warp-core engines mounted on the wings were spooling and drawing in dark energy from subspace. "It's all ready to fly."

The moment those words escaped my mouth, my smile fell. "Oh damn. It's ready to fly."

A Ratter trotted down the ramp, weapon in hand. It immediately saw us and started firing. I dove behind a nearby cargo loader. The giant yellow robot-looking thing might be good at picking up everything from missiles to xenomorphs, but it turned out to be terrible at offering any cover.

Two red-hot bolts of plasma zipped by my head, singeing my hair as they flew by. A third hit the loader in the leg, boring a hole through its shin before deflecting off to the side with a shower of sparks.

"Get away from her, you bastard!" Tolby shouted, returning fire. His shots went wide and harmlessly drilled holes into the other side of the hangar, but they were enough to cause the Ratter to retreat up the ramp.

"Don't mess up that shuttle!" I screamed. "We kind of need it!"

"Why do you think I missed so much?" he yelled back.

A door across the hangar slid open and in poured five more Ratters with rifles blazing. Though their shots were as wild as their eyes, they threw enough of them Tolby's way that he and Jainon took cover inside a nearby storeroom.

I shook my head and vented my frustration to the world. "You have got to be kidding me! Why aren't they fighting Mister Cyber Squid?"

"Because these are the smart ones that know when to abandon ship," Tolby answered. He continued to shoot, and while his next few shots only succeeded in sizzling the air, the fourth nailed a Ratter square in the face. "That's one," he said. "Where's Empress and Yseri?"

"Not sure," I replied.

A Ratter popped out a little more than he should, and I tried to capitalize on it by lining up a shot. But before I squeezed the trigger, I jerked back under cover as a trio of plasma bolts zipped by. I shot back as much as I could, but I didn't hit any of them. A couple of my shots were close enough that two of the Ratters flattened themselves behind a stack of crates. In the brief lull of incoming fire, I spied the other two Kibnali.

"I see them," I said to Tolby. "They're on the shuttle's wing, using the engine for cover. I think—"

My sentence was cut short when more plasma flew at me from downrange, and it was only a combination of divine miracle and Tolby's return fire that kept me from earning a body bag.

"Get out of there!" Tolby yelled, keeping the Ratters suppressed as much as he could.

"Kind of pinned down here!"

"It's not like you have to run!"

I muttered a curse at myself and grinned. After all I'd done and endured, I was still acting like normal modes of travel constrained me. A stitch through spacetime later, I popped out of a wormhole and joined Tolby inside the storeroom.

"Surprised I didn't have to spell it out for you," he teased, popping a few shots off at the Ratters.

"Kind of forgot I could do that," I said. "Funny how a good old-fashioned firefight makes you forget everything."

"Yeah, or your brain is still mushy from using that thing."

Jainon, blade and pistol in hand, crouched. "Open a portal in the other hall. We'll cut them down from behind."

I snuck a peek out of the storeroom and my heart nearly jumped out of my throat. The all-too-familiar red pulse of a Ratter grenade caught my eye as a Ratter gave one a throw. The grenade sailed perfectly into the storeroom, promising to give each one of us a first-class ticket to the hereafter.

Instinctively I opened a portal on the floor and threw the exit across the hangar. The grenade flew through and dropped neatly on its sender's head before exploding. Two Ratters were shredded in the blast, while the other two darted out from their respective positions, screeching with horror. Tolby put the first one down with a well-placed shot to the midsection, while the other one fell to fire from both Empress and Yseri when it made a run for the shuttle and was caught in the open.

I'm sure time didn't actually stop, but it sure felt like it did as I tried to process what I'd done. I'd never killed someone before, and I couldn't help but feel disgusting, as if part of my soul had been ripped away, never to return.

Those thoughts vanished the instant the ramp to the shuttle began to raise. Immediately, I made a run toward it. "Don't let them get away!"

Empress and Yseri were the first to reach the ramp, but they were forced to dive sideways when plasma fire came flying toward them. It closed before the two could regain their feet or the rest of us could make a push.

A high-pitched whine filled the air as the engines lifted the shuttle off the hangar floor. I clenched my teeth, knowing we had only seconds to do something before we'd be stuck on a ship we could never take.

"Send us in!" Empress barked.

I threw out a portal in front of the Kibnali and prayed I had managed to visualize the shuttle interior well enough that the exit would be a good one. Empress and her handmaidens dashed through, blades and pistols ready. My heart pounded twice in my chest and then skipped a beat when two shots of plasma flew out of my portal, carving furrows in the hangar deck.

I hesitated, unsure if I should rush in to help or stay put to avoid my chest catching plasma. Tolby, on the other hand, kept his weapon up and swung behind me to get a view of inside the wormhole, clearly ready to crack a shot at whatever nasty he encountered.

Before he could get a good view, the shuttle wobbled and fell to the deck. The landing gear absorbed the impact, but it hit with such a loud thud, I was impressed that the struts didn't crumple like paper being turned into an origami boulder.

A Ratter flopped out of the portal, chest pierced and deader than a vacuum. A second one followed suit with the same diagnosis. Empress hopped out and wiped her blade on the back of one of her two kills. "That's the last of them."

"Out flipping standing," I said. "I'm ready to go home and enjoy a hot bath and a huge root beer float."

With my dream firmly planted in mind, I jumped through the wormhole with everyone else close in tow. The shuttle was a little smaller than my own ship, but it was three times as nice and best of all, intact. Well, three times as nice if one ignored the recent redecorating with blood. Tolby made a beeline for the cockpit and hopped in the pilot seat. I raced for the spot for the copilot, but Empress stole the spot.

"Strap in," she said, more of a polite order than a friendly suggestion. "We'll take it from here."

I sat in one of the passenger chairs and raised an eyebrow. "You fly?"

Empress drew the corners of her lips back, and there was an aura full of gloat surrounding her. "Eighty-eighth floor has a hundred flight simulators," she said. "I spent a dozen years there nonstop after I tired of learning about extinct flora. I bet I can pilot more spacecraft than you can name."

"As long as you get us out of here in one piece, I'll be more than happy to take you at your word," I said, laughing.

"All right, here we go," Tolby said. "Next stop, anywhere but here."

After flipping a few switches overhead, he reached over and pushed the throttle forward. The shuttle lifted off the deck once again and gracefully spun in place until it was facing the hangar doors, which to my unease, were closed. The brief flutter of butterflies in my stomach turned into a baby critter trying to dig its way out when the doors stay closed after repeated button pushes, switch flips, and dial turns by both Tolby and Empress.

"Would it help if I got out and pushed?" I said with a nervous chuckle.

Tolby threw a frustrated glace back at me. "Yeah. It might."

"Shuttle control isn't responding to our requests," Empress said, working her console.

The shuttle rocked sideways, and I slammed forward in my seat. Tolby furiously worked the controls to keep from spinning the craft into the hangar wall. A klaxon blared inside the cabin, and I opened my mouth to ask the obvious what-the-hell-is-going-on question, but the words got stuck in my throat when Mister Cyber Squid made an appearance.

Perched on top of the spacecraft, the creature leaned over the top of the cockpit. Tolby lunged for the shields and threw them up a nanosecond before Mister Cyber Squid smashed the ultra-plex with his head. Arcs of light-blue energy shot across the shuttle as the kinetic shields absorbed the blow. And then another. And another.

"What in Thrapgar's name did they feed this guy?" Tolby said. "He's going to punch through our shields!"

"Can you throw him?" I asked.

Tolby jerked the stick left and right. Everyone, including Mister Cyber Squid, went for a wild ride that would test any rodeoer's skills. "He's not going anywhere!"

"Buck him harder!"

"Any harder and we're going to punch through to the upper decks."

Mister Cyber Squid traded headbutting the cockpit for beating on it with his tentacles. The shields flickered one last time, and then there was a brilliant flash as they overloaded and collapsed.

"Ram him into the wall!" I shouted.

"It'll ruin the ship!"

Mister Cyber Squid reared back and slammed into the cockpit. The ultra-plex cracked like a spider web, and I added two points of fright to my already full-revved panic engine. "The ship's already ruined! Just do it!"

Tolby shoved the throttle all the way to the stop.

I clenched my jaw as I was pressed into the seat as the shuttle surged forward. A half second later, I was thrown against my five-point harness as the spacecraft, complete with a cyber-squid battering ram, plowed into the side of the hangar.

CHAPTER THIRTY-FOUR

Mister Cyber Squid shrieked, his cry sounding like something between a bull elephant charging and the whine of a dark matter turbine on its last legs. Thick, orange goop sprayed into the cockpit as the ultra-plex caved in. Emergency lights and sirens filled the shuttle cockpit. The spacecraft's engines sputtered and then failed altogether before the ship tumbled down. The landing gear shattered under the combined weight of spacecraft and cyber squid, but thankfully that meant the landing gear absorbed the brunt of the energy from the fall, saving us all from being killed. So here's to you, physics, for being awesome.

"Someone needs new shocks," Tolby moaned, falling over in his seat.

"So does my spine," I replied. I went to unbuckle the five-point harness but stopped with a whimper as pain raced up my back.

Empress was the first to get out of her chair, followed quickly by her handmaidens. "Leave your pain here," she said. "The still warrior is the dead warrior."

I sucked in a breath, wanting to spend an extra moment or two mentally preparing myself for what had to be done. There was an electric pop somewhere in the rear of the shuttle, and smoke poured into the cabin. That was more than enough for me to spring into action, as I had no desire to see my surname changed to Flambé.

I was barely free of the chair with the portal device in hand when the entire shuttle rocked sideways. A deafening explosion left a loud ringing in my ears. Fire raced through the shuttle's interior, and I popped open a wormhole and dove through with a trail of Kibnali behind me.

We flew out the other side, a good meter above the hangar deck, and crashed into the unyielding floor. I rolled and struck my head hard enough so that while I was lying on the floor, catching my breath, I half expected to feel blood after I reached back to feel the damage. There was a knot, and it was tender, but at least there wasn't grey matter escaping my skull.

A calm, distant voice filled the air. "Explosion detected in hangar. Outer hull integrity still maintained. All fire crews report."

"Tolby, we're going to have company!" I yelled. "And I left my gun in the shuttle!"

"We've already got company," Tolby said, eyes wide. "That thing's still alive."

I shot upright. Still pinned between the burning wreck of the shuttle and the hangar doors was Mister Cyber Squid, pissed off as ever. Two of his tentacles and part of his side were trapped in the wreckage, but it looked like he might not be stuck there forever.

"How long do we have before he gets loose?" I asked.

Mister Cyber Squid screeched and jerked against the wreckage, and one of the tentacles ripped off. A second jerk later, he tore free of the shuttle, spraying orange goo everywhere. The monster fell to the floor and stumbled, but he steadied himself within a couple of heartbeats.

"You had to ask!" Tolby yelled.

"Like you weren't thinking the same thing!"

"Enough!" Empress barked. "Run!"

I didn't need a second to the motion to kick myself into high gear. I ran with the others for the hatch across the way, and the sounds of Mister Cyber Squid's heavy charge fueled each of us to near light speeds. Before we could reach the exit, three Ulydian damage-control bots skittered out of the hall on their six spidery legs, with numerous arms popping out of the tops of their round bodies. Right behind them came four Ratters, each armed with pistols.

The bots raced past us and went to tend to the fire. The Ratters, however, came to a halt and raised their weapons. If I had had my weapon, I probably would've started shooting. Thank god I didn't, and thank god the Kibnali were more aware of things than I was—not to mention more understanding of how to use the Ratters to our benefit.

Instead of shooting them dead as the Kibnali had done to all the others, they kept running, albeit it more to the side. This kept the Ratters' attention solely on the behemoth bearing down upon us all rather than on starting a new firefight.

The Ratters shot wildly at Mister Cyber Squid, but their shots bounced off his hide and only succeeded in making them his new chew toy. The monster drove through two Ratters at the same time with his bull charge and sent them flying into the air. The third Ratter was quickly snatched by his tentacles, and despite its squeals and feeble attempts at pulling itself free, it was smashed against a bulkhead and killed instantly. The fourth Ratter backed away from the carnage and quickly joined us in making a run for the exit.

Tolby was the first through, and I came through next. I paused inside the threshold for Empress and the handmaidens to get in before I hammered the control panel, closing the door and locking it. There was a soft thud from the other side as something human-sized hit the hatch. Then there were a bunch of little thuds. Then one big thud that caved the door in a quarter meter.

"Now what?" Tolby asked. "The shuttle was the only thing left with subspace drives."

"Is there another bay?" Yseri asked.

Tolby shook his head. "No."

"Our only choice is the escape pods," I replied. "Hopefully the guns are still offline, and the pods can accelerate fast enough to get us away from whatever star is about to pop through."

"Oh, that's comforting."

The words had no sooner left his mouth when everything shook worse than being at the base of Mount Vesuvius blowing its top. We were tossed into the air and slammed into the wall. The lights flickered once before going out altogether. When the red emergency lighting kicked in, the reason for the new, floating feeling in my stomach was clear. The artificial gravity was gone, and everyone was suspended midair.

"Catastrophic damage to engine rooms, power regulators, air filtration, aft sensor relay, damage-control systems, and hyperspace CAT drive," said the ship's AI. "Hull integrity compromised on multiple decks. Warp fields collapsing. EMP damage sustained. All hands abandon ship. Repeat, all hands abandon ship."

"What the hell happened?" Tolby said, asking what was no doubt on everyone's mind.

I shook my head and offered my best guess. "Museum must be kicking out huge chunks of debris."

"Can you jump us to the escape pods?" Tolby asked.

I shook my head. "I don't know," I said, looking down at the portal device. "That's pretty far for a blind jump."

"Try!" he said. "We don't have much time."

I nodded and sucked in a breath. Once I visualized, aimed, and pulled the trigger, however, I wasn't greeted with a portal, but a mental image of alien words that slowly transformed into ones I could understand. "Unexpected power surge," I said, reading them aloud. "Reboot and reinitialization of prime mover required before further use."

"What?" Tolby asked.

I reread them, swallowed hard, and looked up at everyone. "I can't use the device," I said. "I think that EMP burst fried it for a bit."

"Great," Tolby said with a growl. "For how long?"

"I don't know," I said. "I think I can see something that looks like a progress bar in my head, but it's not moving. And there's something about estimated spacetime distance being zero."

"This changes nothing," Empress said, cutting in. "We can still reach the pods before it's too late."

"At least the guns will stay offline now," said Yseri. "That's something."

That was something, and at this point, I was ready to take all the somethings I could get. No one spoke further as we rushed for the escape pods, which was fine by me, too. I felt we were going to need every ounce of concentration we could muster to get out of this place intact. It also didn't help that the fuel on my EVA suit was registering low. Stupid museum piece. Not even ready for a simple spacewalk.

As such, while the others zipped through the halls with ease, I had to use carefully controlled bursts. The fact that the ship was tumbling in space and I was bouncing off the walls and slamming into corners only added to my problems.

I rounded a corner and entered one of the last halls I needed to jet down. At the other end floated Jainon, who was waving me over. "You'll need to be faster than that unless you want Empress to leave you behind. You don't strike me as the type who likes swimming in plasma."

"I'm trying to go faster," I said. "My fuel is almost spent."

Another explosion rocked the ship, which was followed by three more. Air rushed by, and I had to fight to grab on to something, lest I get swept away by the sudden jet stream. My faceplate latched in place automatically as alarms blared and an announcement came. "Danger: hull integrity at critical levels. Repeat hull—"

And then everything went quiet, and the rush of air was gone. I keyed the radio to Tolby. "You okay?"

"Yeah. Don't take off your helmet."

"No kidding. I'd like to keep my eyeballs from being sucked out of their sockets."

"That would ruin your chances of getting into the Space Ranger Academy," he joked. "Now get up here. We're at the ladder."

I pressed down the hall, feeling better that we were almost there. When I got to Jainon, it was only a dozen meters to an access ladder that led down to one of the banks of escape pods. I reached the bottom, and Empress and Yseri were waiting there next to Tolby, who was currently running a bypass with his PEN on a sealed hatch.

"How long?" I asked.

"Not long," he replied, smiling and tapping the PEN on his helmet. He pressed a button on the control panel and the hatch slid open.

As soon as I hopped through, I gasped. Dozens of Ratters floated limply through space, eyes wide, mouths open. I pushed forward, trying not to think about the corpse that had bumped into my shoulder or the fact that the first three pods we'd passed were already gone. "There's got to be one here."

"I'm not willing to entertain any other thought," said Tolby.

I soon reached the next hatch and choked back tears when I saw that that one was already launched, too. "Gone," I said, trying to sound strong and in control even if I was barely so. "Probably a broken one anyway. We'll get the next."

Despite my demanding statement to the powers that be, Fate was not inclined to give in to my wants. The next was gone as well, as were the ones after that again and again. As we grew nearer to the end of the hall, I found it a struggle to breathe, thanks to my anxiety.

"Still a couple more ahead," Tolby said. He grabbed my hand and pulled, which was enough to snap me out of my momentary daze. When we got to the final two pod bays and found them empty, however, I wished I would've stayed in that wonderful, blissful land of detachment.

"Damnit!" I yelled, striking the wall with the bottom of my fist. The pain felt good, so I did it again and again. "Damnit! Damnit! Damnit!" My body went limp and I floated gently upward. "We just went through this!"

"What else is there?" asked Empress.

I sucked in a breath to recompose myself as I focused on her question. I had to keep it together. Correction, I could keep it together. I'd been through too much to lose it now.

I whipped out the archive cube and brought up the schematics for Pizlow's ship. As I searched, I realized how much I admired the Kibnali matriarch. Even with Death walking to our front door, she was focused, and one day, I hoped to be able to be like that. "Okay, there's another bank of pods, aft, near the engines, but there's no telling if we can make it there, or if any are still left operational."

Empress's face soured. "Probably no good. How far can you throw us back in time?"

I temporarily closed my eyes to concentrate and checked the reboot routine to see where it was. The progress bar that popped in my mind had barely moved, and beneath that mental image sat the spatial and temporal limits which were as low as my hope to see to tomorrow. That said, the limits weren't zero anymore. "I think the most we can jump right now is an hour."

"Then that's what we work with," Empress said.

"Just remind me what's going on when we go through," I replied. "It's going to scramble my brain again and I don't want to wander off."

Tolby squeezed my shoulder. "As if I'd ever let that happen."

"Okay, here we go," I said, closing my eyes again. My mind linked with the portal device and numbers filled my thoughts. Memories of where I'd been and who I was faded, and as I stretched my thoughts into the recent past, exhaustion overtook me. It was all I could do to stay awake, let alone concentrate.

A portal opened on a nearby wall. It started off as the size of a marble but quickly grew. Its edges wobbled, and the bigger it became, the more it felt like a whale was resting on my head. We were teetering on a monumental paradox by jumping back for whatever reason, and I knew the Universe was doing all it could to prevent that from happening. Still, I pushed on as hard as I could, even when the pain behind my eyes felt excruciating.

Ultimately, it proved too much. The portal collapsed as my eyes filled with water and my lungs longed for air. "I can't," I said, panting. "The backlash is too much."

Empress gripped my arm. "Focus, Dakota! Find us a way!"

Digging deeper than I ever had before, I restarted the process. Everything around me fell away as I concentrated on forming the next wormhole. It came to life, but even more malformed than the previous attempt. Despite its shaky nature, it did clearly open into the past.

That view, however, only lasted a split second. As Tolby moved toward it, the last of my safety discs shorted out, and the wormhole collapsed.

"This isn't working," Yseri said. "We make for the aft pods. We've got no other choice."

"Wait," Tolby said. "Dakota, those schematics you were looking at. Are you sure they were the right ones? They looked a little different than the ones I had."

"Mako class cruiser, right? Series 2D."

"Pizlow's ship is a 2D?"

"Yeah, why?"

Tolby shook his head, muttering some obscenities at himself. "I could have sworn earlier you said 2B. That's what I had pulled up. The 2Ds have a modified bridge that can break away from the main ship if needed."

"Are you sure?"

"Yes, I'm sure! Look if you don't believe me!"

I did, not because I thought Tolby was mistaken, but with everything that had gone wrong thus far, I needed to see it for myself. It only took a few seconds for me to bring up the blueprints again, jump to the bridge and cycle through its features. Sure enough, the thing could serve as a giant life raft. It even had a micro-displacement drive mounted underneath for expeditious travel if need be.

My face lit up. "You're a genius!" I shouted. My energy faded when I noticed part of its design. "It'll only separate on the commanding officer's orders."

Tolby held up his PEN. "I guess I'm in for the hack of my life."

CHAPTER THIRTY-FIVE

The race to the *Revenant*'s bridge was filled with rumbles and floating obstacles, mostly in the form of Ratter corpses, though general ship debris came in a close second. About twenty meters away, we passed through a closed hatch. Air rushed out as we moved through the bulkhead, and once through, we closed it behind us.

"That's a little promising," I said. "If this hall still has some atmo, maybe the bridge is in good shape."

"I'd wager the micro-displacement drive is in good shape, too, then," said Tolby.

With a new surge of hope, I flew down the hall with the rest of the Kibnali in tow. At the far side, we found the hatch to the bridge was not only sealed, but the control panel was nonresponsive and only offered a single red word on a blue background: LOCKED.

"Of course you are," I muttered, madly pushing the panel's buttons. When that didn't work, I traded being rational for kicking and hitting the hatch a few times. It made me feel momentarily better, but like the previous attempt, it didn't produce results.

"Damage Control probably sealed the bridge before it went offline to keep it safe for as long as possible," Tolby said. "So unless you've got Pizlow's override codes, it won't open. You'll have to portal us through."

My stomach churned at the thought, and just thinking about trying another wormhole gave me a massive case of vertigo. I tried to push a little more but ended up with a nose bleed. "I think I need a rest and it still needs a few to recharge," I said. "Can you do anything?"

"I can try, but we might not be here in a few minutes." Tolby whipped out his PEN and went to work. Thirty seconds later, Tolby shook his head and stuffed away his PEN. "Pizlow's security is top-notch. I'm not going to be able to bypass it before we're plasma. Tunnel us through."

"I'm not sure I can yet," I said. Though my head did feel a little better, I still couldn't shake the nausea.

"This is about to be a now or never kind of deal," Yseri said. "Make it now."

I conceded the point. More blood oozed from my nose as I tried to make it happen. Invisible claws tore at my eyes, neck, and scalp, but still I pushed through until those lovely numbers popped into mind. Thankfully, a wormhole leading from our position to the bridge popped open a few seconds later, but not before I upchucked in my helmet.

The Kibnali raced through, and Tolby grabbed me by the arm and dragged me along. The moment each of us cleared the portal, artificial gravity slammed us into the floor.

"I've never been this happy about smashing my face on metal," Jainon said with a laugh as she pushed herself up.

"Or as happy about puking on myself," I said, sliding open my faceplate and wiping my face clean as best I could before taking in my surroundings.

The entire bridge was only about four meters long, but it was easily twice that in width. Opposite the hatch we'd jumped through were a pair of chairs flanking the captain's chair. Consoles surrounded each of those stations, and they all faced a large, curved set of ultra-plex screens. On those screens we saw an excellent view of dark space that was occasionally interrupted by gouts of flame shooting out of the museum.

"How do we detach from the main ship?" Jainon asked.

"The controls on the captain's chair should do it," I said, checking the schematics. "Looks easy enough."

"Assuming the computer doesn't lock us out."

"Only one way to find out," I said, making a run for the captain's chair.

I was a single step into my stride when four pops sounded in rapid succession. I spun around to see Empress and her handmaidens collapse on the floor and Tolby stagger. Behind him, Pizlow looked at his stun gun in disgust before tossing it to the floor, which was bad for him, because unlike the handmaidens, Tolby didn't drop.

Tolby roared and charged Pizlow. Sadly, his left side had little strength, and his charge was more of an awkward limp. Still, he had enough fight in him to give me enough time to scoop Jainon's rifle off the floor. By the time I got it up and came around, however, the fight between Pizlow and Tolby was over. Pizlow had Tolby facedown on the floor with a knife digging into the back of his neck.

"Don't you dare!" I yelled.

"You're in no position to make demands," he said with a maniacal laugh. "Funny how you've always been a step ahead but in the end, you needed at least another two more."

Standing more statuesque than one of Medusa's victims, I had no words, at least, not until the sounds of a nearby explosion broke the spell fear had over me. "There's plenty of room for us all in here. No one has to die."

"You're right about the first part," Pizlow sneered. He dug the point of the blade in and twisted. "Drop your gun."

"I'll shoot you if you hurt him."

"You might get me, but not before I sever his brainstem. Now drop it!"

"Shoot him, Dakota," Tolby said, without a hint of fear in his voice or eyes.

I shook my head as my vision blurred and tears flooded my eyes and ran down my cheeks unabated. "Just stop! He never did anything to you."

"That's right. You did. You stole what was mine, tried to feed me to that thing, and destroyed the greatest find in all of civilization." The ship rumbled, and Pizlow threw a glance at the hatch he had come through. "Give me the portal device and get out."

"You'll never get it to work on your own," I said. "Take us with you, and I'll teach you everything I know. I swear."

"This isn't a negotiation."

"Warning, spacetime anomaly detected," the far-too-chipper AI said. "Unknown event approaching. ETA eighty-eight seconds."

Pizlow's brow dropped. "Three seconds and he's dead."

"We'll all be dead!"

"One."

He never got to two. I dropped the rifle and held up my hands. "Okay. It's yours."

Pizlow nodded, but he kept the blade still at Tolby's neck. "Now the device."

Though I'd capitulated, I wasn't about to cave completely into his demands. I had a half-baked idea. "It's yours. But you're not getting it here. You're getting it in the past. That way you can go wherever you want, and we still go home."

Before Pizlow could respond, I shut my eyes and squeezed the last of my tears out. In the self-induced darkness, a landscape of numbers flooded my mind, the last ones I knew I'd ever see if this didn't work. I could only pray the device had enough charge to pull this off.

A portal leading to an hour in the past sprang to life next to Pizlow. Immediately, I tossed the artifact through and straightened as my backbone solidified. "There. We're still in your stupid interrogation room, so go get it now and make sure none of this happens."

"You stupid girl," Pizlow growled. "You think—"

Tolby, taking advantage of Pizlow's distraction, rolled sideways and managed to bite deep into Pizlow's leg. The brute roared and stumbled back, which gave Tolby ample opportunity to scramble away.

At that point, the wormhole started to distort, and Pizlow dashed through. From our view, I saw him try for the portal device, but as he was about to grab it, multiple arcs of electricity shot out of its skin, causing him to jump sideways. The tunnel through spacetime collapsed a split second later.

"You gave him the device?" Tolby shouted.

"It got him out of here, didn't it?"

"But he's got the most powerful artifact in the galaxy!"

I raced for the bridge controls. "It's a paradox if he takes the device and keeps this from happening, so he can't. Now strap in and get ready to fly us out of here!"

Tolby jumped in the pilot's seat and grabbed the controls. "Get us separated!"

"Remember, I want a Viking funeral," I said with a half grin. I turned my attention back to the bridge controls and worked them faster than a grand pianist setting a new record for playing prestissimo. "*Revenant* command," I said, "verify Captain Pizlow is no longer aboard and separate bridge for emergency egress."

"Scanning," replied the sickeningly calm feminine voice. "Please standby."

I drummed my hands on my thighs and bit my lip. The ship rumbled from a distant impact, and I glanced at the timer on my HUD when another gout of plasma jetted across our view of space.

"Come on," I said. "How much ship still exists that can actually be scanned?"

"The percentage of habitable space on the *Revenant* is low. The percentage of working scanners is even lower. Please standby."

"We don't have time to standby! We need out of this apocalypse, now!"

"Engaging in conversation is putting further strain on my limited resources. If time is of the essence, I suggest being quiet."

"Gah!"

Tolby twisted in the chair and captured my focus. "Hey," he said with a knowing smile. "We had a good run."

"Don't you—" I stopped myself from arguing further. Tension melted in my body, and the chaos unfolding around us faded away. "Yeah. Yeah, we did. And I wouldn't have wanted to do it with anyone else."

CHAPTER THIRTY-SIX

It all happened so fast.

The command module separated with the massive boom of three dozen explosive latches going off and the firing of a dedicated ejection rocket mounted underneath. We'd cleared the *Revenant* by a meter at best when the museum melted away, and a rapidly expanding star took its place.

Tolby shot us into hyperspace without thought or calculation.

We didn't go for long before a new problem was sighted on the horizon. "Drop us out before we're lost forever!" I shouted.

"On it," Tolby replied evenly, bringing us back into real space.

One he had, I exhaled the breath I'd been holding for two minutes and sank into the captain's chair. My white-knuckled fingers relaxed their grip on the seat, and I ran them over my sweat-laden scalp and hair. "You okay?"

Tolby nodded. "I'm alive. I think that's all I can ask at this point."

"Same," I said, blowing out another puff of air in an effort to relieve tension. I checked the scanners. A lot of emptiness surrounded us, and beyond that, more emptiness stood waiting.

Normally, I'd find that a bit gloomy since we had no bearings at the moment, but hey, at least we weren't about to be torn apart, and my parents wouldn't spend the rest of their lives wondering what had happened to me. "For the record, none of this was what I had in mind when I said we should find the *Vela*."

"Me either," Tolby replied.

I hurried over to him, wrapped my arms around his neck and squeezed. "And I'm really, really sorry I didn't listen to you more."

"Yeah, well, if you hadn't, we wouldn't have found them," he replied. "But from here on out, you better."

"I will. I promise." I then pulled away and grinned. "Provided you don't turn into some bloodthirsty furball bent on intergalactic conquest. You were kind of scary back there, you know?"

"Only because I had to be," he said. "I have no intentions of repeating past mistakes, or seeing future generations do the same."

"Glad to hear," I said, giving him one last squeeze.

At that point, he popped out of his seat and checked on the other Kibnali. After a moment, he sighed with relief. "They're fine, but probably won't wake up for a bit. How's the ship?"

I brought up a diagnostic screen and carefully went through each area. I couldn't chance speaking first and jinxing us to doom. Once I'd reread everything at least three times, I looked over to my best bud and smiled. "We're in the green. How long do you think it will take for the nav computer to find out where we are?"

"Maybe a couple of hours to get enough data from parallax scans. Couldn't have gone that far."

"Far enough from that star," I said, laughing. "That's all that matters."

"What do you think happened to Pizlow?"

I shrugged. "No idea."

"Still not worried about him getting the artifact?"

I shook my head. "I'm sure he never made it out alive. I could feel that backlash coming the moment the idea popped in my head, and since he's without safety discs, we should probably just be thankful he didn't wipe out this sector of the galaxy trying to take everything for himself."

"You're certain he's dead?"

"I would assume, no? Why? Worried he'll come after us still?"

"No," Tolby replied. "I'm hoping he was part of the group when Hisoshim said at least one who tried to escape would die."

"Oh," I said, biting my lower lip. "Me too, now that you mention it. That must be it, though. I mean, we're all here, right?"

"Right..." Tolby's voice trailed, and he sat back in the pilot's chair. He didn't say anything for a moment, but he did throw a meaningful glance at Yseri and Jainon before he spoke again. "Now that you've got that archive cube, you'll probably want to disappear for a few months."

The corners of my mouth drew back. "I think you do."

"All I'm saying is that I'm sure you've got important things you want to get done."

"You don't have to explain," I said with a playfully dismissive wave of the hand. "Go enjoy your romp."

"I knew you'd understand. And for your continued dedication to the Kibnali, I shall compose an opera worthy of your name."

"I appreciate that, and in fact, I understand so much, I'm going to help," I said as I whipped out the archive cube. My arm tingled as I made the mental connection. There was a melodic pop in my head, and the top of the cube lit up as a holographic menu sprang to life in front of me.

"What are you up to?" Tolby asked warily.

"Well, you can't expect to repopulate your entire species without a new planet, right?"

"Planning on buying us one with that resonance crystal? You still have it, right?"

I fished in my EVA suit and pulled it out. For a moment, I became lost in its sparkle as the fact that I was holding an immeasurable amount of wealth was not lost on me. How I prayed I wasn't about to wake from a dream.

"Yeah, I've got it," I finally said. "But I wasn't planning on buying any old planet, per se."

"Then what? A solar system or two?"

"Too boring."

Tolby snorted. "Owning a solar system is boring, huh?"

"Mhm. A headache, too," I said. "Who wants that kind of stress? Rogue comets. Strange alien invasions. Interstellar taxes. Pirates. Squatters. You name it."

"Don't forget the mysterious black cubes of doom," he said.

"Precisely." I then pocketed the crystal and shot him an impish grin. "Tolby, my dear, have you ever heard of General Chik Tak?"

"Yes. That collection of mythology you let me borrow last month had a bit on him. There's supposed to be a god trapped in his tomb, if memory serves."

I spun the archive cube around so Tolby could get a better view of what was being displayed. Framed in a green circle was the image of a floating island above an angry sea. At the center of the island were a dozen crystalline towers arranged in an oval and stretching far into the heavens. In the middle of those was a mausoleum with runes etched across its surface. To the side of this display was a detailed star map of exactly how to get to this hidden gem of a planet.

"What do you say we see how true the legends are and colonize a new world at the same time?"

(PAGE LEFT INTENTIONALLY BLANK)

(EXCEPT FOR THAT LINE; AND THIS ONE, TOO)

SPOILERS: THINGS GET WORSE

(Dakota Adams Book II)

Time travel is messy.

And I don't mean morning hair after prom, messy. I mean flushing dynamite down the toilet, messy.

Long story short:
Ship, trashed. Food stores, gone.
Ravenous monsters, everywhere.

Worst of all, I have to listen to my best bud and his new harem of space cats constantly "repopulate" their species. I swear to god, if I don't find some earplugs soon, I'm going stick my head in a warp coil.

The silver lining to our predicament is that the abandoned facility we found has some sweet tech we might be able to use to escape— that is if we can bring it back online before we're eaten.

That said, if this is the end of my epic adventures, always remember: if I die, I want a Viking funeral.

CHAPTER ONE

I sat at the edge of a battlefield that was messier than hair the morning after prom.

My initial plans to crush my enemy had been met with disaster. Sure, the big guy has always looked super cuddly with his white, tiger-striped fur, feline face, and sparkling green eyes that could melt the Ice Queen's heart, but beneath that loveable exterior was a vicious persona and a tactical genius. In the span of twelve moves, my army on the game board had been cut in half, while Tolby had suffered only a few minor setbacks.

"Alright, I'm done playing with you," I said, trying to bluff my way out of this predicament. "I'm going to raze your cities to the ground and post the video for the world to see unless you surrender posthaste."

Tolby grinned and kept his playing cards close to his chest. "Worst bluff in history," he said. "Your death is more imminent than a warp core cracked in two."

"Is that a fact?" I said, picking up a piece of ChapStick and moving it to flank his front line battle tanks. "Chew on this."

Tolby cocked his head. "You can't do that."

"I think I just did," I said. "Guess you forgot that gunships can fly over any terrain."

"That's not a gunship. That's a factory. Unless you've got some ginormous engines installed on it I don't know about, it's not going anywhere."

"No, the red-capped ChapSticks are gunships. The blue ones are factories."

"You've got that backward."

"No, you—" I cut myself short when I realized he was right. All I could do was throw up my hands in frustration. "Ugh! This is too confusing without proper pieces."

Tolby shrugged. "It's the best we can do, I'm afraid, given our circumstances. This ship is not outfitted for entertainment."

He had me there. For the last few hours, the navigational computers of the lifeboat we were in had been trying to figure out where the hell we were. Why, you ask? Well, that's another story, but the short of it is we made a blind jump through hyperspace to avoid getting swallowed by a blue hypergiant, and so when we came out of it, there wasn't a recognizable star in sight.

Since lifeboats aren't usually stocked with board games (note to self: this could be a fantastic niche market to corner), we were reduced to scavenging game pieces from the less-than-critical stash of supplies we found.

"Fine, if I can't do that, I'm sending my other nuke," I said, returning my sadly-not-a-gunship factory to its original place and seeing what cards I had in hand. Well, calling them cards is being generous. They were pieces of cardboard we'd pulled off a box of communicators and subsequently scribbled upon with a red marker we'd found in a storage locker.

"You can't do that either," he said. "You didn't research Fast Firing."

My brow dropped. "What? I don't have to do that for nukes. That's only artillery."

"No, that's for both," he said. "Check the rule book."

"There is no rule book! We made the game up like ten minutes ago!"

"Then I'm making an addendum clarifying this point of contention."

"Funny how that addendum helps you. It's almost like—"

Tolby's eyes went from playful to challenging. "Like what?"

"Like you're cheating," I said, not backing down. I crossed my arms over my chest.

"I'm cheating? Me?" he said, rising and fur bristling. "I don't need to cheat to win, Dakota."

Despite the fact that his immense bulk now towered over me, I didn't back down. "Apparently you do."

Tolby shook his head and snorted. "Fine. I'm cheating. I surrender. You win."

It took me a moment to gather my thoughts at the unexpected turn. Recent events that included a multitude of near-death experiences had caught up to each of our psyches, and as such, things were tense between us. I hadn't meant to end the game that abruptly.

"Don't be like that," I said. "Come on, sit. We barely played. We'll figure it out."

"You're making this exceptionally not fun," he said. He then glanced over my shoulder to the door behind me. "I should check on Yseri and Jainon, anyway, make sure they're resting okay."

"You mean you're going to have another romp together."

"I was trying to be discreet."

"Discreet went out the window after your tenth time," I said, filling my tone with ire. Look, I understood that in the last twenty-four hours he'd gone from being alone in the universe, species wise, to being reunited with a pair of presumably gorgeous Kibnali females (I say presumably because they're not really my type, you know, but Tolby seemed to gush over both of them). But I was still his best friend, and I thought I'd been more than accommodating when it came to him wanting to sire a slew of kits. I mean, they could at least wait till after we got home and we weren't all packed together like sardines.

"You could always help the computers figure out where we are," he offered. "That way we both have something productive to do. Your assistance would likely boost efforts by five percent."

"Maybe I could if your two girlfriends weren't louder than a freight train. Seriously, given how vocal they are, the bulkheads might as well be made out of tissue paper." He didn't say anything as he went for the door, so I fired one last shot. "Guess I'll be here—alone—till you get back."

Tolby hit the button for the door and it opened with a hiss. Before he stepped through, he looked at me one last time. "Maybe by then you'll realize it's not the end of the world."

"I don't think it's the end of the world!" I shouted after him, but he didn't hear it. The door closed. I stood, huffed, and shook out the stiffness in my legs before jumping into the navigator's seat near the front and checking the status of the parallax scans and immediately wishing I hadn't. "Daphne, tell me good news."

"Glady," replied the ship's AI. "In the beginning was the Word, and the Word—"

"Not that good news," I said, curling up in the chair and burying my face in my hands. "I mean tell me this screen is lying. Tell me you have some idea where we are."

"Given your respirations, heartbeat, increased sweat production, and flutter in your tone, we both know that would do no good," she replied. "Your mental acuity is beyond such simple trickery."

I sighed. "Are we at least in the same galactic quadrant?"

"No."

"Same galaxy?"

"No."

"Same cluster?"

"No."

"Local group?"

"No."

I went back to burying my head in my hands. It was safe there, warm, and most of all, it was a place I was familiar with, which was exactly the opposite of what the void outside our ship was like. I peeked out of my fingers and dared one last question. "Same super cluster?"

Silence.

I stewed in my seat and waited as more silence settled in. Then, the sounds of Kibnali foreplay drifted into the cabin and lit a fire in my soul. "Well?" I said, anger mounting. "You better keep talking because if I have to listen to that for another hour while also thinking about all the no's you gave me, I'm going to open an airlock and suck sweet, sweet vacuum."

"I'm sorry, but I am unable to answer your previous question."

"Why?"

"My programming will not allow you to be in greater states of distress by any action or omission of action on my part."

"Huh?" I glanced at my cyber arm and wondered if the small bits of brain damage it had caused before during installation and use were now responsible for me not following what Daphne had just said. That little delusion lasted about as long as a batch of Mom's cupcakes when Dad would get a whiff of them. Truth was, I didn't want to follow. "How the hell did we fly out of a super cluster? No one can do that."

"Then I'm happy to say that you're the first," she replied, a little too chipper for my likes. "I suggest putting in for an award when you get a chance. I bet you'd get a lovely plaque as well."

"Is that supposed to make me happy?"

"It would make me happy. Assuming I could be happy. I'm only a program after all. But I could fake it well enough. Would you like to see?"

I snorted. "No, what I'd like for you to be is helpful, and telling me that I should be happy about blindly flying halfway across the universe is the opposite of that."

"Might I suggest that you take an inventory of what you have? I haven't known you for long, and I've been eavesdropping on your conversations for even less time, but it seems to me that you are the clever type and won't be stopped by something as trivial as being lost in space."

At first, I was put off even more by her description that this was all trivial. But as the sounds of rampant Kibnali sex blasted through the bulkheads, pounded my eardrums, and threatened to rip apart my sanity, I decided that focusing on anything else was for the best. To that end, I started making a list of what we had, or rather what I wished we had. "Please tell me you have noise-canceling capabilities."

"I most certainly do," Daphne said, sounding thoroughly insulted that I would even dream of asking. "Shall I take care of your distraction?"

"For the love of all that is good and holy in this universe, yes."

"There should be a headset inside the left panel of the captain's chair. If you put those on I will take care of the rest."

I dove into the panel like a hawk and plucked a sleek, red, and black set of headphones from a compartment. The cushions were big and comfy and offered a snug fit as I slipped them over my head. A moment later, the sounds of their romp was nothing more than a cringe-worthy memory. I sank back into the chair with a happy smile on my face. This was a small victory, but a victory nonetheless. And even if we had a long, long way to go, I felt like I'd just taken my first step forward on a journey I knew we would all complete. Looking back, that was incredibly naïve, but I suppose if I'm being honest, my expectations aren't always realistic.

"I don't suppose you have any good music stored away somewhere?" I said.

"What would you define as good music?"

"At this point, I'll take anything other than neo pop-country fusion," I said with a laugh.

"Going by what I know of you, might I suggest some 7th century PHS Bach or Beethoven?"

I perked in my chair. I couldn't believe my luck. I loved both of those composers, and even if over a thousand years separated us, I'd always felt I had a connection to all of the grand classical masters. Of course, maybe I shouldn't have been that surprised. After all, this ship had belonged to Pizlow, and despite all of his brutish, mobster ways, he did generally have a keen and refined sense when it came to collecting various forms of art. Thus, it should've been a given he'd have the classics available to listen to. "Either Bach or Beethoven would be lovely," I said. "But what would be perfect would be some Chopin."

"How about his first ballade?"

I settled back into the chair with a happy smile. "You're one with my soul right now."

A few seconds later, the majestic start to Chopin's Ballade No.1, Opus 23, resounded in my ears. As the piece went on, I started to follow Daphne's advice and take inventory of everything I had.

First, I still had my best buddy, Tolby. Even if he was currently indulging himself for the umpteenth time in physical relations while we drifted in space, I knew he'd never leave me. That was very comforting, because aside from being a great friend, he was handy in all things tech and good in a fight.

Second, we had a functional spaceship that had enough fuel and supplies to last us for quite some time. Hopefully that meant it could keep us alive until we knew where we were and came up with a way how to get back home.

As I thought about a third point, an itch began to build at the back of my head. I tried scratching it, but quickly realized that itch was deep inside my skull and not on my scalp. This realization sat about as well as the idea of getting a stomach pump done with a garden hose. Thankfully, said itch went away after a few moments.

When I brought my hand down and saw my cyber arm, I easily came up with items three and four on my list of assets.

You see, my cyber arm wasn't an ordinary piece of hardware or upgrade you might buy at an enhancement shop. In fact, this completely kick-ass piece of tech could not be bought at all. It had been installed in me less than a day ago by the remnants of a lost race, The Progenitors, and it served as an interface for both a time-traveling device and an archive cube I'd found earlier. While I no longer had the portal device that let me slip through spacetime, I did have the archive cube the Progenitors had made, and inside that cube I had the most gargantuan collection of information in the known universe.

"Alright cubie," I said, whipping the thing out and turning it on. "Show me what you got."

It didn't answer. It didn't do much at all other than sit in the palm of my hand and cast a warm glow a little above it. A few seconds ticked by and then a holographic screen popped up showing the schematics for the Revenant—Pizlow's ship and the last thing we had been looking at. I flipped back to the main menu, which was a huge page filled with top-level categories and a search bar at the top (apparently, the thing was smart enough to adapt its display to familiar methods of use, depending on the species using it).

I surfed for a while, and though I didn't find anything of immediate use, I found plenty of interest. I read about some far-off planet that traded in dreams and colors, and a culture that believed the only thing worse than death was to be born on the third day of the week. I admired artwork made using solar wind and stared at a five-line poem that repeated four words over and over that had somehow won an intergalactic poetry competition.

At some point, events of the last few hours caught up with me, and my eyes felt heavier than an emo-goth's love letter. My right arm itched, and it felt like creepy crawlies going up my shoulder and neck. I wrote it off as yet another side effect of having alien tech inside me, possibly upgrading (again), and let sleep take a hold of me.

It didn't last.

A thunderous explosion rocked the ship, and my eyes shot open. Status screens across four separate monitors flashed bright red warnings, and a klaxon blared.

Before I could say or do anything, Daphne spoke. "Warning: Explosion detected. Hull integrity compromised. Multiple fires in engine room."

(End of Preview)

ACKNOWLEDGMENTS

As always, I have the usual crew to thank: My wife for putting up with a lot of bad writing over the years, my wonderful editor Crystal for turning slop into something decent, and my kids for giving me endless ideas on what's fun and adventurous.

I'd also like to give an extra special thanks to the fantastic Katherine Littrell who breathed wonderful life into the characters and gave Dakota the voice she needs.

Of course, none of this would be possible without all my brilliant readers, new and old; so here's to hoping you enjoyed this first book and are off to read more.

ABOUT THE AUTHOR

When not writing, Galen Surlak-Ramsey has been known to throw himself out of an airplane, teach others how to throw themselves out of an airplane, take pictures of the deep space, and wrangle his four children somewhere in Southwest Florida.

He also manages to pay the bills as a chaplain for a local hospice.

Be sure to drop by his website https://galensurlak.com/and sign up for his newsletter for free goodies, contests, and plenty of other fun stuff.